the SEASON of YOU & ME

ROBIN CONSTANTINE

BALZER + BRAY
An Imprint of HarperCollins*Publishers*

For Jody, who loved the beach and sunsets and endless nights filled with laughter and friends. Miss you, Empress.

Balzer + Bray is an imprint of HarperCollins Publishers.

The Season of You & Me
 For information address HarperCollins Children's Books, a division of HarperCollins Publishers, 195 Broadway, New York, NY 10007.
www.epicreads.com

Library of Congress Control Number: 2015955107
ISBN 978-0-06-243884-3

Typography by Erin Fitzsimmons
17 18 19 20 21 PC/LSCH 10 9 8 7 6 5 4 3 2 1
❖
First paperback edition, 2017

the SEASON of YOU & ME

Also by Robin Constantine

The Promise of Amazing

The Secrets of Attraction

ONE
CASSIDY

MY NANA HAD A SAYING—"WISH IN ONE HAND, shit in the other, and see which one gets filled faster." I never understood it, because, *duh*, who would willingly crap in their hand?

Then I met Gavin Henley and understood.

I couldn't blame him though—that would be playing the victim, and I wasn't a victim. The reality of our situation was this: I'd been ready to lose myself, to shake up my dull little junior life that consisted of homework, my bakery job, and—well, yep, that was it. One nonrefundable prom dress and too many hours of ugly crying later—I was o-v-e-r him, sort of, but that didn't mean I hadn't spent the last torturous month of school wishing.

Wishing I'd never met him.

Wishing I could be homeschooled.

Wishing I could disappear.

Wishing we were together again.

That's when I finally understood my nana's saying, bleak as it was. Wishing was futile. Wishing was nonaction. If Nana's wisdom had been literal, I'd be buried under a steaming pile, which was pretty much what the fallout had felt like. I was done being buried. Luckily, the escape plan was a no-brainer. For once, my parents' divorce served me well.

"Cass, I know you're, like, tragically heartbroken, but the whole summer with your father? Really?"

Emma was prone on my bed, poring over the pages of the New Jersey magazine where my father's bed-and-breakfast was featured. Her tone said *annoyed*, but her eyes were wide and curious as she looked over the two-page spread that declared Ocean Whispers a gem of the Jersey Shore. That gem was my refuge for the summer.

"I'm not tragic anymore," I said, which was only a tiny lie. I occasionally wallowed in my playlists, vacillating between Adele despair to T. Swift revenge fantasies to total MCR raw emo pain and back again in the month since Gavin and I had broken up. Seeing Gavin daily in school was bad enough, but the looks of pity, the whispers, the rumors of his screwing around—then the photo evidence of it—was worse. I wanted to leave the *planet*, let alone the city. The upside was that Gavin had graduated and would be off to Penn by the time I returned from Crest Haven. I'd never have to see his face again.

Unless I tortured myself on his StalkMe account with photos of all he'd been doing.

Without me.

"Aren't you worried you're going to miss out on everything?"

"Which one do you think?" I asked, holding up two bathing suits and drowning out her question with my fake brightness. "Wait, why do I have to choose? You know, I'm working at a day camp, I'll probably be at the beach every day." I threw them both into my nearly full suitcase.

"Cass." Ems closed the magazine and sat up. "I'm being serious. Are you sure this isn't a cop-out? You don't have to leave town to get over him."

"Why not?" I asked.

Emma shrugged. "I don't know, because isn't facing your problems the mature thing to do?"

I sat next to her. "It's *problem*, singular. And I don't want to face *he who shall not be named*, so what does it matter? I've faced him enough—getting away from him is exactly what I need to do."

"Fine, but you're getting away from me too; that sucks. Sugar Rush will not be the same without you this summer."

"Then break up with Drew, quit the bakery, and come with me. Dad would love to host the two of us," I said, picturing the damage Ems and I could do down the shore. It was all before us—sand, sun, fun, but the twist of her lips and *yeah, right* eyes let me know it was impossible. Emma was with Drew, and they had it bad—like, joined-at-the-hip bad. Drew was a decent guy, and treated Ems like a goddess. His one flaw? He was Gavin's friend, which had been a bestie dream come true when we were together, and was beyond awkward now that we weren't.

She elbowed me. "All I'm saying is you've never spent more than a week at your father's. Why do you want to go now? Don't let Gavin have that power over you. Go for an extra week or something, come back, have a hot revenge hookup with someone, and shove it in his face right before he leaves for school as a final eff-you."

My stomach knotted. I stood up and walked over to my vanity to choose some necklaces to take with me from my jewelry tree. The first one I picked up was the Tiffany heart necklace that Gavin had given me for Valentine's Day. I knew I should have thrown it across the room, but it was so pretty, and sparkly, and oh, crap, I just couldn't part with it. *I saw this and thought of you*, he'd whispered as he put it around my neck. I'd eaten it up. *Silly girl.* I put it aside and chose a beaded choker instead.

"I've declared myself hookup-free for a while. Remember?" I said, holding up the choker to my neck, then adding it to my *take* pile.

It was easier to think of Gavin in big, evil-nemesis terms,

something to be battled and triumphed over, when the truth was seeing him still hurt like hell. I was sick of pretending that it shouldn't.

He'd *known* me. We'd shared secrets. Or at least I had. He'd seen me naked. We'd done *it*. A lot. There was no taking that back. We had plans to be regulars at his parents' condo in Ship Bottom for the summer. Kissing some random guy might have buried those feelings for a moment, but after the initial thrill, they were still there in all their jagged, painful glory. I knew, because I'd hooked up with my boss's son, Nate. It was prom night, and I'd been feeling particularly sorry for myself. He was back from college, talking about how much it sucked to be living with his parents. We held a mutual pity party, finished off the bourbon that was left over from a batch of cupcakes, and then groped each other in the supplies pantry. Huge mistake that made the decision to spend the summer with my father easier. Even Ems didn't know about that one.

"Still, you don't have to run away." Emma's phone went off. She scrolled through her messages, big grin on her face. I didn't need to ask who was texting. I went back to picking out vacation jewelry.

My bedroom door squeaked open. A light citrus scent filled the air. Nana. Her signature Jean Naté always entered the room before she did. She stood in the doorway, holding the cordless phone to her shoulder to muffle noise.

"It's your mother. She's picking up from Jade Garden. Any special requests?"

I shook my head. "Just the usual."

"How about you, Emma? You're more than welcome to stay."

Emma stood up and slid her phone into her back pocket. "No thanks, Nan, heading out soon. Drew's picking me up."

Nan looked between us and chuckled. "You girls need a new hobby."

Ems laughed. Nan put the phone back up to her ear and resumed talking to my mother, muttering something about extra almond cookies as she wandered back to the kitchen.

"Why don't you bail on dinner, come hang out; maybe it'll make you change your mind," Emma said.

"Third wheel to you and Drew? Sure, let me fix my hair."

"I'm not going to stop, you know."

"I'm leaving tomorrow, you know."

"I know." Her face fell and the reality hit me. My first summer without Ems by my side. We'd come a long way from looming bracelets and playing Rummikub, for sure. But no matter what she said, she wouldn't be by my side this year even if I didn't leave town. Her days revolved around coordinating her and Drew's work schedules so they could spend maximum time together. It had been that way for me and Gavin too, so who was I to be annoyed with her? Nana had been right, though—it would be smart to get a new hobby, one that didn't wrench my soul, like maybe knitting or knife throwing. I pulled Emma in for a quick hug.

"You'll come down," I said into her dark curtain of hair.

She laughed. "Yes."

"Without Drew?"

There was a pause before she answered. "Of course."

There wasn't a lot of conviction behind those words, but I chose to believe her.

After dinner I finished packing, by the end tossing in random things like my owl earrings and an extra pair of dressy flip-flops because I couldn't shake the feeling I was leaving something behind. I draped myself across the suitcase to finally get it zipped shut. My life in one large bag and a flower-print duffel. Was I running away? It kind of looked like it. I got ready for bed, but was too restless to sleep.

Mom and Nan were in the living room, watching their usual Friday-night bridal show marathon. I always used to feel a little sorry for them when I breezed through on my way out to see Gavin. I had a life. They watched other people's lives on TV. Lame. Following my breakup though, when I wasn't working, hiding out with them had become my Friday night. Then I understood why they liked it so much. Everything faded away for a while when you got caught up in someone else's drama. Weddings were happy, fluffy, and hopeful events. Everything was perfect and pretty. It was easy to correct someone else's mistakes, even if it was just the awful ruching on a wedding dress. I sat down to join them.

"All packed?" Mom asked.

"I think so," I said, trying to ignore the sudden queasy feeling in my gut. I stood up. "I'm gonna get some air, sit on the porch for a bit."

"Want company?"

"Nah, I'm good."

Mom kept her eyes on me a moment longer, which I took to mean *Are you sure?* I nodded and she turned back to the show. She and Nan had been my own private mental health tag team: if one wasn't asking how I was, the other was offering up some diversion, as if in one moment out of their sight I would derail into hopelessness. That wasn't entirely false. I mostly appreciated it, but sometimes all I needed to do was be still. Let the thoughts of Gavin in, diminishing their hold over me.

I sat on the top step, wrapped my arms around my knees, and looked up to the sky, to the pointed rooftops that formed my view. The night was warm and the air smelled of garlic from the Italian restaurant down the street. I closed my eyes, imagined the low hum and rumble of Gavin's Jeep turning the corner at the top of the block. How many times had I waited for him in this exact spot, hidden by the pines on either side of the walk to the front porch? I used to stand on the second step so we were the same height, and pull him close, memorizing how our bodies felt together, feeling his chest expand with each breath, so when I went to sleep I could imagine him next to me.

Totally love zombified.

I'm not sure we ever formally met; it was more like fate threw us together in the form of Spanish II. I sat in the last row, by the windows—he was one over, not quite next to me because his row was longer. It was hard not to notice him—Gavin didn't just sit in his desk, he owned it, melting into the seat, long legs reaching out past the chair of the person in front of him. Head down, dark hair partially covering his face, he never looked like he was paying attention, but anytime Profesora Butler called on him, he replied *en español* perfectly, grinning to himself when he knew he'd thrown her off.

Sometime in October, the first text from an unknown number came.

Hola hermosa.

I ignored it, even though I thought it was an odd coincidence, seeing as I was getting a text in a language I was currently in class studying. Ems had pranked me so many times I blew it off as a customer service bot she'd signed me up for as a joke. The third time it happened during the week, I finally took the bait.

Who is this?

En espanol, por favor.

So maybe not a bot. I ignored it again, until the following day, when I knew how to answer *en español.*

Quien es este?

Espera

Wait? For what?

The messages piqued my interest, but not for a moment did I think it was Gavin. He gave no signs, no glances my way, nothing to indicate that he even noticed I was across from him. And it's not like I was pining away for him either; he was a body in a chair—a hot body that wore his jeans well, no denying that—but I didn't think about him in any way other than that.

Fate, or more accurately, Ems intervened the second time . . . or *the* time. The night my life changed. She had begged me to come along on her first sort-of date with Drew. He hadn't called it a date—he'd asked her to *hang out, bring a friend*. Emma made it sound like a group thing, but when Drew picked us up at her house in his two-door Mustang—it was clearly not a group thing.

Ems slipped into the backseat first, giggling at Drew, who smiled as he held up the driver's seat and said hey to us. I gave myself a quick mental pep talk—*the ride won't be long, this is the kind of adventure you've been waiting for since freshman year, Emma would do it for you*—and steeled myself to be cramped in the back, then glanced at the passenger, and, whoa . . . there he was, the guy from Spanish, fiddling with the radio and cursing about hundreds of stations with nothing but techno crap. I convinced myself that the jolt I felt was recognition. His eyes met mine and he smiled, but only briefly; once Drew was back in the car, it was all about the lack of decent music on the radio and who was going to be at Meadowbrooke.

Ems leaned forward in between the front seats, sharing in their conversation, laughing at practically everything Drew said; she was so calm, relaxed, sure of herself. I wondered if Gavin and I were there to fill in awkward silences in case things didn't go okay, but Drew and Emma already looked like a couple. I stared out the window, pretending the lack of leg room didn't make me want to crawl out of my skin. In spite of the cramped space and slightly awkward arrangement, I was looking forward to finally going to the place that, every Monday in school, was talked about with hushed tones of epic party awe. As ridiculous as it sounded, Meadowbrooke was legend.

The park was two towns over, adjacent to an abandoned psych hospital that was occasionally visited by ghost-hunter shows. When we first pulled in, all I saw in the dim glow of a partially broken streetlight was a swing set, a metal slide, and an empty basketball court. Far from impressive or legendary. Drew passed the sad little excuse of a playground and made a sharp left turn down a tree-lined dirt path. The ground was uneven and as we bumped along, I hit my head on the roof of the car. I bit back a squeal and turned to Ems, sure she was as weirded out by the scene as I was, but her face was rapt as she looked ahead. Gavin sang along with a song I'd never heard, but which apparently wasn't crap judging by the way he was nodding along to the beat.

The path opened up to a clearing and wide dirt patch with at least ten cars parked askew. People roamed the lot and leaned against rear bumpers. Someone scooted in front of the car, knocked on the hood, and yelled "Drewmeister!" We may as well have been in a car-ride safari park, staring at the jungle life. *Oooh, look, seniors.* I toned down my wide-eyed gawking.

Once out of the car, Drew opened four longnecks and handed one to each of us. Gavin split, leaving me staring at Drew and Ems, who were staring at each other. I took a sip of beer, determined to go along with wherever the night took me. Why not? I'd survived the ride, and there were so many people there, so many *new* people, I didn't need that guy.

"Where's Gavin?" Emma asked me.

I shrugged. Her brows scrunched together. Drew took her hand. "C'mon."

The three of us walked toward a makeshift bonfire that

someone had started in a garbage can. The night was cool, and while a fire was hardly necessary, it added to the mood, made faces more exaggerated, intriguing. What may have looked like one large group was actually several smaller ones, threes and fours, clustered together, all caught up in their own little impenetrable worlds. When I turned to say something to Ems, she was gone. My phone buzzed. I slid it out from my back pocket, grateful for something to do, and tapped for the message.

Eres muy bonita esta noche, Cassidy.

No way, I thought, but must have said out loud, because the person next to me stepped back and said, "What?" My mind blanked; it was just letters on the screen that I didn't understand. I knew *muy* was "very." *Bonita* was . . . "pretty"? And my name. I should have been freaked, but it made me smile. Being called very pretty didn't feel like a threat. I tapped a response.

RU here?

If whoever had been texting me responded with *en español, por favor*, I would have screamed.

Look up.

I slowly tilted my chin and looked up at the sky. What the hell was I supposed to be looking at? Was this an elaborate Emma prank?

"Not *that* up," a male voice called.

I looked across the fire. Gavin stood on the other side.

Everything snapped to focus and sharpened.

Gavin was the one who had been texting me?!

"You?" I asked as he walked closer. Damn, he had dimples.

He raised his hands up. *"Sí."*

"But . . . why?"

"Why not?" he asked, walking past me. His secretive smirk beckoned me to follow him. We sat side by side on the hood of Drew's car, sipping our beer, making small talk about school and the night, until I decided to cut to the important stuff.

"How did you get my number?"

"Emma."

"She didn't—"

"I told her not to."

"Wouldn't it have been easier to talk to me in class?"

"Where's the mystery in that? Besides, you're too serious in class, pen at the ready, open notebook, conjugating verbs and shit."

He thought I was serious? He noticed me in class?

"So, Ems knew you were texting me, and you knew I was the friend coming tonight—why did you disappear when we got here?" I didn't know where this bold Cassidy was coming from, but I felt charged, wanting to get to the bottom of it, and he was too freaking cute close up.

"I got the feeling you weren't interested. You looked out the window the whole way here."

"You were talking about the crappy music."

"It was pretty crappy, wasn't it? I mean, Drew pays out the ass for premium satellite, you'd think—"

"What did the last text say?"

"You take Spanish, you should know."

"I only look serious. You're the Spanish scholar."

"Only because it's my second time taking it. Butler needs to change up her lessons," he said.

I wasn't letting it go; I wanted to hear him say it. He shifted to face me, the glow from the fire flickering across his face. He kept his eyes on mine. So serious.

"You look very pretty tonight, Cassidy."

I blushed at the compliment, laughed, took a sip from my beer. Suddenly there was a loud mechanical *woop* sound. Then there were lights. Blue and red and blue and red.

"Shit," Gavin said, grabbing my beer and tossing it with his toward a nearby garbage can. He took my hand. "Run."

We weren't the only ones scattering toward the woods. I wasn't sure what kind of trouble I was running from, but visions of Nana in her housedress, or worse, Mom, who was out on a date that night, coming to pick me up at a police station, fueled my run. Leaves crunched as we darted through the trees. Peals of laughter, more crunching, *shush*es coming from every direction as kids from around the fire scattered. The woods were cooler, and my face was frozen in a grin, my breath coming out in gasps. I had no clue where we were headed, but I trusted Gavin. I had no choice.

I focused on his hand clasped around mine, pulling me forward. It felt right, comfortable, like I'd found something I'd been missing. My pulse pounded in my head and the last sip of beer threatened to rise on the back of my tongue. We finally reached a clearing, a large field with waist-high weeds surrounding a massive, imposing-looking building with chain-link fences around it. Gavin let go of my hand and stumbled forward a bit, looking up at the sky and laughing. I bent over, hands on my knees, dizzy from the run, my mouth dry. Gavin took my hand again.

"C'mon." He was out of breath too. We sat on the chilly ground with our backs against the trunk of a large tree, facing the abandoned asylum. My breath slowed; my thoughts became more rational.

"Well, now what do we do?"

Gavin laughed. "We wait. This always happens when some jackhole lights a fire."

"Will they come after us?"

"Too much of a hassle; that's why we scatter. Sometimes they have a patrol car over here, but I guess luck is with us tonight. As long as no one causes any real trouble, like setting the woods on fire, everyone kind of goes along with it."

We sat listening until the sounds in the woods died down. The fire was snuffed. The flashing lights were gone. I pulled my knees up to my chest for warmth and stared at the abandoned asylum. "Think it's haunted?"

"Nah," Gavin said, reaching into his pocket and producing an ornate silver flask. "But this would make one helluva horror flick, right? Maybe there's a psycho who got loose right before the place shut down and he's been living in the woods all this time and decides to go on a killing spree because he thinks he's being attacked."

"So we're the first to die, then?"

"Maybe me—you'd be the ingenue, the one everyone falls in love with." He opened the flask and offered it to me. I was about to take it, but stopped.

"Or," I said, "the ingenue gets lost in the woods, but is found by a charming guy who turns out to be the escaped psycho, and he drugs the girl and takes her to his asylum lab to perform all kinds of sick experiments."

He took a swig from the flask. "It's only Fireball."

"And you feel the need to carry a flask?"

"Sometimes. Takes the edge off. Keeps you warm. I won't perform any sick experiments unless you want me to," he said, holding it out.

I took the flask from him this time and downed a sip. Fireball was the perfect name because the liquid burned my throat, but it tasted like cinnamon and, true to Gavin's word, warmed me up. I ran my thumb across the engraved front of the flask.

"GWH—what's your middle name?"

"It's my father's flask; he's George Wallace Henley."

"Wow, that's a flask-worthy name." I handed it back to him.

He laughed. "Sounds impressive, right? I'm Gavin William Henley, so I guess I can pass it off as mine." He took another sip before screwing the top back on. His phone dinged. He reached into his pocket and checked the messages. The screen illuminated his face.

"Drew says coast is clear."

My heart fell. I was sitting in a field of weeds in front of an abandoned asylum and had no desire to leave. Gavin stood up, held out his hand for mine, and pulled me to standing. I stumbled over the root of the tree and gripped his arms for balance. He steadied me, laughing. Even his laugh was sexy. I couldn't stop staring at him, couldn't wait to hear what would come out of his mouth next. How had I not noticed any of this for two months in Spanish?

"I think we'd be the couple who made it out alive," he said. "The one everyone roots for."

I leaned against the tree and pulled him toward me, my mouth reaching for his before I could think, rationalize, stop myself, because the boy with the silver flask was trouble, and

I knew it, but I didn't care. He was momentarily startled, but then made this low rumble of approval in his chest that I felt as he kissed me. His lips were warm and tasted like cinnamon and as his arms crushed me against him, everything around us dissolved. I had an epic story to whisper in the halls of school on Monday.

It was a story I wished I could forget.

And wishing . . . well, yeah, I knew where it got me.

"Hey, Cass, you're a million miles away." Nan held the railing as she settled onto the top step next to me. I shook off the Gavin thoughts, but a nagging question remained, the one Emma had brought up earlier in my room.

"Do you think I'm running away?" I asked.

She wrestled something out of the pocket of her housecoat—a waxed paper envelope with two almond cookies. She offered me one. I was going to pass but figured I'd be missing Jade Garden soon enough. We nibbled on the cookies before Nan said anything.

"You know, I never liked that boy. He didn't eat dessert."

I laughed. "That's random."

"No, a man who doesn't eat sweets doesn't know how to be sweet, in my experience anyway. And I don't mean the superficial fake sweet. I mean the real, deep sweet."

I wasn't about to touch what real, deep sweet meant. I'm sure whatever Nan was thinking was far away from where my perverted mind was taking it. Mom stepped out onto the porch, opened the folding chair, and sat down, putting her legs up on the railing and letting out a long, hassled-sounding sigh.

"Cassidy thinks she's running away."

"I want to run away," Mom said, tilting her head back and looking up at the sky.

"So you think I am?" I asked.

She turned her head to me. "Why would you say that?"

"I don't know. Emma thought maybe it was immature to skip out."

"And Emma's the authority on maturity now," Nan said.

"I know, I know, I just don't want it to look like I'm copping out."

Mom looked dreamily up to the sky again, her face softened. "Copping out of what? Cassidy, you're spending the summer with your father, you're not running away. You're changing the scenery. There's a difference. You're opening yourself up to new experiences. That's all, nothing wrong with that. This will be good for you."

I hoped she was right.

TWO
BRYAN

EYES CLOSED, I COULD IMAGINE I WAS IN THE OCEAN.

I was whole underwater.

Floating.

Still.

In control.

One with the water around me.

Some moments, I could step out of my life. (Step. Ha.)

There was always that point, though, when my brain reminded me that communications between it and my legs were wonky. That it could shout commands all day and my lower half wouldn't listen, as if the nerves in my legs were plugging their ears and singing *lalalalalalalalalala, we can't hear you*, but worse, because there was no undoing it.

I'd never walk again.

Even a year and a half after the accident those words were unreal.

T-10. Incomplete. Numbers and letters that defined me now.

They were unreal too.

In the water though, I could imagine. Remember.

If only some instrumental version of "Radioactive" hadn't been playing under the water, I would have been golden.

"Bryan."

A splash across my face brought me back to the rec center pool. Fluorescent lights instead of the sun. Chlorine instead of salt. I blinked the water from my eyes, shifted the therapy noodle out from under my knees, and paddled upright. My arms ached from my workout. I'd pushed myself hard. I may not have had use of my legs, but I had the upper body of fucking Iron Man. #wheelchairperk

Jena, a rec center noob, stood at the side of the pool and waggled her fingers at me. We didn't really know each other, but knew *of* each other. Wade had her stats down, like he did for every girl who was working at the rec center for the summer. Single. Sophomore. Soccer/swim girl. Liked to party. Her red lifeguard hoodie skimmed the top of her legs. Her long, tanned legs. Legs that could run and jump and kick without a second thought. Thighs that could wrap around me.

She cleared her throat.

"Sorry for the splashing. I wanted to get your attention."

She bent down and grabbed the therapy noodle out of the water.

"No worries. I've had people get my attention in worse ways."

She pressed her lips together. Clearly my material was not charming her.

"We're, um—closing soon."

"Seven already? I'll be right out."

She looked around. Her eyes landed on the pool lift. My first few times in the water, I'd used and hated everything about it, especially needing someone else's help just to take a swim. Six months of training and I was expert at getting in and out of the pool, no fanfare necessary. Although getting help from Jena might have been worth it.

"I don't need that," I said, and made my way toward the end of the pool. She followed alongside as I swam to the end of the lane.

I pulled myself up on the edge and twisted, placing my butt down and centering my weight. Jena handed me a towel. I was about to tell her she didn't need to baby me but nodded thanks and took the towel from her. Hot girls being helpful was definitely a #wheelchairperk. I'd left my wheels close for easy access. She looked at the chair, then me. I smiled.

"It's not as hard as it looks; I can manage."

She played with the string pulls on her hoodie and fidgeted, eyes darting between me, the chair, and the kids who were screaming at the other end of the pool. "Mr. Beckett said to check in with him before you leave. Do you, um . . . need help with anything else?"

"I *am* headed to the shower. . . ."

Her head snapped up and her eyes locked on mine. A confuzzled-kitten look, maybe wondering if she'd heard me right. It was cruel of me to leave her hanging. I knew that. She was vibing off the tragic of my situation, like anyone else who knew of me and my accident. *Oh, he's that guy, the one who liked to surf, the one who tripped and fell and fucked up his life forever. The one they had that fish-fry fund-raiser for over at the VFW hall. Must not laugh around him.*

I smiled. "Kidding."

A flash of teeth and a high-pitched giggle told me she was seriously relieved I hadn't been trying to put the moves on her. Laughter always broke the ice. Even if it was of the holy-shit-I'm-so-glad-you-were-kidding variety. At least I'd made her think of something other than hauling my ass out of the pool.

"You should tell Mr. Beckett he needs to play some better underwater tunes—that instrumental stuff is boring. Something like Neck Deep." I draped the towel over my shoulders.

She laughed again, but stopped when she saw I wasn't. She must have thought I was joking.

"That's a band?"

"Yeah, I know it sounds like—well, I guess it might be

ironic if I was quad, or would that be a coincidence? I always mix that up," I said.

"Quad?"

"—draplegic, you know, paralyzed from the neck down. That would be sort of—"

Oh hell, Bry, why not joke about your daily skin check for pressure sores, wouldn't that crack her up? "I also like Jimmy Eat World and the Story So Far."

"I love Jimmy Eat World. I'll have to talk to Mr. Beckett about it," she said, over-smiling to erase the awkward. The kids at the other end of the pool screamed again, running away from each other. Jena sounded her whistle. The kids kept messing around. She rolled her eyes. "Gotta deal with them. See ya."

"Later," I said as she yelled for them to stop running. They didn't listen.

Good for them.

I locked the brakes on my wheels and hoisted myself into my chair, then pushed off to the showers.

Alone.

"So I hear you don't like my taste in music?" Mr. Beckett stared intently at his computer screen as I maneuvered through the doorway. The rec center was an older building; not much thought had been given to accessibility except in the newer wing with the pool. It was tight, but I managed, positioning myself between the chairs that were in front of his desk. He may have thought it looked like he was working, but I could see in the reflection of his glasses he was playing solitaire. After a few clicks of his mouse, he turned his focus on me, folding his hands on the blotter in front of him. The scene felt oddly formal considering he was my godfather.

"It's great if you want to put everyone to sleep, Owen."

"It's popular stuff though, no?"

"For forty-year-olds."

"Ha, ouch, Lakewood."

"You wanted to see me?"

Mr. Beckett was my father's best friend, best man, fishing buddy, a fixture at our house on Thanksgiving and New Year's Eve. As Mom and Dad and my younger brother, Matt, were working through their own shit adjusting to our new situation, he'd been the first person, aside from my therapist, to help me feel that being paralyzed wasn't some dismal life sentence. He didn't do it with fake enthusiasm. No pom-poms, no clichéd words of wisdom or pity. He did it by being there, in the worst and best moments, offering silent acknowledgment to move forward, letting me feel shitty if I wanted to, but never allowing me to wallow so deep I couldn't get out. From the look on his face, I couldn't tell what kind of moment this would turn into, but I knew he wanted to talk about something. He took off his reading glasses, folded them with more care than necessary, and placed them at the top corner of the blotter before finally leaning forward on his elbows.

"What?"

"How are you feeling about Monday?"

"Good. Ready." Monday was my first day back as a camp counselor post-accident. I'd held the same job when I was fifteen, and figured things couldn't have changed all that much in two years. Six-year-olds were six-year-olds. They ate. Ran. Spilled shit. And didn't want to do much else but swim. Totally manageable.

"Okay, cool."

"It doesn't sound like you think it's cool."

He blew out a long breath and leaned back in his chair, hands clasped behind his head like he was doing a sit-up. He looked at a water stain on the paneled ceiling as he spoke.

"I do think it's cool, and I'm glad to hear you're ready, because I think you're ready too."

"Then what's the problem?"

"Don't you think that looks kind of like Florida?" He pointed at the ceiling, outlining the water stain in the air with his index finger. "There's the panhandle, and see, over there—"

"Just be straight with me. I can handle it."

He looked at me again, sat upright in the chair. "A few of the parents have expressed concern about your ability to take care of the kids in case of emergency."

"Wasn't that the whole purpose of that Q and A session last

week? What kind of emergency?"

"I don't know. Polar ice caps melting. Werewolf bites. The usual stuff parents worry about. I know both you and Wade are more than capable of taking care of your group."

"Then why are you telling me this?"

"I wanted you to hear it from me, not some trickle-down island gossip or mouthy kid. You can handle it—I wouldn't have offered you a job if I thought otherwise—but I know it can be tough dealing with people who don't understand what you're capable of."

"Fuck it."

"Mouth, Bry."

"Who complained?"

"Doesn't matter. I reassured the parties involved, but since this is your first time back to work, I thought I'd give you some options."

"Like what?"

"You know Olivia isn't going to be with Tori in the culinary class anymore. Her father is—"

"Working on an engineering project in Houston and they have to go there for the summer. Yeah, I know." I left out that it was all Tori had been complaining about the past two weeks, pissed that Liv would be abandoning her for the whole summer and worried that Mr. Beckett was going to drop her cooking class and assign her to a group of tween boys.

"This is the first year we're offering that as a special elective. It's been a popular pick, so Tori definitely needs help. I thought I'd offer you the position, let you make the choice if you'd rather stay in one place, help Tori and have the kids come to you, or if you want to stick with the plan. I've hired a replacement for Liv, but I wasn't specific with her assignment so there's still time to switch things around, if you're interested."

The one thing I'd loved about being a counselor was that no two days were alike. I was a rock star with the kids—at least I had been, at fifteen. Keeping them safe had never been an issue—I was always alert and did head counts, and a lot of the time we were in the building anyway. But hearing that people had concerns made me second-guess myself. Fuck that.

"Stick to the plan."

He smiled. "I had a feeling that's what you'd say."

"Anything else?"

"Nah. Hey, remind your dad if he wants to go fishing tomorrow, the boat's pulling out at four thirty a.m."

"You guys are nuts," I said, turning my chair to leave.

"Have a good weekend; rest up—you're gonna need it!"

As I wheeled down the hallway my phone started blowing up in my backpack. I waited until I was out by the Charger before taking a look. Tori. The girl next door. Friend. Meddler extraordinaire.

Where ru?

Liv's last nite!!

Do NOT bail!! We need u!

No, actually, they didn't need me. Liv would be leaving whether I showed up or not. We didn't need an awkward good-bye with buffalo wings and forced smiles, although I didn't think it was her doing. Much ado about nothing was classic Tori, wanting us all to get along. I replied.

Me: Tired.

Tori: Huh? From sitting all day ;)

Me: Yeah. :p

Tori: Wimp

Me: Later

Setting the phone to silent, I tucked it away into the zipper pouch of my backpack; then I opened the car door and transferred to the driver's seat. After my accident, the Dodge Charger had been my incentive, my reason to get out of bed. I'd been working on my probationary driver's license and had my eye on it before I got hurt, but when the full impact of how my life had changed hit me, it hadn't been the first thing on my mind.

After a particularly rough day in physical therapy, my father told me about the car—that the fish fry at the VFW hall had helped pay for the adaptive controls and some of the paperwork. When I was ready for instruction, the lessons were waiting for me. The car was an extension of me now as much as my wheelchair. I loved it and the freedom that came with it.

Learning how to transfer into the seat and adjust everything so I could break down my chair had taken a lot of practice, but now it was second nature.

I popped off one wheel from my chair, then the other, before folding it up and stowing it away, over my shoulder and into the backseat. I pulled the front door closed and revved up the engine with the hand control, turning up Neck Deep on the stereo to obnoxious.

I peeled out of the lot, nose toward home, grinning at the guy I'd cut off as I made my right turn. The population of Crest Haven had tripled since Memorial Day. Tourists.

To him I was just a douche in a car.

I loved it.

The closer I got to home, the more I ignored the burning feeling in my gut that I was, in fact, wimping out. It was too late to turn around, and going there, well, what would it prove? I *was* tired—that was a fact, not an excuse. But if I was being honest with myself, it had more to do with self-preservation. Was it awful to admit I was relieved Liv would be gone for two months? That maybe the time apart would give our friendship a reboot.

Liv had been Liv, always there in our group of friends, hanging out, catching air from a wave or joking in the halls at school with the rest of the guys. She was hot in a tough, take-no-shit kind of way and had a great smile, and when she asked me to prom I said yes. Mercy date or not, it was nice to go. Normal.

We hung out for the month after. Nothing serious, hooking up a few times. Things got weird between us when she invited me over to watch a movie. Going over to people's houses was always a challenge because of stairs and space and carpet. Although I was more practiced at getting around, not every place was prepped to have me as a visitor. Liv had a finished basement right off the garage complete with a forty-two-inch screen and leather recliner couch. It was kind of cool to have a place to chill and watch a movie. With a girl. Alone.

We sat side by side on the couch, the movie on, but my mind was on her tight purple tank top. The way it hugged her. The space between her breasts that I imagined pressing my lips against. Not that I expected much to happen. I never knew if my body would be up to speed. I could get a hard-on in chemistry if my pants brushed against me, but with a girl next to me, when it would actually be useful, I couldn't count on it.

"I always liked you," she whispered, nipping my earlobe.

And . . . lift-off.

Liv straddled me, her tank top off and perfect breasts there, right in front of me, the way I'd imagined. Soft. Her skin smelled sweet, like vanilla. She rocked her hips against me. My fingers fumbled with the button on her cutoffs, when she reached down and undid them herself. It was happening.

And then it wasn't.

"Am I doing something wrong?" she asked.

"No," I said. We kissed some more, but the heat was gone. For me anyway. I stopped, pressed my lips together to turn away, but Liv didn't take the hint. She ran her tongue across my mouth, pecked at my lips.

"Stop."

"Bry, it's okay," she whispered.

"No, Shay, it's not." I turned my face away from her, then realized what I'd said.

That stopped her.

She leaned back, folded her arms across her bare chest. "I'm not Shay, is that it?"

"No," I said, but *was it*? That had popped out of my mouth so unintentionally.

"Tori told me—"

"Tori should shut her mouth," I said.

"Look, she didn't mean—"

"Is that what all of this is? Prom, hooking up—do you want this, or did Tori ask you to do it?" I couldn't even hook up without help. Anger at Tori replaced humiliation. That I could handle. The other stuff—the fact that Liv wouldn't look me in the eye, me fucking calling her Shay after all this time, the inability to get out of there quickly—it sucked.

She buttoned her shorts and slid off me, searching for her bra. I handed her the tank top, then moved to the edge of the couch, ready to transfer back to my chair. The leather was slippery and I face-planted on the floor. Liv shrieked, and was on her knees, ready to help me up.

"I got this," I said, pushing myself to sitting. My wheels were in reach. I hoisted myself up onto the chair. Liv took my hand in hers and sat down on the end of the couch. Minutes passed. There was a shootout on the television. Liv ran her thumb across the back of my hand. She looked at me then. Her eyes gutted me.

"I don't think I'm ready to handle this," she said.

"I'm not asking you to," I said.

I wrenched my hand from hers.

"Can you open the garage?" I asked. She nodded. We didn't speak again.

That.

That had been enough for good-bye.

When I got home, Mom was perched on the couch, book in one hand, coffee mug in the other. During the year, she taught language arts to freshmen at Crest Haven High. Before my accident, she used to teach at least one summer-school class or tutor, but she'd decided to take that summer off because she claimed she needed a break. I thought it was a load of horseshit and what she really wanted was to keep an eye on me. She looked up as I came through the front door.

"Hey, how was your swim?"

"Good; feeling pretty strong."

"Hungry? I've got some leftover chicken parm." She placed the mug down on a coaster and slid a bookmark into her paperback.

"Perfect."

I went to my room, hung my backpack on the hook near the door. One unexpected side effect of being para was becoming a neat freak. I wanted everything within reach. Simplified. No junk on the floor either. When I was in rehab, my parents converted their office into a new bedroom. It was bigger than my old one, but I missed being upstairs, closer to Matt, our late-night chats across our shared bathroom. But, #wheelchairperk—I didn't have to share a shower.

"Don't forget your wet bathing suit," my mother called from the kitchen. I dug into my bag and pulled out my trunks, then met her in the kitchen. She took the suit out of my hands.

"I can do that," I said.

She waved me off as she headed onto the deck. "No, eat before it gets cold."

The chicken parm and a can of Coke were on the table, waiting. Comfort food. I dug in, not realizing how hungry I'd been until dinner was in front of me. There wouldn't have been anything that good at Liv's get-together, more reason to feel better about not going, I told myself. Mom came back in, sliding the screen door shut behind her.

"Hey, got something in the mail today for you," she said,

sorting through a bunch of envelopes that were on the counter. She reached into a large, puffy white package and pulled out a black tee. She fanned it out over the chair to show me. It read "Don't Mind Me, I'll Take the Stairs," and had a wheelchair symbol popping a wheelie down stairs. I smiled. The shirt thing had become a joke between me and Mom, after my therapist gave me a That's How I Roll shirt on my last day of rehab. My dad didn't really like the dark humor—he was still convinced I'd walk again one day, and thought we were thumbing our noses at fate. I looked at it like a small act of rebellion. A way to show people I did have a sense of humor. That it was okay to laugh.

"Thought maybe you could wear it on Monday," she said, taking the seat across from me. There was something in her voice. Something that made me think she knew what Mr. Beckett had said to me.

"Let me guess, you talked to Owen," I said, twirling spaghetti around my fork.

"Okay, maybe I did," she confessed. "He wasn't sure if he was going to tell you."

"I wish he hadn't," I said, shoveling the spaghetti in my mouth.

There was a loud thud outside, then footfalls on the deck. My kid brother, Matt, was about to step into the kitchen when my mother stood up.

"Wait—do not come in the house with those work boots. You'll get mud and manure everywhere."

Matt grumbled as he pulled off his boots, then stepped through the sliding screen door a moment later, eyes large as he saw my food. He reached over and snatched the piece of chicken parm off my plate and inhaled half of it before giving it back to me.

"Hey," I said, but couldn't help laughing.

"All this manual labor works up an appetite." It was Matt's first summer working with Dad in our landscaping business. It shouldn't have jabbed at me, but it did. It was sort of unspoken that one day it would be Lakewood & Sons, and I'd always railed against it, taking the job at the rec center when I was fifteen almost out of spite. I didn't mind helping Dad, but I'd never seen myself slinging manure for the rest of my life. There was more to it than that, but it was never anything that interested me. Until the choice was taken away. And while I could still help now, going along on a job would be challenging.

Challenging. I hated that fucking word sometimes.

"Where's your father?" Mom asked.

"He had to go back out to get gas for the mowers. We have a big job tomorrow," he said, opening the refrigerator door and pulling out the carton of orange juice. He didn't bother with a glass.

"Matty, be civilized; I can fix you a plate," Mom said.

He closed the carton and put it back in the fridge. "No can do, Moms, got plans."

"Oh really?" she asked, leaning against the counter.

"Yeah, I thought you'd be out too, Bry," he said.

"What do you mean?" I asked.

"Liv's going-away party."

"Party? I thought it was a couple of people."

"Started out that way. Nick texted me—they're moving it back to the house, so I'm gonna hit the shower and go over."

Nick was Tori's twin brother. Our neighbor. My friend. Sort of.

"Are you telling me there's going to be a party next door?" Mom asked.

Matt grinned. "Chill, Mom. Nothing to worry about, we're just hanging out; we might come over and use the half-pipe too, if that's okay," he said.

"Who's 'we'?" she asked.

"A few of the guys. It's cool, Mom, really. Bry, you should come."

"Not really in a half-pipe kind of mood, Matt."

"Ha. You know what I mean. Aren't you and Liv, like, together?"

I felt my mother's eyes on me. After the circus that was prom, I'd kept tight-lipped about Liv, avoiding the subject of my nonexistent love life whenever possible. Mom really needed to go back to work.

"No," I said, and I swear it felt like it echoed around the kitchen.

"Bummer," he said. "Later." He thundered through the

house, taking the stairs two at a time. A force. So big and present, it took a few moments for the air to still. Mom sat down across from me. I finished up my plate.

"Why don't you want to go to the party?" she asked.

"It's not really a party, Mom. Anyway, I'm tired. I have a big night of *Realm Wars* planned."

"Look, Bry, it's none of my business, but it's summer and I think you should try and maybe . . ."

"Maybe what?"

"Get out a little more. That online game was fine in the beginning, but I hate to think—"

"Look, if I wanted to go I would. I just don't feel like being around anyone right now. Don't read more into it."

She nodded. I felt like shit.

"About before, what do *you* think about what Owen said? Do you think I can't handle the kids in case of emergency?" I asked.

"Bry, I worry about a lot of things. Every time you get into your car, or I know you're swimming, I say a prayer. It's automatic. A mom thing. You, being a camp counselor? No worries at all."

"Not even a Hail Mary?"

She smiled. "Okay, one. That's it. You're going to be great."

It sounded so easy when she said it.

I WOKE WITH A START, A NECK SPASM SENDING A jolt of pain down my right shoulder. There was a breeze in the car, fresh air carrying the salty scent of the ocean. I sat upright, still disoriented. Mom had the windows down, which must have meant we were off the parkway, close to my father's. I kneaded my neck, rubbed the sleep out of my eyes, and blinked a few times.

"How long was I out?" I asked.

"A good two hours—lucky; this ride always feels about an hour too long." Nan fanned her face with a stack of advertising mailers from every casino in Atlantic City. This was a multitasking journey. After they dropped me off at my father's, Mom and Nana were hitting the casinos on the way home.

It was a gorgeous blue-sky day. We were about fifteen

minutes away from the causeway that crossed over into Crest Haven. Fifteen minutes to sun, fun, and adventures that would wipe Gavin out of my memory. Kind of like a lobotomy, with sunscreen.

But I couldn't shake the feeling of dread.

Sometime in the middle of the night I'd realized I was making a huge mistake. *Spending the summer with my father?* All I'd thought about was getting away from Gavin, but being faced with the reality of the trade-off made me want to barf. Why hadn't I listened to Emma?

We saw my father about three times a year. There were never set days; it was more like whenever my mother had a feeling too much time had passed between visits, we'd jump in our car and take the three-and-a-half-hour trek to Crest Haven.

It hadn't always been this way.

I had sketchy, almost dreamlike memories of what life was like when my parents were actually married. Some good, like pancake breakfasts at the diner, walks in the park where they each held my hand and swung me every few steps, even one Christmas Eve when we strung our small tree with decorations we'd made out of photos and construction paper, then sat in the dim glow of the lights. Some terrible: Mom and me waiting and waiting at a restaurant for Dad to arrive, epic yelling matches where my father would storm out and Mom would end up crying.

One Saturday morning, about a month after first grade started, I woke up and my father was gone. Saturday had been our jam. Cartoon Network and scrambled eggs, the one meal he claimed he could make really well. I would whisk as he broke the eggs into the measuring bowl. That morning I'd taken out the bowl and whisk, but when I went to wake him up, my mother told me he was gone. "We'll be fine, Cass," she'd said, as if that was enough of an explanation. At the time I hadn't really understood it was permanent.

After that, we moved in with Nana Shirl, and she became my afterschool companion. She taught me to play gin while we sipped weak tea and ate dollar-store hot-pink sugar wafers. My mother went from job to job: waitress, retail sales, check-out person at the grocery store . . . nothing seemed to stick. If I thought the fights between my mother and father were epic, the throwdowns between Mom and Nana made them seem like casual conversation.

During those fights, I'd hide in my room to block it out, since I didn't really understand how my mother had ruined her life, which is what Nana would inevitably say. I'd imagine calling my father, asking him why no one had asked me where I wanted to stay. And while I saw my father at least twice a month on Saturdays, I never had the nerve to ask him why he left. I just enjoyed being his pal in the moment.

It wasn't until Dad married Leslie that I spent weekends with them in Hoboken. And even then it was only a handful of times. Leslie had a job in public relations, which sounded important and glamorous, and we got to see a lot of movies for free before they even came out. Mom never seemed jealous or angry, never made me feel like I needed to choose sides. After Dad remarried she went back to school to train as a dental hygienist, and then found a steady job with regular hours. The fights between her and Nan died down. We settled into normal.

At first Dad was in the picture for the big stuff—birthdays, holidays, an occasional outing to the zoo or the beach—but soon after Leslie had my half brother, Hunter, everything changed. Dad traded his human resources job for teaching and they bought the bed-and-breakfast and moved to Crest Haven. Getting together, even for the big things, was a hassle with the distance. Over time, we just fell out of seeing each other, and once I hit high school, I'd dodge his invitations purposely. Part was allegiance to Mom and Nan, part was I didn't want to deal with feeling not quite at home. I could get away with most of it, except for my one week during the summer. That was his.

It wasn't terrible. Dad and Leslie did their best to make me feel at home. Having a little brother as a sidekick for a week was kind of cool too. I had my own room, painted a dusky blue color that I'd picked out, white wicker furniture we purchased at a specialty store, and a bulletin board with shell-shaped pushpins. Dad had even given me an old-fashioned three-speed bike to get around the island. All of this was supposed to make me feel like I had a place there.

There was always a musty, not-lived-in smell in my room when I first arrived. The top of the vanity stayed pristine. No hollow in my bed to snuggle into. Nothing that said *home* to me. I was always "on" at Dad's house. My best behavior. Conversation light. At least it felt that way. I knew my mother had told him the reason for my sudden desire to spend the summer, but I didn't anticipate any heart-to-hearts. Maybe that was part of the appeal.

My mouth went dry as we passed the bait shop I used as a landmark on the way to Dad's. *ETA—five minutes.* There was a massive shark jawbone hanging above the door. Today it felt like I was driving into it, helpless. Was it too late to turn around? Now that I was out of school, avoiding Gavin would be easier, Ems had been right . . . but then there was Nate, the baker's son from Sugar Rush . . . *Don't shit where you eat.* Another one of Nan's favorite sayings. I was screwed.

We turned the corner of my father's street, only to get stuck behind a horse and buggy, the driver holding on to the reins as she spoke to her passengers and pointed toward a row of brightly colored houses on the street. One of my first years visiting, Dad and Leslie had sprung for a kid's carriage ride where the tour guide explained the architecture of Crest Haven. We learned about conical witches' hats roofs and widows' walks and gingerbread trim. I loved the way the town looked, like a place out of another century. My mother tapped the wheel with her index finger and sighed.

A few moments later we pulled up in front of a big white Victorian monster of a house, complete with gingerbread latticework and a mansard roof. The sign out front read, "Ocean Whispers . . . A Seaside Retreat," which sounded like a rehab clinic to me, and there I was, checking in to get over Gavin. A small iron fence surrounded the property, setting it apart from the other inns on the street. The wraparound porch had a row of white rocking chairs, which were vacant but moved gently back and forth in the breeze. Dad sat on the top step, but stood up when he saw us. Mom maneuvered into a spot reserved for check-ins and cut the engine.

"I don't know about this," I said, watching as my dad and Hunter trotted down the steps. Hands tucked in khaki shorts, lime-green polo with the collar up, my father looked like he just walked out of a Vineyard Vines ad—dressed to impress. Hunter was at his heels, holding a toy airplane over his head, dipping and weaving it through the air as they walked.

Mom and Nana both turned back to me. "What?"

"I think . . . I'm not sure I want to stay."

"Well, you picked a heck of a time to tell us," Nana said.

"Ma, not helping," my mother said, then reached for my hand. "Hey, you're here now. Give it a week—like normal, okay? If you want to come home after that, we can talk about it. I have a feeling you won't want to."

I nodded. Hunter peered into the car and grinned. He'd grown so much since Easter break. I smiled back at him, the feeling of dread lifting a little. Mom and I stepped out of the car. Nan rolled down the window and waved at Dad. That was the most greeting he would get from her.

"Cassidy," Dad said, opening his arms as I walked over to the sidewalk. Before he could hug me, Hunter got between us and flew his airplane right into my abs with a dramatic-sounding "Pppsshhhwwwrr." The plane dropped to the ground and he jumped back, making hand gestures that I guess represented a crash. He gave me a once-over.

"Your hair got long," he said.

"And you grew about ten inches," I said, tousling his mop top.

"Did not," he said.

"Okay, maybe two," I said. He threw his arms around me and squeezed. Hunter gave good hugs. He finally let me go, picked up his toy plane, and walked toward Nan, who was waving out the window for him to come over. My mother joined us at the back of the car, opened the trunk.

"Much traffic?" Dad asked, stepping off the curb to get the bags.

"Nah, I think we were ahead of it."

Mom tugged the duffel out of the trunk. I took it from her and slung it over my shoulder. Dad had my suitcase in his hand. This was really it.

"Leslie made some lunch. There's more than enough if you and Shirley want to stay for a bit."

My mother closed the trunk and crossed her arms. "Shirl's fingers are itching to get at the slots. We're staying over in AC tonight. Making a mini break of it."

"You're always welcome here. Owner's discount."

Mom chuckled. "You know how I feel about B&Bs."

"It's really not so bad," my father said, smiling. A beat passed between them, a shared memory, maybe? Something I wasn't privy to. Not long ago, after Mom had one of her seasonal decluttering episodes, I'd found a black-and-white photo strip of them in the trash. The kind you used to be able to get from an arcade photo booth. They must have been at the beach—Mom was in a bikini top, Dad was shirtless. They both looked so young and happy. They were even kissing in one of the shots, which should have skeeved me, but it made me sad. Now they stood before each other, pretty much strangers with one thing in common—me. Did anything last?

The front gate to the inn creaked. Leslie trotted over to where we were standing. She was younger than Mom, but not by much. Once it was clear that Les was in the picture for good, she and Mom became friends—not like me and Em were friends, maybe more like distant relatives who were pleasant with each other at the yearly family reunion.

"Sorry, was just finishing up a check-in," she said, giving Mom a loose hug. Mom patted her back before they pulled apart. "Are you staying for lunch?"

"Thanks for the invite, but no. We have to get back on the road before traffic gets too heavy," Mom said.

"We're so happy Cass is staying with us for the summer," Les said, giving my hand a squeeze. Mom opened her arms to me. I dropped my bag and wrapped my arms around her. Her mouth was right by my ear.

"Remember, I'm a phone call away."

"Yeah," I whispered.

"You're going to have a great time."

"I hope so," I said. I made my way around to the passenger side of the car. Nana sat like the queen in the front seat, fanning herself with the mailers. I bent over to kiss her cheek. She grabbed my hand and slipped something scratchy into it.

"Enjoy yourself, but not too much," she said, winking.

"Will do," I said, opening my hand. Two twenties.

And they smelled of Jean Naté.

We watched and waved as the car sputtered around the corner, then we went inside. Dad carried my suitcase. I carried my duffel. We climbed up the three flights of stairs to my room. I shouldered open the door and was greeted by the not-lived-in musty smell, even though the curtains billowed in the breeze. The bed was made, the wardrobe was open with empty hangers waiting to be filled. My stomach lurched as we tossed the bags on the bed. *You chose this, Cass,* I reminded myself.

"Why don't we leave this and have some lunch. You must be starving after that ride. We have chicken salad. Your favorite."

Leslie's chicken salad with pecans and red grapes *was* my favorite, but my eyes tingled with the threat of tears. I needed a moment to collect myself, take it all in.

"Um, I'd like to unpack first, if you don't mind," I said, stalling.

I walked over to the vanity. My name, CASS, was spelled out in a mix of blue sea glass and broken clam and scallop shells. I ran my finger along the C and laughed.

"Hunter did that," Dad said.

"I love it."

"You'll have to tell him," he said. "Take as long as you need to unpack, we'll be downstairs." I waited until he was on the second-floor landing before closing the door. I pulled out my phone and called Emma. She picked up on the second ring.

"Come home," she said.

"I, I . . . Ems." My throat closed up around her name. I leaned against the door and slid down, hand on my forehead. *The whole summer; what had I been thinking?*

"Cass?"

I took a breath. "I think I made a huge mistake."

Our late lunch became an early dinner, and after, I asked my father if it was okay to take the bike out. Hunter heard and begged to come along. I bit my tongue. I knew the polite thing would be to say, *Sure, come along*, but I wanted to be alone. I widened my eyes at Dad, hoping he would understand. He nodded.

"I need you to stay here, Hunter," he said.

"But why?"

"I can't finish the chocolate peanut butter ice cream on my own. Cass will be back soon."

"Can we have a game night then?" he asked. Dad looked to me—this was the bargaining chip to bike solo. Game night didn't sound like complete torture.

"Sure," I said. Dad checked the tires and filled the back one with air, and then I was off. It was still too early to ride my bike on the promenade—only pedestrians were allowed during the busy hours—so I rode alongside it on the street, going all the way down to the end, replaying my conversation with Emma in my head. She'd talked me off the ledge, or at least helped me come up with a game plan. Of course I was freaking out; getting over someone was not as simple as changing the scenery. It was a start, but I needed more direction.

You have to do something symbolic, she'd said. *Something physical to represent that it's over, something that will begin a new thought pattern.*

Emma's mom was on her third marriage, and she'd been through enough breakups with her to have some opinions on what worked when it came to moving on. She also had access to a self-help-book gold mine that could rival any library's.

I was ready for a new thought pattern, that much I knew. I had something in mind that would kick-start it. I pumped the bike harder, standing on the pedals to put more power behind it.

The streets were thick with pedestrian traffic. There were sun-kissed people toting beach bags and umbrellas, lumbering across the road after a day on the sand. Others were already dressed and heading out to dinner. Families lined up for mini-golf. The occasional horse and buggy clomped by. There was no reason not to be excited that Crest Haven, a place where people came from all over to enjoy the beach, the food, and the quaint atmosphere, would be my home for the summer. Was I ready to move on? Yes, but I needed to be far away from the crowds. The symbolic physical thing didn't need an audience.

I rode out farther than I ever had, to a beach at the end of a long straightaway. There was tall grass on either side as far as I could see, and the briny scent of the ocean got stronger as I pedaled to the end of the road. I was on the west side of the island, a place where locals hung out. The beach wasn't as pristine; the sand was more rocky than powdery, but it was empty and the water only lapped gently at the shore. I had a feeling it was Crest Haven's version of Meadowbrooke when the sun went down, but for now, it was the perfect place for my symbolic gesture. There were a few cars in the parking lot, and someone whistled as I locked my bike to the rack by the beach. I ignored it. Blinders on to everything except my mission to obliterate Gavin from my mind.

I kicked off my flip-flops and left them by the start of the path that cut through the beach grass. The sand was cool beneath my feet and I sank into it as I made my way toward the water, my heart still pounding from my ride. My legs ached, I was a sweat ball, but the exertion felt good. Purposeful. The only other people on the beach were a small family who were packing up, and two older guys who were sitting on lawn chairs next to a few fishing rods. I went a little farther down the beach and sat near the shoreline, letting the water lap over my feet. Thoughts of Gavin bubbled up without any effort. It was like the moment I got quiet, he was there.

You don't have to do this, Cassidy. It was one night.

The final straw had been the picture of Gavin and that girl, the one I probably wouldn't have seen except that she had tagged him in the shot and posted it on StalkMe. *How could he have been so careless? If only I hadn't seen it, would we still be together?* There were other clues—a card addressed simply to *Dimples*, which somehow crushed me all the more because those dimples were *for me*; times where he blew off answering me when I asked him where he'd been when I couldn't reach him—things I chose to ignore because I loved him, or at least I thought I did. Maybe I loved the *idea* of him, of having someone to walk down the halls with, someone to go to prom with, someone to make summer plans with. Was I really willing to put up with the constant doubt and questioning, wondering if he was telling the truth, all so I could have someone to hang with on a Saturday night?

Not anymore.

When I'd visited Ocean Whispers at Easter, I'd taken a walk on the beach by myself, deliriously happy because I'd discovered the secret of life, of love. Gavin and I were solid then, or at least it felt like it. Prom was a dream, like summer and Gavin's graduation, end-of-year parties . . . we'd even talked about how we were going to stick together in the fall when he went away to Penn. Defy the odds. It seemed possible. I'd knelt in the damp sand then and wrote "Cassidy Loves Gavin," whispered it to the ocean. I made a wish that it would be forever, and when the ocean swallowed up our names, it felt like something heard me.

Wish. That word.

I knelt in the damp sand again now and etched "Goodbye, Gavin" with my index finger along the waterline. I sat back and waited for the ocean to swallow it up, to take it in, to make it real, permanent.

Any moment the water would just rise up and erase it.

I waited.

And waited.

Maybe the tide was going out.

Or maybe as far symbolic physical gestures went, this one sucked.

What if I took a picture of it and posted it on StalkMe; maybe it would be like, *eff you*?

Lame, Cass.

There was something else I could do, something I knew would be tough to let go of, but wasn't that the point? It needed to be tough to mean something. I traced the Tiffany heart pendant around my neck with my finger. The one I'd put in the don't-take pile, the one I'd changed my mind about as I was leaving. I couldn't get rid of it this way, could I? I undid the clasp and let it drape over my hand for a moment before closing my fingers around it. It was the first piece of jewelry a boy had ever given me. It meant something, or it had at one point. Now it was just a reminder, wasn't it?

I saw this and thought of you, how lucky we are to have each other.

How lucky could we have been if things ended so badly? Had he given other girls a necklace? Told them the same thing?

Fueled by those thoughts, I tossed it into the water.

"Good-bye, Gavin," I whispered.

There. I could cross "symbolic gesture" off the getting-over-Gavin to-do list.

I stood up and wiped the sand off my butt, turned back toward the parking lot.

I walked a few steps before I froze.

My face flushed hot.

What the hell did I just do? It's a freaking silver Tiffany heart necklace! I spun back toward the ocean, stood at the water's edge, and scanned for anything sparkly. My pulse pounded in my ears. It had to be there, I'd only thrown it moments ago. The edges of my vision blurred. Tears.

I stepped into the water. The ocean was clear, calm, practically like bathwater. I treaded lightly, ignoring the pinch of the shells beneath my feet. The necklace should have been there, but I couldn't see it; the shells and pebbles close to the shoreline made it hard to differentiate anything. I walked out to smoother sand, the water just below my knees, and turned toward the beach—I hadn't thrown it any farther than where I was standing.

Nothing.

I went back to the beach, ignoring the looks from the old guys fishing.

Ignoring the snot running down my face.

The salty sting of tears on my cheek.

The necklace was gone.

Only it didn't make me feel better.

It was like I lost something all over again.

I took the path back to the parking lot, stopping to put on my flip-flops, shoving one foot, then the other into the thongs. The sun was about to set. The sky looked unreal, a burst of orange and pink with thin wispy clouds. So pretty. I needed to get back home before it got too dark. My legs ached.

I crouched down to undo the lock.

And then I lost it.

Total ugly cry, right by my bike.

I put my face in my hands.

It was over, it was really fucking over, and by leaving I made damn sure there wouldn't even be a chance to talk about it. This was for the best, wasn't it? Then why did it feel so crappy?

"Hey, hello?"

I looked up.

There was a boy sitting in the driver's seat of a black car parked a few feet away. He waved, gave me a small concerned smile. I swiped the tears and snot away from my cheek with the back of my hand and acknowledged him with a nod.

"Everything okay? Need help with the bike?"

"Oh, um, no, I'm good," I said, standing up. Of course he was cute, and there I was probably looking like I had the map of Europe across my face in blotches. Not that I really cared; I wasn't trolling the parking lot for a date.

"You seem upset," he said.

Nosy much?

"No, just you know, the sunset, it's so pretty," I said, gesturing toward the sky but realizing he probably didn't buy it. He laughed. The smile lit up his face. There was something about the tilt of his head, the way his hair fell, his pale-blue eyes—he looked familiar, but that was sort of impossible since

I was pretty sure I'd never seen him before. And fate and love and déjà-vu chance meetings were total and utter romantic bullshit.

I hopped on my bike.

"Be careful," he said, which sounded ominous.

Maybe I'd seen him on *America's Most Wanted*.

"It gets dark pretty quick, no lights on that road."

"Thanks for the tip," I said, pedaling away. I pumped fast, trying to outrun the setting sun. I couldn't shake the feeling of having seen the boy in the black car before. If he was so concerned about me and my bike, why hadn't he gotten out to help me? Was he some whacking-off parking-lot perv who wanted to lure me closer? Was he there to watch the sunset? Why was I thinking about a boy? Nan's words echoed in my head.

You girls need a new hobby.

For once, it was wisdom that I understood completely.

FOUR
BRYAN

I WATCHED IN MY SIDE MIRROR AS THE GIRL RODE her bike toward town, back along South Ferry Road. If she picked up her pace she'd probably make it before it got too dark. Tourists usually didn't venture to Crescent Beach. Most locals didn't either, unless they wanted to party, fish, or search for Crest Haven diamonds, which weren't exactly diamonds but quartz pebbles you could polish up to shine like gemstones. She wasn't local, that much I knew. What had she been crying about?

"Duuuuuude."

I startled. Matt laughed, pulling open the door and sliding into the passenger seat. He put his skateboard between his knees and adjusted his seat belt.

"Christ, could you be any louder?"

"Thanks for picking me up, bro. Was going to tell you to come over and say hi but I saw you were otherwise occupied. Who was the hot girl with the bike?"

I ignored him and started the engine.

"You reek of pot, Matty. Don't you have body spray or something?"

He sniffed his tee. "Shit, really? Maybe we could hit up CVS and I can bum an Axe tester. Grab some Combos while I'm there."

I made a K turn out of the lot. Matt yelped to the group of kids at the end of the parking lot. There was a reciprocal yell as we pulled out. I kept my eyes on the road.

"Seriously, you should have come over. Are you too good for us now? Nick, Tom, and Jake were asking about you," Matt said. He had his hand out the window, letting it go slack against the breeze as I drove.

"I didn't feel like hanging out, so what's the point?"

"The point is they're your friends too."

"We don't have a whole lot in common anymore," I said. The truth was Tom and Jake had stopped coming around after I got hurt, as if being para was contagious, but it wasn't like I'd ever been super close with them in the first place. Nick on the other hand had been a regular at my house, along with Wade and Tori. He was closer to Matt now than me. They didn't ignore me or anything, but once we were outside of school, we didn't hang out much. I got that they didn't know what to say, but there really wasn't anything *to* say. "I'm kind of over hanging out in a parking lot."

"Whatever, I still think you should trick out your chair and try the half-pipe. What about surfing? Are you gonna get back in the water? Did you see that video I sent you? I think we could do it. We could help you out."

Yes, I'd seen the video he sent me. And the one Wade sent. And the one Tori had sent me too. Inspirational videos with paraplegics doing *amazing* things. Jumping out of planes, scuba diving, snowboarding. Things I could do too if only I set my mind to it. They meant well, of course. People always did, but I wasn't about to do something I wasn't ready for. I wanted to surf again, but I just wasn't sure I wanted the help he was offering.

"Yeah, cool, maybe. Why couldn't you get a ride home with Nick?" I asked, changing the subject.

"He wanted to stay. Gotta get home for the raid tonight. You in?"

Was I in? *Realm Wars* raids were my life at the moment.

"Yeah, I thought you forgot, you know—"

"Holy shit, there she is," Matt said. We'd caught up to the sunset girl. She stood on her pedals and coasted for a bit before she began cycling again.

"Man, I could bury my face in that ass," Matt said.

I backhanded him in the arm. "Matt."

He undid his seat belt. "C'mon, Bry, slow down. I just want to talk to her."

I felt protective of sunset girl for some reason. Whatever she'd been crying over, she didn't need to be hassled by my horned-out stoner brother. There were no cars coming in the other direction, so I slowed a bit and moved halfway to the other lane to go around her. Matt took that as a sign to chat her up. I pulled him back by his tee.

"Dude. Don't. Really."

"C'mon, it's summer girl season, Bry. I'm just having a little fun," he said, leaning out the window again.

Sunset girl turned her head toward us, her eyes wide when she saw Matt hanging out of the car. The bike wobbled and she came to a stop, putting her feet down. Matt opened his mouth to speak but I pulled back on the gas and we sped off, peeling out. He braced himself on the window frame as we picked up speed, his hair blowing back, big stupid grin on his face. He finally pulled himself in, hooked his seat belt, and leaned back in his seat.

"I fucking love summer," he said.

Monday morning I was even more nervous than I'd been going back to school for the first time. As much as I'd known I could handle the kids when I talked to Owen on Friday, being faced with the reality of it was a different story. I sat in the multipurpose room, waiting for Wade and checking over my roster for the bazillionth time. Which parent didn't think I could handle this? Would I be able to tell? Of course they were right. What did I think I was doing?

Wade strolled into the multipurpose room five minutes before we were supposed to be at drop-off. He was shirtless, camp polo slung over his shoulder and still wearing sunglasses. He scarfed down a bagel as he crossed the gymnasium floor, nodding and waving to the other counselors with his free hand. By the time he reached me, he had finished his breakfast and was busy shrugging on the polo. His wet hair hung down to his shoulders; he pulled it back with one of the elastics he kept around his wrist.

"Lake, I think you can lose the clipboard."

"I think it makes me look like I know what I'm doing."

"You do know what you're doing." He finally took off the shades and slid them into the front of his polo. He grabbed the clipboard from me, eyes scanning our camp roster.

"Why are you letting ten rug rats get you so torqued up?" He handed it back to me.

"Don't know. Maybe because that's ten lives we'll be responsible for the entire summer."

He flinched in mock surprise. "Man, when you put it that way."

It was a move that was supposed to make me lighten up, but I white-knuckled the hell out of the clipboard anyway. I hadn't told Wade about my conversation with Owen, and didn't plan to, but my mind kept flipping between confidence and doubt, and at the moment doubt was winning. I hadn't been nervous when I held the same job at fifteen. At fifteen I'd been like Wade. No worries. Work was just a few hours to pass the time before hitting the surf and checking out the summer girls.

Wade ran his hand in front of my face a few times. "Geez, you really are wound up. Bry, the first time you pop a wheelie for these kids you'll be their superhero. C'mon."

We made our way out to the blacktop for drop-off. Campers had already started showing up. A lady stood in our designated area holding hands with a blond boy who looked like he might cry at any moment. He had an Avengers lunch box dangling from his clenched fist.

"Hey, who's your favorite?" I asked.

The kid looked up, eyes darting over my wheelchair, then back to the woman who I assumed was his mother. She nodded at him and smiled. "Go ahead."

He swung the lunch box back and forth and stared at the ground again. "My favorite is Captain America. That's who I was for Halloween."

"I think Iron Man could take him," Wade said, crouching down to the kid's eye level. His mom glanced at me fast, then back at Wade.

"Name?" I asked.

"Colby Somers," she said. I scanned the list, all the while wondering if Colby's mom was the one who had voiced her concern. Was she giving me the side-eye?

"Yep, right place. Hi, I'm Bryan."

"I'm Maggie Somers. He can be a little shy at first, but when he warms up he'll probably talk your ear off. Hey, Cobes, I'm leaving now, okay?"

Still in an Avengers debate with Wade, Colby barely waved at his mom. She smiled at me before heading out. I put a check mark next to his name. *One down, nine to go.*

"Since my man Colby-Wan here was first today, he gets to be line leader. Sound cool, Bry?" Wade asked. In five minutes Colby had changed from constipated little dude to beaming model camper when he heard Wade's nickname for him.

Maybe things would work out fine.

"Hey, Bryan!"

I turned toward the sound of my name.

"H-bomb! Didn't know you were going to be here," I lied. Hunter Emmerich was my chem teacher's son and had been my afterschool buddy on several occasions during the year when I helped Mr. E. take stock in the lab.

He scrunched up his face. "You did too."

I pretended to go down the list. "Hmmmm . . . no H-bomb here."

"Really?" He looked panicked.

"Yeah, oh wait, here you are." I high-fived him and all was right with the world. Mr. Emmerich smiled.

"He could not get here fast enough."

"Bryan, this is my half sister!" Hunter pointed to a girl

who stood behind Mr. Emmerich's shoulder. She had her arms crossed and was looking in the opposite direction. Mr. E. tapped her on the shoulder. She turned. I nearly dropped my clipboard.

Sunset girl.

Her eyes flashed with recognition, then lowered, taking in my wheelchair. From the furrow between her brows I figured it was the last thing she expected to see. I'd never gotten out of the car that night.

"This is Bryan—he spells it with a *y*, isn't that cool? This is Cassidy; she screams in her sleep. She's working here this summer too."

"Hunter," she said. Her cheeks reddened.

"You're working here?"

Cassidy nodded. "I don't actually scream in my sleep, by the way, only when someone wakes me by getting all up in my face." She bent over and tickled Hunter's side. He shrank back, giggling.

I smiled. "I do spell my name with a *y*. Nice to meet you, again."

"Again?" Mr. E. said.

Cassidy studied me, the corner of her mouth turned up slightly. "Yes, I sort of met Bryan the other night when I was out riding my bike. He practically ran me over with his car. Guess I'll be seeing you around." She crossed her arms again and walked away, leaving me with a confused Mr. Emmerich.

"I didn't practically run her over, sir," I said, wondering why she'd . . . of course. She had no clue that was my brother's idea to hang out the car and drool, or that I was trying to save her from his awkward advances. I laughed. Touché, Mr. E.'s daughter.

"Later, Dad," Hunter said, giving Mr. E.'s legs a squeeze before joining Wade and Colby. Mr. E. waved and walked toward the rec center, jogging a bit to catch up to Cassidy.

"Who was that blond chick?" Wade asked.

"Mr. E.'s daughter. Cassidy."

"No chance of her name being on our roster, eh?"

"I'm surprised you didn't know she was going to be here," I said.

"Me too. I'll have her info by the end of the day," he said.

Of course he would.

The rest of drop-off was easy. Too much went on for me to even worry about which parents had complained. When all the kids were accounted for, we herded them back to the gym for morning sing-along. As we passed Owen's office, he called my name.

"I'll catch up," I said to Wade. He saluted me, as did the rest of the line. Twenty minutes into camp and the kids were already his minions.

I wheeled into Owen's office, and right there in my line of vision was the ass my brother had wanted to bury his face in. Total unintentional #wheelchairperk was being able to get an eyeful of a girl's rear view without seeming like a perv. I looked away quick. I was already on uncertain ground with her and wanted to at least apologize for the other night before getting caught checking her out. She stepped aside to make room for me, still wearing the same little upturned half smile/half smirk from when she met me at drop-off.

"Bry, could you show Cassidy where Tori's room is? I have to get to the multipurpose room before the masses revolt."

"Um, yeah, sure," I said.

"Great." Owen grabbed a whistle that dangled from a hook on the wall and shuffled around his desk to our side. He motioned for us to go out ahead of him. Cass went first. I followed, purposely looking anywhere but at the fray on her cutoffs.

"So, it's this way," I yelled over the noise of the hallway, motioning with my chin and pushing off ahead of her. She had her camp polo slung over her arm, her eyes scanning the hallways, looking everywhere but at me. We turned the corner into a longer, less chaotic hallway. The test kitchen was at the end of it.

"Hey, about the other night," I said. "I didn't . . . well, I wasn't trying to scare you or anything, you know that, right?"

She stopped. I reversed so I could look her in the eye.

"Then what were you and your cretin buddy trying to do?"

I laughed. "That cretin is my brother, and I was trying to . . . well, he thought . . . that was his way of flirting. I sped away because I was trying to stop him from embarrassing the hell out of himself. Sorry if we made you feel uncomfortable."

"That's his idea of flirting?"

"Yeah, I know. He's fifteen, kind of clueless."

"Well, okay, apology accepted, but tell him he's a little scary."

"I tell him that all the time."

She smiled then, not the little side-smirk one, but full on. It was distracting. For a moment I thought she was going to say something else, but we resumed our trek toward Tori's room. Cassidy took a breath in, and this time I didn't imagine it. She was about to say something but pressed her lips together instead.

"What?" I asked. She stopped and looked at me.

"You used to surf, didn't you?" she asked.

It was the last thing I anticipated her asking. My face must have shown it. Her brow furrowed again, a little line right between her eyebrows. "That was awkward . . . was that awkward? Sorry. It's just, you looked familiar the other night and I couldn't place you, but when I saw you this morning . . ."

"Have you seen me surf?" I asked. There's no way I would have not remembered meeting Cassidy Emmerich.

She shook her head, ran her fingers across the polo that was slung over her arm.

"Then what?"

"I was here last summer when they had that, um, fish fry

for you, to raise money. They had a big display of photos and stuff, a video too . . . of you surfing . . . that's why you looked familiar. I wasn't sure at first, but when I saw Mr. Beckett, I remembered meeting him there too, and it all kind of clicked."

"Wow."

"I hope it was okay that I brought it up. I mean, it was kind of driving me crazy where I'd seen you before."

"I'm so sorry," I said.

"For what?"

"That you had to sit through something as lame as a fish fry. You know, if I'd had anything to do with that, I would have made it a burrito fest or something. Fish fry just sounds so sad, so very, very sad. And I hate fish."

Her smile rearranged the atoms in the hallway. *Damn.*

"Is that . . . well, is that how you got hurt? Surfing?"

"No, nothing that exciting. So you've been to Crest Haven before? How is it that we've never met? Your dad was my chem teacher." I began pushing down the hallway again, hoping my vague answer wasn't a turnoff. I just didn't feel like rehashing my accident at the moment, not after I'd made her smile that way. Not after we were actually getting along.

"I guess I've always sort of kept to myself, done things with my dad's family. I visit a few times a year, but I usually spend a week in June. This is the first time I'm down here for the whole summer."

She was here for the whole summer. I could get used to seeing her every day.

"Cool. What made you want to work here?"

She shrugged. "Don't know, change of scenery, I guess. Or maybe it's this fashion-forward polo and goofy logo. Do you think any self-respecting manatee would ever wear a beanie copter hat?"

"No, I don't."

Just then, Tori opened the door to the test kitchen, her eyes darting between Cassidy and me, as if she'd caught us in the middle of something suspicious.

"Are you my help?"

"Co-counselor, yes," Cassidy said. "You must be Tori."

"And you're ten minutes late."

Cassidy bristled.

"Tori, this is Cassidy. Owen asked me to show her around; it's my fault she's late."

"Whatever, look, we have, like, no time before we have to get to the sing-along, so whenever you feel like getting in here to pitch in, that would be awesome." She spun and went back in the room.

"What's her deal?"

I knew exactly what Tori's deal was, but Cassidy didn't need that baggage this early in the morning. Anyone who'd be taking Olivia's place was toast, even though it wasn't intentional.

"First day, lots to do," I answered.

"Well, thanks for the escort," Cassidy said.

"Anytime."

She was about to go in, but turned back. "I'm sorry if I made you uncomfortable before."

"You didn't."

"So, we're cool then?"

"Totally."

"Oh, and it's Cass. My friends call me Cass," she said. Tori appeared again, shaking her head as she reached for the doorknob. Cass waved and scooted into the room in front of her. Tori leveled me with a look.

"What?"

"Really, Bryan? You are so basic sometimes."

With that she closed the door, leaving me in the hallway with a stupid grin on my face. If that was being basic, so be it.

Cassidy Emmerich remembered me from my picture . . . which meant she'd thought about me . . . which meant—well, I really didn't know what it meant, except that I suddenly felt as high as my brother must have been the other night when he'd been hanging out the window. I made my way back to the multipurpose room.

I fucking loved summer.

FIVE

CASSIDY

"SO YOU AND BRYAN KNOW EACH OTHER?" I ASKED as Tori closed the door.

"Yeah, since, like, forever."

"He seems cool."

"He's a great guy. My friend is sort of seeing him. She was supposed to be my co-counselor this summer," she said, looking right through me. There was an edge to her voice, not nasty exactly, more protective. I'd been employed for all of ten minutes. How could I be on someone's bad side already?

"Your friend was supposed to have this job?" My father had mentioned pulling strings, but I couldn't imagine he had that much influence to knock someone out of their position. He was just a chem teacher slash bed-and-breakfast owner. Not exactly the summer camp mafia.

"Yes, but she had to leave for the summer, so it's not really your fault or anything, just, you know, kind of a bummer for me."

"Look, I'm sorry I'm late; my dad told me to go to the office first. I had no clue what position I had. I'd never want to take someone's job from them," I said. Her features visibly softened. She closed her eyes, took a deep breath, and seemed to reboot herself.

"Let me try this again . . . Hey, I'm Tori, welcome to Camp Manatee. Sorry I'm being a total bitch. I'm in the middle of a crisis, not what you want to walk into the first day."

It was a relief the source of her annoyance wasn't me. "I'm Cassidy."

She motioned for me to follow her to the front of the room. The test kitchen was large and bright with rows of tables facing a long island at the front of the room that had a sink and stovetop built into it.

"Do you have any experience in a kitchen?"

"Actually, yeah, my last job was in a bakery. And I do a lot of cooking at home, fend-for-myself kind of stuff. Nothing fancy." I didn't add that my bakery job was mostly working the cash register or adding embellishments to cupcakes, but at least it sounded impressive, and for some reason I wanted her to like me. It would be nice to have an actual friend. Ems and I had been texting like crazy, but I craved real conversation with someone other than my six-year-old half brother.

Adorable as he was, I wasn't sure I had much more to add to his constant shark chatter.

"Wow, cool. It's not like I'm running the cordon bleu of camp programs or anything, but any experience is helpful. We're icing and decorating cupcakes today, thought I'd keep it simple. We can't do anything really cool, like chopping or range-top cooking, due to insurance issues." She crouched down, opened a large drawer, and pulled out two cupcake tins.

"So, um, what's the crisis?" I asked, following her to the far end of the island. She placed the tins down on the counter next to a shiny silver KitchenAid mixer and lifted the beater back. Chocolate cake batter dripped from it. My stomach growled. I'd missed out on the breakfast part of bed-and-breakfast that morning.

"I had three dozen cupcakes ready to go today, packed them up last night, but my brother and his stoner friends had a midnight snackfest and there were only eight left this morning. I made those suckers from scratch too. It killed me to use box mix for these, but there just wasn't time."

I stifled a laugh at the "brother and his stoner friends" comment. Funny as it sounded to me, I didn't think Tori would appreciate it. She unclamped the bowl from the base and was about to pour the batter into the tins when I stopped her.

"Wait, don't you have to grease them?"

Tori gasped and placed the bowl down. "Damn, thanks,

good call. I don't know where my head's at today. There should be cupcake liners over in that far cabinet."

I walked over to the row of cabinets and opened a few until I came across one that held supplies. Napkins. Straws. Enough plastic wrap to encase the Empire State Building. Tinfoil sheets . . . and finally, cupcake liners. I stood on tiptoe, knocked them off the shelf, and caught the box in my other hand. Tori held up her hand for me to toss them. I did and she missed, laughing.

"We make a great team," she said, picking them up.

There was a crackle over the PA system. "All counselors report to the multipurpose room for morning rally."

"Oh shit," Tori said.

I grabbed the cupcake liners from her hand. "I'll line, you pour. Do we have to go to . . . what was it . . . morning rally?"

She picked up the batter bowl and followed while I frantically lined the tins.

"Since we don't have a set group of kids, no, not all the time, but Mr. Beckett wants everyone there on the first day and Fridays; that's when he makes announcements and stuff."

"And what about the camp shirt, do we have to wear those?"

"Only mandatory for the special electives counselors on field day."

We finished lining and pouring and Tori popped the tins in the oven, then we went off to morning rally.

The multipurpose room was writhing with kids. I spied

Bryan. He was slightly apart from his group, glancing at a clipboard and then the kids around him, holding his index finger in the air, like he was doing a head count. He looked so much more serious than on our walk to Tori's room.

I couldn't believe he was the same guy from the other night at the beach who almost ran me over. Maybe that was exaggerating—the car did sort of swerve out of my way—but the guy hanging out. *Ugh*. Boys. The apology was welcome. I was so relieved he didn't press me further about the night, like why I'd been bawling my eyes out, and I hoped I hadn't overstepped by asking him about how he was hurt. At the fish fry the year before, there hadn't been any mention of how it happened exactly, just the pictures and talk of his progress. When I saw him in the wheelchair at drop-off, it jogged the memory of where I'd seen him before. He seemed like an upbeat, laid-back guy for having had such a shitty thing happen to him. *And* he was seeing someone.

Good for him.

"Cassideeeeeee!" Hunter yelled, and waved wildly. I waved back as he tugged on the shirt of the tall boy standing next to him, a counselor I hadn't met. The dude with the dark-blond man bun. His eyes followed the reach of Hunter's outstretched arm until they landed on Tori and me. Tori lifted her hand in greeting. He trotted toward us. Tori fidgeted, her mouth twitching into a barely there smile, as if she didn't want to seem happy but couldn't help it. It wasn't hard to see why.

Man-bun dude was hot and he knew it, but not in a cocky way, just the way he carried himself, broad shoulders back, chin lifted. Everything about him said, "Hey, world, I'm here, enjoy me." He even made the ridiculous camp polo look good.

"Hey, I'm Wade," he said, holding his hand out to me.

Firm, confident grip. Charming green eyes. Must. Stay. Away. That and the way the hint of a smile disappeared from Tori's face when Wade introduced himself to me. She had a *thing.* Subtle, but it was there. Wonder if he realized? Lots of girls probably had a thing for Wade. I would not be one of them, no matter how tempting. *New hobbies.*

"Hunter's told us all about you."

"That kind of scares me," I said.

"Nah, nothing too bad. Don't let this one boss you around." His eyes went to Tori.

"Funny," she said, in a way that let him know it was not funny at all.

"C'mon, Tori, first day of camp, help me make a good impression on the new girl." He jabbed the air in front of her, bouncing from one foot to the other.

Tori rolled her eyes, but she smiled. "Would you just grow—"

The lights in the multipurpose room flickered off and on, and loud, thrumming bass spilled out through the sound system. Wade and Tori stopped their exchange and we turned toward the front of the room. Someone had started the kids clapping along with the music. I folded my arms across my chest. Just when I thought things couldn't get any cornier, a six-foot manatee entered the room.

A six-foot manatee wearing a beanie copter hat.

A six-foot manatee *shuffled* in, that was actually the best word. It waved and bopped along to the music. Mr. Beckett held up one of its fins as they danced their way to the middle of the floor.

"Did you know about this?" Tori shouted at Wade. He shrugged and clapped along, straight-toothed grin lighting up his face as he walked back over to Bryan and his group. He was one of those guys who could make anything look cool, like we were the weird ones for not wanting to join in.

"Is this a new thing?" I asked. She nodded.

I caught Bryan's eye. He put his clipboard over his face then took it away, shaking his head and grinning. Synchronized clapping with mascots wasn't his thing either. For some reason, that was comforting, like I had an ally. The music died down and Mr. Beckett tapped his handheld mic before speaking.

"Welcome to the first day of the rest of your summer!"

A cheer exploded through the room.

"We've got so much in store for you! Bur first, let's give a warm welcome to our new camp mascot, Monty!"

"It has a name," Tori said, covering her eyes.

"On the count of three, 'Hello, Monty!' One, two, three—"

Mr. Beckett held his microphone out to a very uninspired yelp of *Hulllo, Monteee*. Some of the younger kids didn't look so enthused about a gigantic fake manatee being in such close proximity.

"You can do better than that . . . again, let's give a warm welcome to Monty!"

It was now or never, I thought. Just jump in and accept that this is what I'd chosen to do for the summer. Goofy as hell, but kind of exciting—new. Different. And about as opposite from Gavin, with his indie-rock, flask-carrying, floppy-haired existence, as I could get. When the count of three was over, I joined in, adding my voice to the chaos:

"Hello, Monty!"

Camp had officially begun.

By the time Friday rolled around, I was more than ready for the weekend. The first week of camp was fun, but being Tori's second-in-command was intense. She was type A squared and had plans for each and every group that came in. The first week was all about baking, and ended with a craziest-cupcake contest that we judged. The following week was going to be nutritious snacks. If anyone could make it fun, I supposed it could be her. She even seemed to be warming to me, as long as I kept up with her.

And I kept up with her, but now I was ready for two days of freedom.

Well, sort-of freedom. I'd already promised my dad and Leslie that I'd babysit for Hunter that night so they could go to a wine-tasting dinner. My Friday night would be chilling with Hunter and unwinding with a game of Hedbanz. Winning at life and Gavin free! That was me.

I grabbed my backpack. "See ya Monday!"

Tori looked up from her phone. "Wait, where are you going?"

"Um, home, why?"

"Our first staff meeting is in fifteen minutes."

"Oh crap, I'm supposed to babysit at seven."

"Relax, you'll be home long before then. Mr. Beckett can talk the bark off a tree, but he usually keeps these short and sweet. C'mon."

Tori packed up her bag. We did one final sweep of the test kitchen to make sure we'd put everything away. She locked the door and we walked to a room at the opposite end of the hallway. Wade and Bryan were already there and waved us over. Chairs were arranged in a large circle, which always meant, ick, *sharing*. Tori took the seat closer to Wade. I sat on her other side, took out my phone, and texted Dad I'd be late but not to worry.

"What are you doing here?"

I looked up as Tori spoke. A boy with dark hair and a backward baseball cap sauntered over to her.

"Nice to see you too, Tor." He glanced at me. Tori sighed.

"Cass, this is Nick, my brother."

He tilted his chin in greeting as if it were too much effort to do anything else.

"The cupcake stealer," I said.

"My reputation precedes me." He grinned as he slumped into the seat next to me, manspreading enough to make me feel claustrophobic.

"No, really, Nick, why are you here?" Tori talked around me. "Staff meeting, right?"

"What?"

"Maybe you two should sit closer," I said, getting up. Tori scooched over and she and Nick continued to hiss at one another. I took the empty seat next to Bryan. I barely noticed his wheelchair. It was compact and almost sporty.

"Checking out the wheels, eh?" he said. My face flushed.

"Uh, I just . . . was thinking how you looked like you were in a folding chair. I didn't really see your wheels until I was right here. That's weird to say, isn't it. Please stop me before I stay something else stupid."

He smiled—the same friendly, laid-back grin he'd given me from his car that night we met at Crescent Beach.

"So you survived your first week," Bryan said.

"Yeah, how about you?"

"Piece of cake, but I'm ready for the weekend."

"Tell me about it," I said. "Any plans?"

He shook his head. "Nothing big. Some of us are getting

together right after this at Sip N' Freeze a few blocks over. You should come."

"Sip N' Freeze? Let me guess, ice cream?"

"They have thirty-two flavors of slush too. Pretzels. Me," he said. "It's not strictly about the ice cream. It's mostly to talk about whoever doesn't show up."

"Sounds fun, but I can't—I'm babysitting tonight."

"Babysitting? After a week of this, that's hard-core, Cass," he said.

"That's me, hard-core."

A cheer went up as Mr. Beckett arrived. He raised his hands for us to quiet down.

"What an awesome first week of camp. Thank you, guys, for being so enthusiastic and thank you for staying after. For starters, I'd like you all to go around quick and introduce yourselves with an adjective that begins with the same letter as your first name."

Groans.

"Guys, really, I won't keep you long; the sooner we get through the corny ice breakers, the sooner you'll be on to your weekend. Promise. We're a team, and knowing each other's names is important. The alliteration will help you remember—I swear, there's a purpose. I'll start—hey, I'm Optimistic Owen."

Just let me die. Now.

My mind went blank. White noise. An adjective that began with the letter *C*?

Cool? Crazy? Corny? Catty? I didn't want to be known as catty. Maybe everyone had played this game before, because my turn seemed to be coming up way, way too quickly. I didn't imagine Nick would come up with something that fast. *Think. Think. Think, Cass.*

"Notorious Nick."

Even he had a good one.

"Trendy Tori."

"Warped Wade."

"Badass Bryan."

All eyes were on me. Deer in the freakin' headlights. *C* is for cookie . . . oh damn. I cleared my throat, my brain desperately searching for an adjective.

"Um . . . Catastrophic Cassidy?"

Mr. Beckett grinned. "Is that a warning?"

Laughter. My cheeks burned, but thankfully it was over.

After everyone had been introduced, Optimistic Owen went over a few basic camp procedures—policies for drop-off, that cell phones could be used only during breaks and in emergency situations, discipline issues. It was pretty basic, mostly like school, but with goofy polo shirts and a paycheck.

"And one last thing," he said, holding up a stack of paper. "This year's scavenger-hunt clues. Take one as you leave, or if it's easier you can download it from the rec center website. If you're not familiar—each year we run a scavenger hunt for the counselors. Yes, more team building, but with prizes. I promise, guys, this is a good one. Once you guess all the answers correctly, each word will be a hint toward what the grand prize is. The only way you can enter is to answer everything. And the only way you can win is if those answers are right. Work in teams of two. If you need a partner, let me know, I can hook you up," he said, eyes directly on me. Great. That's what I got for calling myself Catastrophic Cass. Wade leaned over to me.

"Cassidy, wanna partner up?" he asked. I doubted he heard the word *no* much. I probably should have been grateful—maybe he was just being nice, but I noticed Tori was casually watching our convo unfold. My allegiance was to her, and if turning down green eyes kept me in her good graces, then I'd do it. I also didn't want to make the Sugar Rush Nate mistake again. If Bryan was dating someone, then he wouldn't be looking for a hookup. He was safe. A friend. I just couldn't tell with Wade.

"Oh, thanks, I was actually going to see if Bryan wanted to team up. What do you say?" I turned to him.

"Sure, I'm in," Bryan said.

Mr. Beckett clapped to get everyone's attention.

"That's it, meeting adjourned—if you're a special electives counselor or not assigned to a specific age group, please see me before you leave. Otherwise, go enjoy the weekend."

"That means us," Tori said.

We walked up to Mr. Beckett, along with a few other counselors, including Nick.

"We're a little understaffed this summer, and since you guys don't have a set age group, there's a few odd jobs that need to be delegated. If you end up working extra hours, you'll be compensated," he said, giving us another handout with our names and a job description next to each.

"What's towel duty?" Tori asked.

"Just stocking the towels in the pool in the morning. I thought you and Cass could alternate."

"I do a lot of prep in the morning," Tori said.

"I can do it. I don't mind," I said to her.

"Really?"

"Yeah, sounds good."

"Great, Cass," Mr. Beckett said. "You should come in about a half hour earlier, starting Monday."

Tori pulled me aside.

"Are you sure you're okay doing all that work? I mean, I can do it once in a while; I don't want to sound like a diva. I just don't know how I'm going to make time in the morning."

"How hard could towel duty possibly be? I've watched you all week, all the prep work you do for the class. I don't mind pitching in like this." I didn't add that I would have helped her with her stuff too, but she seemed to want things the way she wanted them, so I backed off.

She looked a little skeptical, but smiled. "Okay then, have a good weekend."

"You too," I said. I passed Bryan on the way out. "Have

fun at Sip N' Freeze. Don't talk about me too much, partner."

He smiled. "Can't make any promises unless you're there."

"Next time," I said, surprised at the warm rush his smile induced.

Maybe being around him wouldn't be as safe as I thought.

SIX
BRYAN

FROM APRIL TO OCTOBER, SIP N' FREEZE WAS A Crest Haven institution. It had been that way for as long as I could remember. My parents had even hung out there when they were in high school—there was a picnic table near the back where they'd etched their initials in their sophomore year. A few years ago, when they updated the rotting picnic tables with an eco-friendly recycled-wood substitute, my father had gotten the board with their initials and had a new mantel for our fireplace made. It was a reminder of how deep our roots were in Crest Haven. It was a staple. A constant. And it was ground zero for scoping out summer girls.

I got there before Wade and Tori and found a spot. Parking was a definite #wheelchairperk. It was early enough in the night, so there were no hordes of tourists or lines that stretched out to the street. I pushed myself up to the window to order. No menu necessary. Every summer, every time, Coke float and a soft pretzel. My only issue these days was that the counter made me feel like a five-year-old because I had to strain to look over it. I learned to stay back a bit; it was easier to make eye contact that way. Besides, I knew most of the people who worked there and everyone was cool about it.

When my turn came I wheeled up, my order practically out of my mouth before I saw her. Shay Foster. Wearing the tight little uniform shirt that had also given the place its nickname of Nips N' Tease. Her dark hair was back in the ponytail she preferred for field hockey season, but I used to love it when it was down, windblown and crazy from a day at the beach. The sight of her made my brain go wonky, my regular order forgotten.

"You work here?" I asked finally.

She leaned on the counter, putting her face partially through the open order window, red-lipped glossy smile greeting me.

"Yeah, started last week."

"Cool. You like it?"

"It's fun, but it can get so crazy with benny season. How about you? I hear you're working at the rec center again."

I laughed. Benny was slang we used for tourists, especially when they were acting like, um, tourists. "Yeah, I'm a counselor. So far, so good."

We sat in a second of *now what do we talk about* silence. It wasn't like it was the first time I'd seen Shay since we broke up, but every time was hard, even though it had gotten a little easier too. She was the biggest *what if* I still tortured myself about. What if I hadn't taken that dare and damaged myself forever? Would we still be together? Have our initials carved somewhere? Last I heard she was dating some college-guy douche canoe who'd been two years ahead of us in school.

"So let me guess, Coke float and a soft pretzel?" Yep, that's how long that had been my regular order. Even she remembered. She leaned in, fingers poised to punch in the price at the register.

"You know what, make it a root beer float," I said. Her eyebrows went up.

"And can you put it in a larger cup with a lid on it? Makes it easier to carry."

"Sure thing."

It took a few minutes for my order to be ready. I wished I had more to say to her; small talk seemed so—small, especially after what we'd shared together. That was before, though. So much had changed. Shay appeared at the window again.

"I can walk this over to your table if you want?"

"No thanks. I got it," I said, grabbing the float. The Styrofoam cup had little give and fit neatly into the large mesh side pocket of the backpack I had slung over my push handles. That was the only thing I liked using the handles for these days. When I got my next chair, I'd get one without them. At least they folded in when I didn't need them for my backpack. She gave me my pretzel and change with a smile.

"It was great seeing ya, Bry."

"Yeah, you too."

I was already half finished with my float by the time Wade and Tori arrived. They went up to the counter to order before sitting down. Wade came back juggling a drink, a hot dog, and two pretzels, while Tori had her usual small lime slush. I was at the head of the picnic table, like a king. #wheelchairperk. They each took a place on either side of me.

"It's about time you got here," I said.

"Are you okay?" Tori asked.

"Yeah, why?"

"We saw Shay. Didn't know she worked here now."

"It's fine. I'm fine. It doesn't bother me to see her," I said.

"Good, because I don't think I could give up Sip N' Freeze," Wade said. "But for you, buddy, I would."

"No need to do that."

"You are never going to freaking believe who Monty is," Tori said.

"Do we care?" I asked.

"It is pretty funny," Wade said before chowing down on half a hot dog in one bite.

"Nick."

"Wait, no way, as in—"

"Yes, my slacker twin. Leave it to him to find the one job on the island that is a grand total of one hour a week."

"Is it even that much?" I asked.

"It's too much if you ask me. Why do we need a mascot anyway? Knowing Mr. Beckett and his love of rounding up losers and rallying them to do something meaningful, he probably created the job for Nick. When he's not in costume he'll be doing janitorial duties. He gets a pointy stick and everything. He loves it, the weirdo. A no-brainer job with more time to slum and surf."

"Hey, if he's happy doing it . . . ," Wade said.

"Who says your job is supposed to make you happy? Are either of you happy at Camp Manatee? I mean, like, really happy?"

Wade shrugged. "It's a decent gig. What's not to like?"

"Same," I said. "Why? Aren't you happy? You practically begged Owen for the cooking workshop."

"I know, and it's cool, but it would be way cooler if I didn't have Benny Barbie as my second-in-command. I miss Liv."

"Benny Barbie? Harsh, no?" I said.

"I thought her name was Cassidy," Wade said, which earned him a balled-up napkin to the face courtesy of Tori.

"I guess she's okay, she's just not Liv, and it would have been nice if I had some say in the matter. I could have offered it to Miki or Danielle, someone I knew. She pretty much got the job because Mr. E. and Mr. Beckett are buds at school. She just pops in out of nowhere, no interview process or orientation. Don't you think it's weird we didn't know she existed before now? I mean, Mr. E. is our chemistry teacher, wouldn't he have casually mentioned he had a daughter our age at some point?"

"You must have been out sick on our Cassidy unit—I think it was between pH levels and the greenhouse effect," I said.

Wade snorted. Tori scowled at him.

"Well, she must have some common sense, since she turned down your invite for the scavenger hunt," she said.

"Dude, I knew that was bothering you. She called herself catastrophic, she seemed kind of nervous. I was being nice."

"Sure you were," she said.

"Tori, please, would you be my partner for the scavenger hunt?"

"Why, so I can do all the work like last year?"

"We made a great team," he said.

"Heeeey, looooooooosers!" someone yelled from the parking lot.

Tori looked over my shoulder and rolled her eyes. "Speak of the manatee."

I turned my head just as a silver pickup swept into the parking lot and took the first speed bump pretty hard. Its occupants howled. Matt and Nick were in the flatbed with their surfboards. I recognized Jake Matson's truck. Tom was most likely riding shotgun. My guess was they were on their way to the cove and stopping in for a slush. At least that's how it was two summers ago, when I was carefree enough to travel in the flatbed and it had been Jake's older brother who'd been driving.

The truck came to a stop and they all got out. Laughing, shirtless, as loud as gulls swooping down to steal some food. They greeted us as they walked past, only Matt stopped and eyed the remaining half of my pretzel.

"May I?" he asked, and before I could answer, he scooped up the pretzel and shoved it in his mouth.

"Geez, Matt, it's like you haven't eaten in days," Tori said. Her eyes lingered on his bare chest a moment longer than necessary. Working with my father had given Matt the kind of muscles you couldn't get from playing video games or skateboarding. Even Wade noticed.

"Matty, look at you, all ripped and shit," he said.

Matt swallowed the pretzel and flexed his bicep.

"I know, right? The physical-labor workout. Hey, Bry, can I bum a five off you?"

"Doesn't Dad pay you?"

"Every two weeks. Come on, I need to try Nick's slush flavor."

"What did you say?"

"Sip N' Freeze is naming a slush after him, didn't you

know?" Matt said as I reached into my backpack and grabbed a five for him.

"Is it hash flavored?" Tori asked.

"Ha, wicked. Nah, pineapple and cinnamon or something like that. We're heading to the cove; you guys should, you know, come hang out," Matt said.

"Working tonight," Wade said. "Picking up a shift at my aunt's restaurant."

"How industrious," Tori said.

"No, more like how the folks want me to pay for my own car insurance and I'm poor. Would much rather be shredding," he said.

"Matty, whatcha want?" Jake called. Matt jogged over to them.

The three of us sat in the wake of his enthusiasm, just looking back and forth at each other. I could feel what was brewing.

"What?"

"You should go to the cove, Bry," Wade said.

"To do what? Sit in the sand? This chair really isn't built for that," I said.

"Okay, we know, but I don't think it would hurt to consider it—you've been swimming, you're strong. That surf program is in July; we could go with you," Tori said.

They had this idea for me to get back in the water. There was an organization that helped people with disabilities surf, and they were going to be visiting a nearby town to run a program for a weekend. I'd checked out the website, and had to admit it looked cool and all, just not for me.

Surfing had always been my time to chill, let my thoughts wander. I couldn't see myself doing it assisted. Couldn't imagine that it felt the same way. Having Wade carry me out to the water. People watching my every move. I wasn't ready. Maybe someday, or maybe never, but I wanted it to be my choice. My terms. My board. Not because it was an inspirational thing to do.

I wanted to do it for me, not them.

I didn't feel it yet.

"Maybe when you get rid of that thing on the top of your head," I joked. Tori raised her hand. I slapped it.

"Do not dis the top knot. I think the benny chicks are gonna dig it."

"Not the ones with taste," Tori said. "That has surpassed man bun into rat's nest. Do you wash it?"

"I will have you know, I take extremely good care of it. My sisters turned me on to coconut oil. Twice a week," he said, taking out the elastic and running a hand through his hair. He leaned over the table and held the ends out for Tori to inspect. I covered my drink with my hand. Tori shook her head, but leaned toward him and touched it.

"Take a whiff," he said. She laughed and brought the lock of hair up to her nose and sniffed. Wade looked at me.

"Ah, no, dude, I'll take your word for it."

Wade turned back to Tori, who still had his hair up to her face, like a bizarre fake mustache. They both laughed. Their eyes and mouths were inches apart, and there was this moment: a flash sort of exchanged between them that made me feel like I'd walked in on something I shouldn't have. It was only a second. Tori let go, and Wade sat back, gathering his hair in a top knot again.

"Yes, smells nice," Tori said. Her cheeks flushed pink and she took a slow sip of her slush. I was thankful when the guys came back over on their way out to the parking lot, balancing out the weird vibes with their loudness.

Nick straddled the bench next to Tori and held out his slush.

"This is the Nick Bardot, want a taste?"

"You're going to have to name it something else," Tori said, wrinkling her nose.

"C'mon, Tor, it's pretty cool," he said.

"Sure, it's cool. You win," she said.

"Tell Mom I'll be in late," he said, getting up. He acknowledged Wade and me with a nod. Matt slammed my change down in front of me as he passed.

"See ya," he said.

As they walked by, heading to the truck, so much envy bubbled up inside that I could feel it collecting in the back of my throat. I wasn't sure why. Maybe it was the way they moved: able-bodied, tall, sauntering along like they had all the time in the world—the way I used to, the way I'd taken for granted. Watching them had made me restless, itchy, wanting something to start. Whatever that meant. The summer felt thick with possibilities.

I just wasn't sure what ones were for me.

SEVEN
CASSIDY

"ARE YOU SURE EVERYTHING'S OKAY? YOU STILL sound so sad."

The moment I heard Mom's voice during my weekly check-in call, I got teary. I don't know why. I wasn't sure what my mother expected; it had only been a week. When I was in camp, busy, I barely had any time to think of home or Gavin, but the weekend brought with it long hours of staring-at-my-ceiling time, which made me miss home, Ems, the way things used to be.

"No, I'm fine. Promise. I just . . . you know, I miss you guys, my stuff, that's all."

"Cass, you're at the beach—or maybe I should ask, why aren't you at the beach?"

"I know I'm *at* the beach, Mom, but it's different than being *on* the beach. We don't really go there with camp. It's crowded on the weekends. Dad and Les keep saying we'll go, but it's been busy; that magazine article has really helped business." *I don't have anyone to go with.*

"Haven't you met any kids your own age at work? Anyone to hang around with?"

Kids my age with a history together.

"I'm trying, Mom."

"So, you're staying, then?"

It would be so easy for me to tell her to come get me. She would, I knew it, but then what? There was this tiny, insistent voice inside that told me, *Hold on. Give it a chance.*

"Yes, I want to stay."

"I'm glad. Not that we don't miss you around here."

"I know."

Let me talk to her, I heard Nana say in the background.

"Nan's taking the phone now. If there's anything else you know you can—"

"Call you, I know, Mom. Love you."

"Love you back."

Nan got on.

"Cassidy, please tell me you haven't been hiding out in your room like you did here. You know 'change of scenery' meant more than a different house, right?"

I laughed. "Yes, Nan, I know."

"Stop feeling sorry for yourself, kid. Put on some lipstick and hit the boardwalk."

"They don't really have a boardwalk here. It's called a promenade."

"Then hit the beach, the pavement, something. Just get yourself out there."

"I will."

After I hung up, I sat in my wicker chair and stared out at the triangle of beach that I could see between the rooftops. Crest Haven had amazing sunsets. The sky was lavender. For the briefest of moments I contemplated taking the bike out, but remembered I had to get up earlier than usual for camp. I watched as the sky turned an even deeper shade of purple, then dark blue.

"I'm going to see a sunset and be happy before I leave here," I declared to no one. It was empowering, though. Why was I just sitting there? I looked around the room. *My* room. The empty bulletin board. I went over to my backpack and pulled out handouts that Mr. Beckett had given us. There was a camp calendar there, and I took one of the seashell-shaped pushpins and stuck it onto the board. It wasn't much, but it was a start. I did have a life here, if I wanted it. The scavenger hunt sounded sort of fun.

My phone buzzed. I checked my messages.

How I wonder where you are.

I tossed the phone onto my bed as if it had given me an electric shock. Maybe I'd read it wrong? I picked it up again. Nope.

Same thing. Gavin. *Gavin*. Why hadn't I blocked him? *Because you didn't want to, remember?* The phone buzzed again.

Miss your face.

I called Ems. She picked up. "Come home."

"Gavin just texted me."

"Get out!"

"What do I do?"

"What do you want to do?"

"If I knew that, I wouldn't have called."

"Cass, you know what you wanted to do, otherwise you wouldn't have called me to delay doing it."

I sat on the bed. "You're right. I was going to text him. I don't want to, Ems, I really don't want to."

"Then don't."

Don't what? I heard Drew in the background.

"Oh, God, you're with Drew. I'm sorry, I'll let you go."

"Please," she said to me.

Your boy texted Cass, she told Drew.

And, so?

Tell him to stop.

"Ems? Hello?"

"Yes, I'm here, what did he say?"

"He misses my face. I mean, why can't he just say 'Hey' or 'What's up'?"

"Because he's a selfish prick who knows you eat that up."

I sighed.

"Listen, I think you've been going about this all wrong. Disappearing without a trace. Are you still on . . . what did you call it . . . a StalkMe fast?"

After torturing myself with Gavin's feed, I'd deleted the app from my phone. Good riddance. It had made a difference. Out of sight . . . mostly out of mind.

"Yes, why?"

"Well, it ends tonight. You need to start documenting yourself doing all sorts of incredible things."

"But I'm not doing incredible things."

"Half the people on StalkMe are not doing incredible things, it just looks like it. Take some selfies during sunset. Put yourself in that bikini, the blue one that makes your boobs look huge. Find some surfer boys, take a pic, and mention how you love your new view. Show Gavin what he's missing, what he screwed up, that you are fine without him."

"How do I know Gavin would even see it?"

"He's totally stalking your feed."

"He is?"

"Drew told me."

Pathetic as it was, it felt good to hear.

"I don't know. It sounds like a lotta work," I said.

"Are you even having fun? You should be hooking up left and right, screw the celibate thing," she said.

Cass is celibate? I heard Drew say.

No, she's screwing half of Crest Haven, make sure you tell Gavin that.

"*Ems!* Don't tell Gavin that."

"Why not?"

"I don't know, maybe because I'm not!"

"This is war, Cass. You may as well start acting like it."

"Okay, I will. Tomorrow. I promise."

The next morning I woke up, showered, changed, and put a quick side braid in my wet hair. My father and Leslie were already awake; I could hear them puttering around the kitchen getting ready for the breakfast service. It was six forty-five, earlier than I needed to be at work, but I couldn't sleep. Gavin's texts and Emma's *this is war* proclamation all swirled around in my head as I tossed and turned. I had to put my phone on the other side of my room to charge, so I'd be too tired to get up and obsessively check it. Gavin hadn't texted again. Thankfully. I grabbed my backpack and headed downstairs.

Smells of something sweet and appley got stronger as I descended the stairs. Leslie was busy piling huge crumb-topped muffins on a glass platter as I walked into the kitchen.

"Mornin', Cass," Dad said, pouring coffee from a glass carafe into a fancy silver urn.

"Cass, could you take this out to the dining room and put

it on the sideboard?" Leslie held out the glass platter to me.

"Wow, that smells good," I said, resting my backpack on a chair and grabbing the platter.

"I have a few set aside if you'd like one."

I pushed through the swinging door to the inn part of the house. The dining room was empty, but everything was set and ready for that morning's guests. It was a pretty room, with floral wallpaper and dark wood and a gilded mirror on the far wall that helped make the room look larger than it really was. The table was covered with lace and a few small silver bowls that held jam and what looked like whipped cream. Two floor-to-ceiling windows let in natural light. I placed the platter on the sideboard and nearly ran into my father as I turned to leave.

"Whoa," he said, sidestepping me and holding out the urn at arm's length. I helped him place it down next to the platter of muffins.

"Thanks, Cass. That would have been a disaster."

We stood facing each other. I said the first thing that came to mind.

"Nan said she never understood why anyone would want to stay in a place where you had to eat breakfast with a bunch of strangers."

To my surprise, he laughed. "That sounds like Shirl. It's not for everyone, but it's really not that bad. People like to relax on vacation. It's okay to let your guard down with a bunch of strangers. No pressure."

"Oh. I never looked at it that way before," I said. He followed me out to the kitchen.

"You're up extra early."

"This is my new start time," I said. "I have to help out at the pool in the morning."

"Owen's not overworking you, is he?" Dad kidded. I didn't want to tell him the busier I was, the less I thought about things.

"Nope, I volunteered," I said. There was a muffin on a napkin waiting by my backpack. I shouldered my bag and took a bite of the muffin, crumbs falling down my chin. Totally as good as it looked.

"Would you like something to wash that down with?" Leslie asked.

I shook my head as I made my way toward the back door. "No, I think I have an extra water in my backpack. I better get going."

Hunter suddenly rounded the corner of the stairwell, his hair sticking up every which way. Shark pj's slightly askew.

"You're leaving without me?"

"Cass has to go in early, buddy."

"And I'm going to be late if I don't leave now. See you at camp, Hunter."

The screen door slammed behind me as I heard Hunter say, "No fair, she gets to take her bike to camp. Why can't I go with her?"

The hero-worship thing was kind of adorable. I'd have to

take him to the arcade one of these days.

My bike was propped up against the side of the house. I took out my phone and snapped a picture. The way it was parked made it look like it was waiting for me to take it on all sorts of adventures. I uploaded the image to my reinstalled StalkMe account with the caption "My beach bum ride. Going where the day takes me." Maybe not as sexy as a bikini-top picture, but I'd work on that later. For now, boom . . . the war had begun.

By the time I reached the rec center, my thighs burned and my mouth was so dry it wouldn't have surprised me if I spit sand. I regretted not taking Leslie up on her offer of something to wash down my breakfast with. I locked my bike on the rack and found Mr. Beckett in his office.

"Cass, wow, you didn't have to come in this early," he said.

"It's cool, I just wanted to, um, get started," I said, which sounded better than "I need something to do so I don't obsess about my ex-asshat-of-a-boyfriend's texts that he sent me last night." *Miss your face.*

Just. No.

Mr. Beckett walked me down to the pool and introduced me to Jena, then directed us to the ladies' locker room.

"You just need to fold and roll, like this." Jena demonstrated. As I suspected, no special skills needed. I looked at the mountain of white.

"So . . . all of them?"

Jena nodded. "Sorry, I know, but it goes fast. When they're folded you can leave about a third in here, some out by the pool, then just park the bin by the men's locker room door. Someone else will put them in there. They don't have to be perfect, just look neat. Gotta get back out there. Thanks, Cass."

I reached in and began the task at hand, fanning out each towel, joining the ends, and rolling them up. Half an hour later, I had a pyramid of towels ready to go. I stacked some in the ladies' locker room, then rolled the bin out to the pool deck. I didn't see the rack at first and walked up to Jena in her lifeguard chair.

"Where do I put the towels . . . Bryan?"

At least I thought it was him. He looked blissed out, eyes closed, face relaxed like he was sleeping. He had one of those long pool noodles under his knees, and held another one across his chest and under his arms.

"I think he's meditating or something," Jena said. "He does that after he swims laps."

"He swims laps?" I asked. I didn't mean to sound surprised, it just wasn't something I realized he could do. He also looked pretty damn good without his shirt on. I got an eyeful of his broad-shouldered, muscled upper bod before he opened his eyes and completely snagged me looking.

"Yes, he does, and his hearing is fine." He grinned.

Jena and I laughed. I kept my eyes on his, not sure where

I was supposed to be looking. He pulled the pool noodle out from under his knees and pushed it over to the side. Jena hopped off her stand to get it.

"What time is it?" he asked.

"About ten to eight," I said.

"Oh shit," he said, letting go of the other noodle. He turned in the water. His legs were strapped together—another flotation device was between his thighs. His calves were noticeably thinner, less developed than his upper body. I looked away.

"Where do these towels go?" I asked.

Jena pointed down to the end of the pool where Bryan was headed. I rolled the bin, catching up to him next to the swim lane. I walked slower, mesmerized by his arms slicing through the water. Had he always been able to swim like this? It must have been hard for him after his injury, but he made it look effortless. When he reached the end of the lane, he pulled himself up with one swift move and spun, landing on his butt and leaning forward slightly. He unhooked the strap that had been around his legs.

"Towel? Freshly folded by yours truly?" I held it out to him. He smiled and took it, putting the flotation device to the side.

"Is it cold?" I asked, kicking off my flip-flops and dunking a toe in.

"Nah, not really," he said.

I sat down on the side of the pool and let my legs dangle in the water.

"What are you doing here this early?" he asked, running the towel across his face, then wrapping it around his shoulders like a cape.

"Oh, towel duty, part of my job now."

"Really?"

"Yeah. Do you swim laps every day?"

"Uh, yeah, mostly I guess. I try to anyway, but sometimes I'll have a bad morning and have to skip."

I nodded. I wasn't sure what he meant by "bad morning" but was afraid to ask. I didn't want to embarrass him or anything. I could hardly imagine getting out of bed, taking a shower, going to the bathroom . . . all those things I took for granted must have required so much more effort for him. Did he have help? He seemed to be doing fine on his own for the swim.

"I get leg spasms sometimes, not so much anymore though. I just never know what my body's going to do. It was worse in the beginning. Still kind of learning."

"Well, it looks like you've got the swimming thing down pretty good."

"Yeah, took a while to get strong enough to be here on my own, but I love it. I got Jena and the other lifeguards to look out for me. Sometimes I just want to pretend to drown to see if she's paying attention, she's so chill."

I laughed. He pulled his legs up, one at a time, and hugged them in closer to his chest.

"Do you need help?"

"Ah . . . yeah, could you put a towel down on the seat of my chair? I forgot to do that this morning."

I grabbed a towel, went over to his wheelchair, and fanned it out to cover the cushion, then held the chair steady while he gripped one of the wheels. He propelled his body up and into the seat with his other hand. Then he placed his feet, pulling one, then the other, onto the footplate.

"Thanks. Hey, could you hand me my pull buoy?"

"Huh?"

"That," he said, pointing to the strappy flotation thing he'd been using. I picked it up and handed it to him.

"Well, I guess I'll be seeing you in the morning then, if, you know, we're here at the same time," I said.

He rubbed his hair with the towel that had been around his shoulders, making it stick up every which way, like Hunter's had been this morning. It was endearing. He smiled.

"Sure hope so."

I laughed, at a loss for what to say all of a sudden. Was he flirting?

"I'll just, um, get back to the towels. Later, Bryan."

"Later, Cassidy."

I WAS SUCH A LIAR.

A white lie maybe—it had been too sweet to pass up—no, actually, I didn't swim *every* morning. I shot for three to four times a week; it was necessary to keep myself toned and to help with my eventual goal of getting back into the ocean. There were days I slacked off, though, took the extra time at home, then went in the afternoon. And sometimes I did have bad mornings, but not lately. The fifteen minutes I spent with Cass each morning had become my incentive. I hadn't missed a day all week.

On Friday, Cass was at the rec center before me, already stacking the towels on the pool deck when I came in to do laps. It bummed me out because I thought maybe she would leave without sitting with me during my cooldown, but maybe Tori needed her for something. I put in a good workout, even though between *stroke, breathe, stroke, breathe* I thought—*What should we talk about today? Maybe I can ask her to time me, pretend I'm trying to train harder. Or maybe I should look extra pathetic and ask her to help me with drying my hair?* Looking pathetic occasionally got me extra fries in school. The lunch ladies were suckers for the wheelchair. #wheelchairperk

I'd lost track of where she was when I turned for my last lap, and then what I saw nearly made me go under.

Cass.

At the end of the swim lane.

Wearing a blue bikini.

And smiling.

At me.

Stroke. Breathe. Stroke. Breathe.

I stopped midlane to watch her, as she first dipped a toe, then sat on the side and shimmied in, shivering when she hit the water. She held her arms up as she shuffled toward me. When she saw my face she flinched.

God, I hoped I wasn't staring.

"It's okay that I'm swimming, I mean, I just assumed . . . the pool's open to everyone, right?"

It was wicked to leave her hanging, but she was too cute. I tried to keep a straight face as I held on to the ledge and reached for my swim noodles, which Jena kept for me at the base of the lifeguard stand now.

"No, it's only open this early to seventy-year-olds and people who don't have use of their legs. You have to get out."

She raised her eyebrows as she looked to the other side of the pool and saw the senior citizens in water aerobics class hoisting weights over their heads, then back at me—working it through—until she narrowed her eyes. She flicked her fingertips across the top of the water and splashed me.

"Ha, you almost had me. Oh, man, I thought you said it wasn't cold."

"This is cold? You must not go in the ocean much."

She shook her head, took a breath, and plunged under the water, popping up with a splash.

"What made you come in?" I asked, maneuvering the one noodle behind me to slide under my knees. Cass grabbed the other noodle off the ledge and handed it to me.

"Thanks," I said.

She sank down into the water until it was up to her shoulders. "It's your fault, you make it look so fun. That, and I thought it might be good to burn off all the junk I've been eating at the inn. There were cinnamon rolls this morning."

"And you didn't bring me one?" I teased.

"If I'd known you liked them, I totally would have snagged you one. Maybe next week."

Next week was way too far away. I'd never been so disappointed about it being the weekend.

"I'm kidding, but you know, I'd never say no to cinnamon rolls."

"Noted," she said. "Hey, so when are we going to start the scavenger hunt thing?"

"So you didn't just ask me to partner up as a way to say no to Wade? Don't want my wheels to slow you down, you know."

She laughed. "I've seen you, I doubt you'd slow me down. Besides, you were the first person I met, why wouldn't I ask you?"

"Oh, right . . . Mr. Beckett's office."

"Actually, at the beach that first night. I met you before I even knew you. Not sure if that makes sense."

"Right," I said. I remembered how she seemed to just appear off the beach. She was hard not to notice, the way she put on her flip-flops like she was pissed with them . . . and crying. *Why were you crying?* The question was on the tip of my tongue, and maybe she sensed it too because she dunked herself under the water. She smoothed her hair back when she broke the surface again. *Just say it.*

"Why were you crying?"

"What?" she asked.

"That night, at Crescent Beach—you were upset. It wasn't just because you thought the sunset was that beautiful, was it?"

She laughed. "No. I was . . . um, homesick. I mean, I want to be here, but I miss my mom and Nana, and my friend

Emma. She might come down to visit soon. At least I'm hoping she will. Maybe we can hang out."

"Yeah, that'd be cool."

"Hey, guys, it's almost eight o'clock," Jena said.

"Wow, already?" I asked.

"I better hit the shower," she said. "This was fun."

"Yeah, we should definitely do it again," I said.

"Definitely."

As I sat in the shower, I replayed our conversation. Maybe I shouldn't have brought up the beach thing. Maybe she was homesick, but then why go to the beach by yourself? And that beach in particular? Was she forced to be here for the summer? Why did I even care? I had no business wanting anything from Cassidy Emmerich . . . but I did. At that moment she was just a wall away. Naked.

Maybe the summer did hold possibilities for me after all.

"We should do something tonight," I said.

We were outside, on the blacktop—the kids running crazy on the playground in the midafternoon heat. Our little guys were playing a rule-less version of kickball with a group of six-year-old girls. We were basically keeping watch. On Friday afternoon, even Owen was lax on organization. One more hour until send-off. For some reason I was pumped.

"Dude, I'm working, remember? I get off at ten—after that maybe?" Wade said.

"Maybe."

"Why don't you call Nick and those guys? They're probably up to something."

"Nah."

"You need to stop avoiding them, Bry."

"I'm not avoiding them; what am I supposed to do with them? Hang out in the parking lot and watch them do stupid shit?"

"You used to be leader of the stupid shit, remember?"

Did I remember? I'd never friggin' forget.

I dare you, Lakewood.

"And look where it got me."

"C'mon, I didn't mean it like that, I just meant . . . you need to do more than *Realm Wars*, dude. It's time."

"Thanks, Mom."

"Since your mom is cool, I'll take that," he said, punching my shoulder. Just then one of the bigger kids from another group grabbed the kickball and threw it away from the game.

"Aw, shit, can't these kids just chill?" Wade said, and trotted toward them. I pushed over to get the ball, but someone came out from behind the Dumpster to retrieve it. Nick. He palmed the ball and threw it with one hand to Wade. Then he noticed me.

"Oh hey, sorry, Bry. I didn't see you."

I dare you, Lakewood.

I'd been mouthing off, throwing shade about Nick's recent

obsession with parkour. The Dumpsters were close together, the tree branch right there. I'd watched him do it. I knew I could do it better.

The tree branch had been in front of me when I jumped out. I'd calculated the distance. My fingertips grazed it.

You used to be the leader of stupid shit.

"No worries, I get that a lot," I said. He laughed, came closer. Nick had taken my fall the worst. Blamed himself. *I dare you, Lakewood.* I knew it wasn't his fault. He knew it wasn't his fault. But things had been strained since then. As close as Tori and I had become, Nick kept his distance.

"So, you're Monty, huh?"

"Hey, shhhh, have to keep my identity on the down low. You know, like Peter Parker and Spider-Man. Right now I'm just, you know, janitor, doing my daily walk of the grounds. Or as I like to call it, lying low until the weekend."

"Right."

Cass walked out of the building carrying a large plastic garbage bag and headed for the Dumpster.

"Duty calls. Later, Bry." Nick jogged over to the Dumpster and opened the top for Cassidy. She smiled at him and laughed at something he said. My jaw clenched watching the exchange, I wasn't sure why—nothing extraordinary was going on between them, but all I could think was *I knew her first.*

No. Nope. Nuh-uh.

Falling for her would be asking for annihilation. I had to admit, though, when she talked about being homesick that morning, I'd noticed she didn't mention a guy.

I'd been stoked.

"Think he's making the moves on your partner?" Wade asked.

I wheeled around. "No."

"You should go for it, Bryan."

"I don't know."

"What's to know? She's here for three months—she's perfect. A summer rental."

I couldn't think of Cassidy in those terms, but I smiled. I didn't want to look interested for fear Wade would get involved. I didn't need to be fixed up. If something was going to happen between me and Cassidy, I wanted it to happen on its own.

Colby dashed up to us then, holding his hand over his left eye, tears rolling down his cheeks. Hunter was by his side.

"He got hit in the face." Hunter turned to Colby. "It's okay, you're not bleeding, Colby."

Colby wailed.

"C'mere, let me see," I said, pushing closer to him. After being around him for two weeks, I got that Colby was the kind of kid who needed to have the seams of his socks lined up exactly or he would pitch a fit. He was beginning to come out of his shell though, which was cool. He stepped closer, his breath in quick gasps.

"Okay, buddy, listen, can you take a deep breath for me? Just one, real slow, then let it out." He tried to do it, but couldn't.

"I'm going to look at it, okay?" I pried his hand, which was surprisingly strong for a little kid, away from his eye and saw . . . nothing. He was red, but it didn't look like it would bruise. I hadn't been paying the best attention—what if something worse had happened? Maybe parents were right to worry about me.

"Oh, no, Colby-Wan, I think you're going to need major surgery," Wade said. Colby paled. "Yeah, you know, like a bag of ice or something."

"Everything okay?"

Cass.

She knelt down so she was eye level with Colby and Hunter.

"I think we need some ice," I said. She stood up.

"I'll get some; hang tight, okay?" Colby nodded while she ran off toward the building. Nick followed Cass inside.

"I don't like kickball," Colby said.

"Me either," I said. "I always miss kicking the ball."

Colby and Hunter looked at each other, then back at me, eyes scanning my legs. I could see them working it through.

"But . . . you can't kick," Colby said.

"Yeah, kind of a bummer, but that's not why I don't like it; I just like volleyball and basketball better."

"You play basketball?" Hunter's eyes widened.

I smiled. "Yep, but I'm not very good at it. I'm pretty decent at volleyball."

"And he can do more chin-ups than me," Wade said.

"Really?" they said together.

"No, he lets me win."

"Not true, wanna go?"

I dare you, Lakewood.

"Not today," I said.

"Awww," Colby and Hunter moaned.

"But hey, watch this," I said, popping up and balancing on my wheels. I didn't usually like performing, but my diversionary tactic of doing a wheelie so Colby would stop thinking about his eye had worked. Popping was one of the first things I learned to do, even though my mom went ballistic. It wasn't the cool factor, although for some reason people found it impressive. #wheelchairperk. It was practical for going up and down curbs that weren't accessible. I'd even handled stairs that way. I did it a few more times when I saw Cass emerge from the building.

"Coool," Colby said. Cass jogged over, a little breathless. She was holding a baggie with ice and two cake pops in her hand. She knelt down again.

"Here," she said, putting the ice bag on Colby's eye. He reached up to keep it in place. She held out the cake pops to both Hunter and Colby. They each grabbed one.

"Keep those pops quiet," Cass said, putting a finger to

her lips. "Tori doesn't know I swiped them." Hunter nodded, already half finished. Colby took a smaller bite, wide grin spreading across his face.

"That was pretty cool of Cass to swipe those for you. What do you say, guys?" I said.

"Thank you, Cassidy."

"You're welcome," she said, standing up. Hunter swallowed the rest of his pop, handed Cass the stick, and took off for the game. Colby nibbled a bit more and handed it back to her half-finished, then took off after Hunter. Crisis over.

"Hey, you mind?" Wade grabbed the half-eaten cake pop out of Cass's hand before she could even answer. "I love Tori's cake pops."

"Why does that sound dirty coming from you?" Cass asked.

He laughed and scarfed down the pop.

"Hey, um, what are you doing tonight?" Wade asked.

Cassidy blinked fast, looked at me. I had no idea what he was up to.

"My dad is taking us out to a lobster place. We have to get there early or else there's like a three-hour wait or something. I don't even think I like lobster, but you know, I have to go."

"Bummer. Bryan here was looking for something to do."

Friggin' Wade.

"Oh, um . . . I'm not sure when I'll be back, but maybe . . . what about tomorrow afternoon? We could look for that first scavenger-hunt clue? I'd really like to do something other than hang with my family."

"Um, yeah, that would be cool," I said.

"Great, I better get back before Tori realizes I'm gone. See ya."

We watched Cass jog away.

"Hmm, that was pretty cool of Wade to pump Cass for info and get her to ask Bryan to hang out tomorrow, wasn't it, guys?"

I shook my head, but could not contain my smile.

"You can thank me later."

"CASS, IT'S NINE—TIME TO GET UP," HUNTER SAID.

I opened one eye to see him standing in the doorway, hands cupped around his mouth. It was a good thing I didn't like to sleep naked.

"Do you know what knocking is?"

"I did knock. You were snoring."

I rolled over to face the wall. "I don't snore."

"Yes, you do, like this," he said, and as if I didn't know what snoring was, he proceeded to demonstrate by snorting and huffing. Loud. I laughed and rolled over to face him.

"I do not sound like that."

"Yes, you do."

"Hunter, it's Saturday. Don't you like to sleep on Saturdays?"

"Sleep is boring."

"You have so much to learn," I said, pulling the blanket over my head.

"Dad sent me up. He made eggs. Scrambled. Your favorite, like me."

I peeked out of the top of the blanket. "With cheese?"

He nodded.

"Did you help him?"

"Yep."

There was a tiny flare in my gut, a momentary flash of whisking eggs with Dad. That had been *our* thing. It's not like I wanted to do it now. That would just be odd. But I still thought about it as Hunter stared wide-eyed at me. Waiting. I'd been his age when Dad left. Seeing Hunter, I knew there was no way he could understand if Dad just up and walked out now. He'd be hurt. Confused. Just like I'd been—even if I couldn't voice it at the time.

Dad wasn't going anywhere in Hunter's life.

I wondered what that felt like.

"Well, now you talked me into it," I said, throwing back the blanket and getting out of bed.

"There's also a box downstairs for you."

"Really?" I grabbed my floral kimono and threw it over the leggings-and-cami ensemble I wore as pj's. I followed him downstairs to the kitchen. There was something sweet baking—it seemed there was always something sweet baking, but it made the kitchen warm and cheerful. Easily my favorite room in the house. Dad and Leslie were sitting at the table. He was chuckling at something she said. She got up and squeezed his shoulder as she grabbed the kettle off of the stove. I'd never say it out loud, but it was kind of sweet how they made a point of eating together. I don't remember Mom eating breakfast with us on Saturdays. She wasn't a fan of eggs.

"Morning," I said. Dad looked up and smiled.

"Cass, sit, I'll get you a plate," Leslie said.

Everything was lined up on the counter and the stove. Even their personal breakfast time was organized.

"No, that's okay, I'll do it," I said. I took a plate from the cabinet and spooned a generous portion of scrambled eggs on it. They were light and fluffy and I could practically hear Dad's instructions as the steam tickled my nose.

You want to take them off the heat when they're not quite done. They still cook when you take them off, but they won't overcook. If you overcook them, they get too stiff.

He made them with milk, not water, a pinch of salt, and a dash of black pepper. Maybe he didn't always send my birthday cards on time, or get me Christmas presents that weren't practical, but there, on that plate, he had the dad thing down to perfection.

"So do I really have a package?" I asked.

Dad wiped his mouth with a napkin. "Yes, from your mother. It's in the office."

"Can I help open it?" Hunter asked.

I smiled. "Of course."

"After breakfast," Leslie said, sitting down again.

"Any plans today? Hunter and I were going to fish at the pier if you're interested," Dad said.

"I think I actually might be doing something."

"Oh?" Leslie and Dad looked at each other.

"Yeah, nothing definite; I have to call," I said, realizing I didn't even have Bryan's number. I thought I remembered seeing a contacts sheet in the handouts from Mr. Beckett though.

"Cassidy, come on, we want details," Leslie said.

"There's this scavenger hunt. A camp thing. Bryan Lakewood is my partner."

"Bryan?! Can I come?"

"You'd be bored, Hunter," I said. I hated how disappointed he looked when I turned him down for something, but I craved a bit of *me* time.

A chime pinged. Leslie put down her tea cup and got up from the table.

"Early check-in this morning. Jeff, could you make sure those sweet rolls . . ."

"I'm on it," Dad said. Leslie ran her fingers through Hunter's hair as she went out to the registration podium in the front hall.

After breakfast, Hunter and I went into Dad's office to open my care package. The desktop was spare, except for a stapler, a basket with Ocean Whispers brochures, a flat-screen monitor, and a stone coaster with some inspirational saying about walking confidently toward your dreams. I picked up the box and sat in Dad's desk chair.

"Dad keeps the scissors in his top drawer," Hunter said, sliding it open.

"Thanks."

Hunter ripped off the brown paper. I used the scissors to slice through the packing tape that held the sides together. I'd barely finished cutting as Hunter pulled open the flaps, and we both rummaged through. His first find was a cellophane bag tied with a hot-pink ribbon.

"Boring," he proclaimed, and put it aside.

"Boring? This stuff is the best!" I said, grabbing it. My favorite coconut body wash and a loofah. Hunter pulled out a bikini top and giggled. The box also contained a pretty sundress and a huge bottle of sunscreen, SPF a million. There was an envelope in the bottom of the box marked *Cass.* I ripped it open. Inside was a note and three twenties.

"Hunter, here—thanks for helping," I said, giving him a twenty.

"Really?"

"Yeah," I said.

"Daaaaad!" He ran out of the room with the bill in his hand. I read the note.

Cass,

We miss you! Hope you enjoy your goodies.

Don't forget to slather on the sunscreen!

Talk soon!

xoxo,

Mom

PS Go buy yourself some lipstick and kiss someone silly!

xo Nan

Kiss someone silly? Did she forget a comma? I laughed.

My father came in with the twenty I'd given to Hunter in his hand. "Cass, did you give this to him?"

"Yeah," I said.

"Are you sure?"

Hunter was by Dad's legs looking a bit pouty.

"Yes, Nan sent it for him," I lied.

"See, told you."

Dad smiled and handed him back the bill. "Go put it in your bank."

Hunter raced upstairs, the house practically shaking.

"That was very generous of you, thanks."

"Well, maybe we can use it at the arcade or something. I feel a little bad telling him no."

"Cass, stop. He's happy with any time you give him. You're here to have fun too. I'm glad you might do something with Bryan this afternoon. You should be getting out."

"Hey, Dad, do you know the Lakewoods?"

"Yes, I work with Bryan's mom."

"Would you happen to have their number?"

"I can do better than that," he said, coming around to his monitor. He clicked the mouse a few times and the screen came to life. "Bryan helped me in the lab last year; I'm pretty sure I have his number here somewhere."

"Thanks," I said, collecting my stuff.

"Here it is," he said. He grabbed a small pad from his top drawer and scribbled down the number. He ripped it off and handed it to me.

"Do you know what happened to him?"

"What do you mean?"

"How he got hurt."

My father shut down whatever file he'd been looking at and stood up, hands in pockets. "I'm not entirely sure—I know it happened in the Crescent Beach parking lot; the kids skateboard there. He fell somehow."

"That sucks." *Nothing that exciting*, he'd said. A fall? Something as simple as that and his life was altered forever. No wonder he didn't want to talk about it.

"He has a great support system though, integrated well in school. He's a good kid."

I thought of him speeding down that road with his brother the night he saw me at Crescent Beach. *Good kid, ha, with a wild side.* "Thanks for the number, Dad."

Upstairs, I flopped down, package and all, onto my bed. I took the note from Mom and Nan and pinned it to my bulletin board, along with Bryan's number. I reached for my phone. A message from Emma—*Pictures, gurl!! This is war! Boobs, please!* I laughed, tapped in Bryan's number. The call went to voice mail, and his message was so polite and serious, I had to smile. Most guys I knew barely said, "Yo, leave a message!" Meanwhile he was all, "You've reached Bryan Lakewood. I can't make it to the phone right now . . ." Cute. I cleared my throat. "Hey, Bryan Lakewood, it's Cass. Cassidy. Emmerich. From camp. Thought we could hook up to search out that scavenger-hunt clue. I'm desperate to get out of this place, but . . . oh . . . wait . . . I mean that in a good way, not like I'm desperate, or you're desperate or anything, I just think it would be cool to hang out. Call me."

I hung up and stared at the ceiling, surprised at how much I wanted him to call.

It would be nice to see the beach.

To be out in the sun and maybe start a base tan.

To see him with his shirt off.

Wait, what?

Safe. Bryan was safe. Seeing someone.

He didn't flirt like Wade, or leer like his brother.

I could talk to him.

I liked it.

More than I wanted to admit.

"DAD, HAVE YOU SEEN MY SURFBOARD?"

I'd been up since eight, helping my father plant red, white, and blue annuals in raised beds around the perimeter of the patio in preparation for our Fourth of July barbecue the following week. Not the raddest form of Saturday entertainment, but it was already eleven and I felt accomplished. Matt was still asleep. We were taking a break, Dad tinkering with his home-brew kit in the garage.

"What?"

"My red board, the quad fish—it's usually up on the pegs in the shed, but it's gone."

He took off his Lakewood Landscaping baseball cap and wiped the sweat from his forehead with his sleeve. "Dunno . . . I didn't touch it. Matty might know."

"Matty might know what?"

We both turned to see Matt, wearing boxer briefs and nothing else, standing in the doorway that connected the mudroom to the garage. He had lines from his pillow across his cheek. My phone was in his hand.

"My fish, what did you do with it?"

He frowned, absentmindedly scratching his abs. "I didn't do anything with it."

"Liar."

He stepped into the garage and closed the door behind him.

"Fine. I didn't think you'd care if I used it."

"Matty," Dad said.

"It's still my board," I said, pushing back so I faced him.

"The surf was mushy last week; the fish rides better in the small waves. Sorry, I should have asked, I just . . . didn't want to make you feel left out."

The truth was appreciated, but still hurt. "Where is it now?"

"You missed a call," he said, tossing me the phone.

I caught it, but ignored the message, pinning Matt down with my eyes. "Where's the board?"

He looked at Dad, then down at the floor. "Over at the Matsons'. I ended up crashing there the other night and Dad picked me up in the morning for work, and I knew I'd be with the guys later anyway, so you know, I just left it there. And, well . . . yeah."

"Left it there?"

"What do you think Jake's doing with it?" he asked, defensive, like I was the one who was being unreasonable.

"I don't care, all I know is that it's mine, and it's gone, and you should have asked. You'll probably ding it up."

"It's not like you're—"

"Hey, stop," Dad said.

"No, say what you were going to say, Matt," I said. He looked at the floor again. *It's not like you're even using it.* I knew that, but I liked to see the board, run my fingers across the smooth glassed surface, close my eyes, and remember what it was like. Imagine what it might be like again. I'd paid for it with my own money. It was *mine.*

"Bry, I'm sorry."

"Just get it back," I said.

"Hey, Matty, think you could put on some pants and help me with the mulch? Bryan did the bulk of your share this morning with the zinnias."

Matt groaned. "I thought the weekend meant rest."

"Come on, it'll go quick with the two of us—then I'll let you taste the latest home brew."

"That's incentive? The wild blueberry beer kind of sucked, Dad, no offense."

"Trial and error, kid. Come on, I'm working on a stout for the Fourth, could use some taste testers. Game, Bry?" It wasn't like we sat with Dad in the garage and got shitfaced, but he let us taste test now and then. Matt was right, the blueberry beer had sucked.

"Uh, maybe," I said, tapping to check my voice mail. I held the phone to my ear and suddenly Cass's voice filled my head.

"What are you grinning at?" Matt asked.

I shook my head, played the message again. And again. Studying the way her voice went up and down, the slight laugh after she'd said the word *desperate*. I kind of figured she was blowing off meeting up, that she'd just been making plans to be polite, but she called me. That's what made me grin.

"Matty, the mulch?" Dad said.

"Yeah, I'll help with the mulch, but I need some Frosted Flakes first," he said, heading back inside.

"And pants," Dad called after him. He looked at me. "Are you up to helping this afternoon?"

"I think I might have plans," I said. I wheeled to the driveway for more privacy and pressed the call button, my pulse pounding in my ear. She picked up immediately. Hearing her voice made me grin again.

"Desperate, huh?"

Two hours later I pulled the Charger into a spot along Beach Avenue, right in front of the promenade. I unfolded my chair, popped my wheels in lightning fast, and made my way toward the access ramp. Cass's bike was chained to the rack. She was waiting on the promenade, wearing the blue bikini top and white shorts. She leaned against a bench, her hair loose, blowing across her face in the breeze. As I got closer, she brushed it back and smiled. All I kept thinking was, *She's there for me. For me.* I made a conscious effort to slow down. My heart pounded with the effort.

"Wow, you're pretty dangerous in that car."

"What? Why would you say that?"

"You practically screeched into the spot."

"Did I? I like to drive. Can kind of forget myself there."

"Yes, I think I've witnessed you forgetting yourself before."

The South Ferry Road incident. "Will you ever let me live that down? I told you, I was protecting you from my brother."

"Maybe if you give me a ride someday."

Cass in my car? Yes, please. I laughed. "Yeah, I'd like that."

"So, did you read the first clue?"

Clue?

I didn't want to tell her that once she called, the prospect of spending time with her had knocked any rational thought out of my head. I had no idea what the first clue was, and she saw it in my eyes.

"Hmm, is that how it's gonna be, Lakewood? Lucky for us I downloaded it from the website," she said, scrolling through her phone. She crouched down next to me, our arms touching. The wind blew her hair into my face.

"Ugh, sorry," she said. "Hold this, please." She handed me

her phone, gathered up her hair, and took a purple band from around her wrist. In a few quick moves it was up in some twisty way that reminded me of the top of a pineapple. The strings of her bikini were tied in a bow at the nape of her neck. Two delicate little strings I could untie with my teeth. How would I ever focus on a scavenger hunt?

"Okay," she said, all business. "Here's the clue. *At the foot of this street, stripes the color of banana—you'll be made in the shade, in a private cabana.* So it sounds like some specific spot on the beach—where cabanas are? I guess if we find that, then we'll find the street."

"Makes sense," I said, but thought *bikini top.* She widened her eyes at me.

"You're the local—where are the cabanas?"

"In front of the Lexington Hotel—that's a bit of a walk that way," I said, pointing down the promenade.

"Then I guess we better get going," she said.

Crest Haven didn't have the kind of boardwalk tourists visited for fun, but it was still heavy with foot traffic. There were no rides, just a long stretch of walkway that ran along most of the beach. The main section had a few restaurants and a conference hall for events, a store for beach clothes and towels, a small arcade, and another shop with fifty different flavors of saltwater taffy and fudge. Navigating the crowd was a little challenging—by the time people saw me they were usually ready to trip over me—but once we passed the last restaurant, it thinned out.

"All right, what's the deal with the fudge shops? Do people hit the beach and suddenly think, you know what, I've done Crossfit and quit carbs all winter to fit into this bikini, but screw it, I'm craving fudge, where can I get some?"

"You've never tried rocky road."

"Should I get us a sample? May as well have the full Crest Haven experience." She jogged back toward Croft's. The girl out front with the samples tray smiled as Cass took some fudge and came back. She held one out for me.

"No rocky road, but she said this white-chocolate cookie dough is insane." We popped it into our mouths at the same time. "Wow, that's like a carnival in your mouth," Cass said. "And to think I could have been working there."

"You could have been a Croft's girl?"

"You make it sound like something I should have considered."

"Nah, just . . . they have a rep for hiring hot girls."

"So do you think I would have fit in?"

Was she flirting with me? *Yessssssss.*

"What if I just said I'm glad you chose Camp Manatee, corny mascot and all?".

"I guess I'll take it," she said.

We continued down the promenade and finally made it to the Lexington Hotel. Cass looked at the street name.

"Cartwright Street?" she asked. "Or do you think it's the one on the other side?"

"Maybe you should take down both names and when we

have all the clues, we'll know which one it is because it will fit in with the rest of them."

"So you *are* thinking about this," she said.

"I'm very competitive. We need to win," I said.

"I think this discovery deserves a celebration."

"What did you have in mind?"

She pointed across the street to a retro-looking silver cart with a bright-red umbrella. A stand-up sign next to it read "Shore Pops—Five fresh flavors! Different every day!"

"C'mon, my treat. I'll go get them," she said.

"Okay."

She walked toward the stairs that led to the street, then turned before heading down. "Flavor?"

"Lemon."

"Very nice, and if they don't have that?"

"Surprise me."

I pushed my chair over toward the railing on the beach side. Typical Saturday at the shore. No open spots of sand. An army of brightly colored umbrellas standing at attention. The surf was mushy, slow flat waves, barely any white water, like Matt had mentioned. It still looked perfect to me. Translucent, green, the sun reflecting off the surface. I closed my eyes. Could almost imagine it washing over me.

"Okay, good news or bad news?" Cass was back, cellophane-wrapped ice pops in each hand.

"How can there be bad news about ice pops?"

"Well, they had lemon, so yay, but it's artisanal lemon infused with lavender and mint. Think you can handle it?"

"I love lavender. Very calming," I said.

She laughed and handed me the wrapped ice pop.

"Hey, would you mind taking a picture of me?" she asked, fumbling with her phone. She opened the camera function and handed it to me. I placed the pop and the phone between my leg and side guard and reversed away from the railing. She climbed on the bench, sitting on top of the part where people usually put their backs.

"Okay, move over that way, your face is sort of in shadow," I said, motioning for her to move to her right. She slid across, sat up straight, and arched her back. *Damn.*

"With the ice pop or without?" she asked so seriously I had to laugh.

"What's this for?"

"Um . . . to show someone on StalkMe I'm having the best time in the world without them."

"With, then," I said. She ripped open the pop and stuffed the wrapper into her front pocket, then resumed the arched-back sex-bomb pose, this time with the ice pop. I snapped a few before she said, "Oh, wait," and pulled her hair down, running a hand through it and letting it trail down her back.

"I would like to have this ice pop before it melts," I said, even though I wouldn't have cared if it were melting all over my chair pad and attracting bees. Having an excuse to stare at Cassidy was sweet.

"Just a few more," she said, grinning.

"Work it, baby," I joked. She burst out laughing and hopped off the bench.

"Let me see."

I handed her the phone and finally unwrapped the ice. It was already dripping in the heat. She scrolled through the photos, smiling.

"So I look like I'm having fun?"

"Totally," I said.

"Okay, your turn, cameraman."

"With the ice or without?" I teased.

"With, of course."

I mugged for the camera and put the ice pop in my mouth. My taste buds were expecting lemon but what I got was much more than that. I winced at the unexpected soapy flavor of lavender. Cass continued taking my picture and laughing.

"No fair," I said.

"Okay, now both of us," she said, crouching down and getting closer to me. Once our faces were framed on the phone screen, she took a few more shots.

"Bryan?"

We both looked up. Standing a couple of feet away from us was Shay and her douche-canoe college-guy boyfriend.

"Shay, hey, what's up?"

Cass stood up and slipped her phone into her back pocket, holding the pop in her mouth as she twisted up her hair again in the elastic. I took smug satisfaction in the way both Shay and douche canoe looked Cass up and down. *Yes, we're together.* It didn't even matter we weren't *together* together.

"You remember Tyler, right?"

Tyler, aka douche canoe, aka guy she'd been with since she broke up with me? Of course I remembered him.

"Yeah. Stockton?"

"Yep, just finished up my second year."

"This is Cassidy," I said. "We work at camp together."

"Oh," Shay said, "did you just move here?"

"Only for the summer."

"Cool."

"Her dad's Mr. Emmerich."

"I had him for chem," Tyler said.

"Nice," Cass answered.

"How do you like it here?" Shay asked.

"It's been fun, better since Bry has been showing me around."

I could have kissed her.

"Oh, great," Shay said, looking to me.

After more convo about the beautiful day and the surge of bennies for the Fourth, Tyler put his arm around Shay and said they had to get back to their beach blanket.

"Guess we'll be seeing you around, then," Shay said.

"Yeah, bye," I said.

Cassidy and I made our way back to where we'd met up. She waited until we finished our ice pops to grill me.

"Back there—friends of yours, I guess?"

"Something like that."

"They seemed nice."

"Not that nice. That was my ex-girlfriend," I confessed.

"I did sort of get that vibe," she said.

"Really?"

"Yeah, she checked me out a little too much," Cass said.

I laughed.

"How long have you been exes?"

It felt like eons ago. Another life. It hadn't even been a year.

"She broke up with me in September of last year."

"So you were together . . . before your accident?"

"Yeah, just about a year; things got a little complicated after that."

We went a bit without saying much. Cass finally said, "Well, that's awful."

"I probably would have broken up with me too. I had a hard enough time getting used to my body, so I couldn't expect her to be down with it too. It was tough though. I wasn't the most upbeat person to be around my first few weeks home. She just, you know, couldn't handle it. I don't blame her."

"And now you're seeing someone else?"

"Um . . . no."

She stopped. "You're not?"

I shook my head.

"Oh, Tori said—"

"Tori said?"

She looked as if she was sorry she'd brought it up. "She mentioned you were seeing her friend . . . Liv? The one whose place I took at Camp Manatee?"

I had no idea what Tori had said, but whatever it was, it had given Cass the wrong impression. "We hooked up a few times, went to prom, but that's it. I'm not with anyone at the moment. Well, except you, here."

"Oh," she said. We continued down the promenade. Had I shared too much? I hadn't anticipated having a conversation about my exes.

"So what about you? Who are you trying to show you're having the best time in the world without them?"

She sucked the corner of her lip in thought, then looked toward the beach. For a moment I thought I may have asked too much but, screw it, I was curious.

"A guy. Gavin. My ex. He's sort of the reason I'm here this summer."

Thank you, Gavin.

She continued.

"The pictures are my friend Emma's idea. Kind of a 'screw you, this is war'—I mean, I used to love StalkMe, until . . . well, that's how I found out he'd been, you know, with other people. He has this flask—"

"He carries a flask?"

"I know, pretentious hipster bullshit, right? It's not really even his flask, it's his father's, but anyway, he left it somewhere, and the person he left it with decided to take a picture and tag him, and me, and, well, then it just got messier. And yeah, here I am, trying to forget him and his stupid face."

"That . . . sucks. Sorry."

"I went to see the girl too. I was so humiliated by the whole thing and how it was just there for everyone to see and laugh about, and I was prepared to rip into her—it was someone he worked with, how cliché can I be here?—and then . . . when I saw her, I just couldn't. There was something sad about her. She's a year younger than me, and she looked so . . . like this had been the biggest thing that ever could have happened to her, and when she saw me she was scared, like I was going to tear her hair out, and I didn't want to be that person. Of course Gavin swept her up in his special Gavin-ness. He's good at it. I just hate how much the whole thing makes me doubt everything. Makes me doubt myself."

"Wow," I said.

"But, you know, it's nothing, compared to . . . I know I'm making a big deal out of nothing. . . ."

"It's not nothing, Cassidy. Breakups blow, no matter what happened."

She laughed. "I guess."

"Hey, can I see those pictures?"

She took out her phone and pulled them up, handed it to me.

I scrolled through the shots, each one better than the next. Then I found it, my favorite one. It was the least posed, the wind blowing her hair away from her face. She had this cute, natural smile—like she had just taken a bite of the ice pop and was laughing at something someone said off-camera. It was perfection.

"Here, post this one, that will get to him," I said. She took the phone from me.

"Really? I was thinking more like this one," she said, showing me one of the arched-back pouty ones.

"Can I be honest?"

"Um . . . okay, I think."

"No denying this is hot, but it looks almost too—"

"Posed? Like I'm trying too hard?"

"Kind of."

"Okay, agreed, the other one it is," she said, pulling up the StalkMe app and chuckling. She read the caption to me. "'Sea-salt caramel ice and the summer sun, another day in paradise.' Sound good?"

"Perfect."

Something had shifted between us, I wasn't quite sure what—this wasn't a date, it was hanging out, and maybe that's what had made swapping stories about our exes easy, comfortable. Every time I was around her, I wanted to know more about her. I wanted to study her face, find out what I had to say to make her smile.

"By the way, what I meant before—you would have totally fit in at Croft's. I'm just glad, you know, you chose camp instead."

She looked up from her phone and smiled.

"Me too."

ELEVEN
CASSIDY

THE FOURTH OF JULY WAS INSANELY BUSY. EVEN though I had off from camp, I'd been working all morning at Ocean Whispers. I helped Leslie make two batches of "Independence Muffins," filled fancy glass bowls with homemade clotted cream, strawberry preserves, and blueberry jam, draped red, white, and blue bunting along the railings, hung the No Vacancy sign underneath the regular one, watered flowers, and made raspberry lemonade from scratch, which was chilling in the fridge for afternoon tea. By eleven, I was ready to go back to bed. Instead I settled for hanging with Hunter and his kiddie pool in the yard, while catching up with Ems on the phone.

"Cass, well done with the bikini shot, but you need to be posting something like that every day. The picture of your feet in flip-flops or a giant manatee mascot does not have the same effect."

"You know I'm not a selfie person."

"Pretend you are; keep 'em coming," she said, the sound of hangers slapping together in the background as she searched her closet.

Hunter splashed me. "C'mon, Cass, come in."

"I think I'll pass on the ankle-deep water, thanks." For some reason he found this hysterical and convulsed into a fit of giggles.

"Hey, I'm putting you on speaker, okay?" Emma said, her voice far away as she continued. "So, what fun, exciting thing are you going to be doing today? Please tell me your toes will be in the sand."

"Nope, it's wall-to-wall bennies down at the beach," I said.

"Cassidy, you better scope out the fun places to hang out, because when this benny gets there in a few weeks, we are not going to be sitting around some sleepy little B&B, got me?"

"Yes, Ems. What are you doing today?" I asked.

She remained silent, but it was one of those very full, *I really don't want to tell you what I'm doing* silences. It must have involved jerkface.

"You can tell me, really. I know it's unavoidable."

I heard drawers opening and closing. Emma was probably searching for the perfect outfit. My stomach ached with envy. Not because I wanted to be around Gavin, but because I missed being around people and places I knew, was comfortable in. I missed Ems. I missed knowing I would always have something to do.

"The Henleys are having a pig roast today; apparently it's a thing they do every year. I really don't want to go, but Drew can't stop talking about it."

Gavin had mentioned the Henleys' annual pig roast to me before, how much he hated it. How the whole thing always felt like it was more about his father trying to impress his business associates than just a family barbecue. How he used to have nightmares that the pig was still alive when they put it in the pit. How much he hated that it still looked like an actual pig.

"Sounds barbaric. Are they roasting Gavin?" Ems laughed.

"Yeah, well, there's a pool and Drew and a martini fountain, so I'm going to focus on those things, and stay away from the pit. You're not pissed, are you? I hate situations like this."

I wanted to hug her for playing it down.

"Why would I be pissed? It's not like I'm there and you're bailing on me."

"Are you sure?"

"Yes. You should wear the red halter top with the white stars, you look hot in that," I said.

"Get out! I have that exact top in my hand, Cass; what are you, psychic?"

"If I were psychic, I think I could have avoided a lot of heartache," I said.

"Ha, right? Gotta run, Drew will be here in, like, five minutes and I'm still not ready. Make sure you take more selfies! Hot ones! No more feet!"

"Sure, bye."

Maybe I was a little pissed. Pissed that she was so excited, and I was sitting in a yard, two feet from a kiddie pool. I did have on my new bikini. Selfie time.

I slipped my shades back on, sat up, tilted my face toward the sun, and started snapping away. Hunter splashed me again.

"Please come in, Cassidy."

I sighed and put my phone on the patio table. Maybe I wasn't doing anything, but at least I had the cutest date. I scooted my chair closer to the pool.

"Hunter, I'll take up the whole pool. Would you settle for this?" I asked, plunging my feet into the six inches of water.

"Yay!" Hunter sized up what exactly my feet and legs would serve in his imaginary world. In no time, his action-figure great white shark was swimming around my legs. I closed my eyes. The lazy sound of buzzing bees from the garden lulled me toward sleep. Who needed a pig roast and martini fountain anyway?

"Wade likes you," Hunter said, not missing a beat with the shark, who he now had swimming toward a floating pirate island. I put my hand up to shield my eyes from the sun.

"What are you talking about?"

"He said you were pretty and stacked."

"Wait, he said that to you?"

The pirate island overturned; Great White lunged for the pirates.

"No. To Bryan. What does stacked mean, anyway?"

"Um, tall. Does he know you heard him?"

Hunter shrugged. A screen door rattled shut. I turned to see Leslie coming down the deck stairs with a towel.

"Did Bryan say anything to him?" I asked. This was what my life had come to . . . grilling a six-year-old about guys.

"Nope," he said, tossing the toy shark up in the air.

"Hey, buddy, time to get ready. Cass, is that what you're going to wear?" Leslie held the towel open for Hunter.

"Wear? What do you mean?"

"We're going to the Lakewoods' this afternoon; didn't your father tell you?"

"No, he didn't. How much time do I have?" I was sticky with sweat and sunscreen.

"About half an hour."

I raced upstairs to change.

The Lakewoods lived about twenty minutes from the main part of town. The roads were a little more winding, without many stops, and everything was so green. We passed farm stands selling tomatoes, fresh-cut flowers, home-baked bread—some even using the honor system, which would never fly back home. This was another world entirely.

"I feel sick," Hunter said.

"We're almost there, sweetie, can you hold on? Do your breathing."

Hunter squeezed his eyes shut, took a deep breath, counted to five on his fingers, and let the breath out. Then he repeated it. I found myself following him as he continued. My stomach was queasy from the bumpy ride too. Finally Dad pulled down a narrow paved road lined with trees that opened up to a sprawling green lawn and a small yellow house that could only be described as cheerful. There was a porch with a swing and a ramp and so many hanging planters spilling over with brightly colored flowers. Several cars were scattered around on the grass. I spied Bryan's car and felt a little jolt that put me on edge. Maybe it wasn't the roads I'd been queasy about.

I helped Hunter out of his car seat and adjusted my shorts and halter top, the same top I'd told Ems to wear, only in blue, which I suddenly felt self-conscious about. *Why didn't I wear a tee? Less skin showing.* Hunter grabbed my hand, or maybe I grabbed his—new things, new people, simultaneously exciting and scary—and we walked through a vine-covered archway that led to the backyard.

"Jeff! Leslie! You made it!" A woman with dark hair, Bermuda jean shorts, and a white blouse that tied in a knot at her waist came up to us. She tousled Hunter's hair and gave me an approving once-over. "Cassidy?"

"That's me."

"I'm Angie Lakewood, Bryan's mom. Well, Matt and Bryan's mom, but I think you know Bryan from camp."

I smiled. "Yes, I do."

She took the serving dish from Leslie. "Will's cooking brats and burgers, and if you're at all interested in home brews, he made one special for today." She looked over her shoulder and then back to us, lowering her voice. "I hear it's sort of sour, so don't feel bad about turning him down, lots of other options. Hey, Cass, would you put this in the kitchen on the table? Leslie, it smells amazing."

"Her famous blueberry crumb cake. I can vouch for its amazingness," my father said, putting an arm around Leslie's shoulder. She turned bright red.

"Family recipe."

"I hate blueberries," Hunter exclaimed, then took off toward a group of little kids who were playing keep it up with a beach ball.

Mrs. Lakewood handed me the blueberry cake. "Bryan's over there, honey."

I searched the crowd for a familiar face. Mr. Beckett was there, looking more like an aged surfer dude than a polo-wearing camp director. Bryan was in his wheelchair and sitting with some people I didn't know. I saw Tori with a few girls, and there was another group of guys and girls near a half-pipe on the far end of the yard watching someone on a skateboard do tricks. And there I stood, alone, holding a blueberry cake. I walked in the direction Mrs. Lakewood had pointed and climbed the deck stairs two at a time.

I slid open the door and stepped into the kitchen. A tall, sandy-haired boy stood there with a cookie in his mouth, looking as if I'd caught him doing something he shouldn't. I laughed, then realized who I was looking at. Last time I'd seen him he was hanging out of Bryan's car. He bit into the cookie and smiled, putting a finger up to his lips. I placed the blueberry cake down on the table with the other desserts.

"Hey, I'm Cassidy."

He swallowed. "I'm Matt, Bryan's bro—"

"Brother who likes to hang out windows of cars and scare girls. We've sort of met before, haven't we?"

"Oh, um, that," he said, averting his eyes and finishing the cookie.

"Yeah, that."

It was hard to be angry anymore. Face-to-face, in the kitchen, he was just a guy with a cookie in his mouth. He seemed smaller and definitely not as creepy. He resembled Bryan, but with more angular features, lighter hair. I was having fun making him squirm.

"Just my way of welcoming you to town."

"You should really work on another way," I said.

"I will," he said.

I stepped back outside and did Hunter's count-to-five

breathing trick. Bryan spotted me and waved. His smile was a beacon in an alien sea. I trotted down the steps and walked toward him.

"Hey, Cass," Wade said, getting up. "Take a seat."

Next to him was Tori, whose tight-lipped, quiet hello made me think twice about sitting down, but Wade's outstretched hand and insisting smile wouldn't have it any other way.

"What are you drinking?" he asked.

I blanked and shrugged. "Um, Sprite?"

"Sure; anyone else?" he asked, looking around before heading off to the table with the drinks.

"Didn't realize you would be here," Bryan said.

"Neither did I," I said, smiling maybe a little too much. It was nice to see him. My body wanted to spring up and move closer, but I felt obligated to stay in the seat Wade had given up. Wade came back with my drink and another folding chair. He handed me the soda, then parked himself near Bryan.

"I hear you guys are kicking our ass with the scavenger hunt," Wade said.

"I don't know about kicking ass, but we did find two more clues this week," I said. We were taking them one at a time. They'd been easy ones, in and around camp. One had led us to a towel, which we figured out pretty quick, and the other was about Monty. I kind of hoped the others would require more effort, like the day Bryan and I went to the promenade. It had been fun hanging out with him.

"It's all Cass, I'm just there to write it down," Bryan said.

"See, Tor, we gotta get moving," Wade said.

Tori was busy scrolling through her phone. She looked up after Wade spoke.

"*We?* Really? Why don't *we* just wait until the last minute like we did last year, and I'll figure them all out."

"We could work together," I said to her.

She looked at me. "I think that's against the rules."

"I don't think there are any rules," Wade said.

"Whatever, we'll figure it out," Tori said. "Hey, by the way, everyone, Liv says hello. She's in Galveston today."

She scrolled through a few more messages. "And she's going to Austin next week. She's so lucky."

"Why would you want to be anywhere else but here for the Fourth?" Wade said. "We have the better beaches."

"She says a special hello to you, Bry," Tori said. Bryan raised his eyebrows in surprise. "Should I say anything back?"

"Sure. Tell her I said happy Fourth."

Tori shook her head and laughed, tapping away on her phone. Bryan looked at me. He'd told me the truth about Liv. I wasn't sure why Tori kept this up, but it was suddenly clear that she wanted me to believe that Bryan was involved with Liv, even though he really wasn't. I just didn't understand why. Did she not think I was good enough? Not that I wanted to be involved with Bryan in any other way than friendship, but it still got me a little steamed. I'd done nothing to Tori, had even gone out of my way to be nice, and she still kept me at arm's length.

"Here, look, Cass, this is Bryan and Liv at prom," Tori said, handing me her phone.

Liv was pretty in a bodycon cobalt dress, her light-brown hair in a curly updo. Bryan wore a black suit with a tie that matched her dress. She was sort of draped over Bryan in his wheelchair. They were on the dance floor and they both looked like they were having a great time. Tori reached over and scrolled to a group shot. I recognized her and Wade and even a few of the kids at the barbecue now. My throat tightened. I shifted in my chair.

"Did you and Wade go together?" I asked.

"No," she said, a little too forcefully. Wade flinched.

"Sheesh, Tor, if I'd asked you would it have been that bad?"

Tori blinked a few times, then whispered, "Yeah, right."

"What?" Wade asked. She turned her face to me and ignored him.

"You look really pretty. I had the same color dress," I said. *I just never wore it.*

"Got any pictures?" she asked.

I was about to lie. It would have been easy just to say *no, I have a new phone* or something, but I didn't care about the awkward anymore. "No, I ended up not going."

Her face scrunched in confusion. "But you had a dress?"

"Yep, you can figure it out from there," I said, getting up.

I walked toward the group near the half-pipe. I wouldn't have to talk to anyone, could just stand there and watch. I didn't even look back.

The half-pipe was entertaining, but the best part was I'd been right; everyone stared ahead and took turns and didn't say much more than *cool* and *all right. Had Bryan ever skated like this? Was that how he'd gotten hurt?* All my father had said was he took a fall. One day I'd ask him. Maybe he'd tell me.

"Cass!" I turned to see Jena, the lifeguard from the rec center.

"Hey, what are you doing here?"

"Nick invited me," she said, motioning with her head to look behind her. Nick was there, his skate helmet unhooked. His eyes followed the guy on the board now. He turned and saw me. "Hey."

"Hey." I took out my phone to snap a picture. I'd never hung out around a half-pipe before, probably way cooler than a pig roast.

"Jena, come on, take a picture with me," I said. Jena, Nick, and a few other kids gathered around and grinned for the camera. I posted it to StalkMe with the caption:

Awesome time celebrating the 4th with some new friends!

At least it looked like the truth.

TWELVE
BRYAN

"FOOD'S OUT, COME ON, EAT!" MY MOTHER CALLED.

"No one has to tell me twice; want anything?" Wade asked. Getting waited on was a #wheelchairperk I wasn't in the mood for at the moment. I needed to tell Tori to cool it with the Liv stuff.

"Nah, I'll get something in a bit," I said.

"Can't promise there'll be any potato salad left by the time I'm done." He wandered off toward the food. Tori was about to follow when I tapped her arm.

"Can we talk?" I asked. She frowned slightly and moved to let some of the others who'd been on the patio go past her. She pulled up a lawn chair next to me.

"Why so serious?"

"Why did you tell Cassidy that I'm seeing Liv?"

She looked down, inspected her fingernails. "I don't know, it just came out. I saw the way you were looking at her on the first day of camp. And . . . just, no."

"No? Since when do you care who I . . . wait, what do you mean, the way I was looking at her?"

"Let's just say, if you were a cartoon character, your eyes would be stars, maybe hearts at this point."

"C'mon."

"That's what I saw. That's what I always see this time of the year. All of you get a little stupid over the summer girls."

"Cassidy isn't a summer girl. It's different. We're just friends anyway."

"Then why do you care so much if I tell her you're seeing Liv?"

"Because I'm not seeing Liv."

"You could be. Benny Barbie is going to be gone at the end of the summer and Liv will be back and she actually lives here and cares about you."

I thought about the last time I'd seen Liv, what she'd said.

"No, Tori, she doesn't."

"Yes she does. Look, I know what happened."

"What?"

"I know she told you she couldn't handle it."

The blood left my face. I knew Tori and Liv were tight, but I didn't want to think about what else she'd told her. About what had happened in her basement that night. In the beginning, after my fall, I had no choice but to have people talk about me as if I were an object, touching me, prodding me, speculating about my ability to take a piss or get a hard-on as if I wasn't even in the room. Part of me learned to laugh about it, but this was different. Personal. I didn't need Tori or anyone else trying to fix my life anymore. Her stare was a white-hot spotlight on my face. I made a conscious effort not to physically react to what she said.

"I wish she hadn't talked to you about that."

Her expression softened. "She didn't tell me specifics, Bryan, just that you left and you haven't talked since. She's felt bad about it."

"She's had time to talk to me about it. She never did," I said.

"You never really let her, did you?"

"Tori, she told me the truth that night, and it's fine, because maybe I couldn't handle being with her either."

"What's that supposed to mean?"

"It means that even if that didn't happen, we probably wouldn't be together. I think we had other problems besides me being in this chair."

"Like what? You guys were pretty perfect together."

"I don't like her like that, okay? Never did. I tried and I think she's great. I just don't want to be with her, so stop trying to fix it. Why are you all over me when you don't even have the balls to tell Wade how you feel?"

My words stung. She opened her mouth to speak, then closed it again, looked away. "How do you even know that?"

"You, um, have some stars too," I said.

She put a hand to her forehead. "Oh, God, it's that obvious."

"To me; maybe not to him."

She sat back in the lawn chair, crossed her legs. "Of course, it's summer, I'm invisible."

"I think you're exaggerating."

"Really? Because it's all I hear him talk about. Benny chicks, summer girls, tourist babes—I can't compete with new and no strings attached."

"You should just tell him."

"That's asking for disaster."

Wade came back with a plate piled high with food, balanced on a red party cup, and sat down across from us. He looked at Tori, then me as he put the cup on the ground next to his feet. "What'd I miss?"

"Everything, as usual," Tori said, standing up. "Want anything, Bry?"

"Nah, I'll go over there in a minute."

She shot Wade a look before walking away. Definitely one with no stars.

"What's her problem?" he said, practically inhaling his chili dog.

"She likes you."

He puzzled while chewing. "Well, duh, it's Tori."

"No, dude, think about what I just said."

He flinched, looked over toward her, then back at me. A series of expressions—disbelief, wonder, shock—lit up his face before he finally picked up his chili dog again. He stopped midbite and put it down. "Nah . . . really?"

"Yes, really. Now you know, so do something about it. Or not," I said.

I scoped the yard for Cass. She was headed our way with Jena and Nick.

"Cass!" I called. She said something to them, then broke away and came over.

"Hey."

"Do you think you could help me over at the food table?" I asked.

Wade looked up from his food and grinned. He knew this was something I'd never do normally, but acting helpless was such a helpful #wheelchairperk, especially when flirting. And that's what I was doing. Taking my own advice. Going for it. She smiled.

"Okay, sure. I'm starving."

Later, when the sun finally set, we gathered out front to watch the fireworks display that my dad and Owen put on every year. It wasn't as big as the ones near the beach, but they did have enough artillery shells and repeaters to make it impressive. Cass was busy helping Hunter catch fireflies, a huge grin on her face as she closed her palms around one. She opened her hands to let Hunter take a peek.

I knew Cassidy Emmerich was a summer girl. Tori was right—she'd be gone at the end of the tourist season, but as I sat there watching her, I didn't care. I liked her. I did. There was something about Cass when she didn't realize anyone was watching her. She was sincere. That's the best way I could describe it. I saw it when she helped the kids in camp, when she laughed with Jena at the pool in the morning, and now with Hunter. And in that moment, as she held out her hand to let the firefly loose, I realized that I didn't care whether she was in Crest Haven for four minutes, four hours, four days, or four weeks. I wanted to be in Cassidy's life, to know her, and whatever time we had, it would have to be enough.

She caught me looking and smiled.

"Is your father really setting off fireworks? Can he do that?" She came over and crouched down next to me.

"He does the mayor's lawn."

"Ah, so he has an in."

"Well, that and the cops wouldn't know where to look; once it gets dark it sounds like a war zone around here. As long as no one gets hurt, everyone's cool."

"That's good. Wouldn't be the Fourth without fireworks."

"About that—did you read the latest clue on the scavenger hunt?"

"Yep. How did it go . . . ?"

"Look up at the sky on this holiday night, rain will come down, burning so bright."

"I think I know what it means. How about you?"

Her eyes held mine. God, could she see the stars Tori teased me about? I could look at her all night.

"Fireworks," we both said.

"Seems too easy," she said.

"I don't think they're all supposed to be hard. We have to put them together; that'll be a challenge."

"I think we're going to kick ass," she said.

The first firework went off, a bright-red artillery shell that caused a couple of the kids hunting for fireflies to stop and look up. Someone said *Wow*. Another went off, then another. Cass pulled out her phone and snapped a few pics. I wondered if they were just for her, or if she was going to post them to bother her ex.

"Cass, we have to head out after the last one goes off," Mr. Emmerich said, walking up behind us.

"Nooooo," Hunter said. "Why do we always have to leave in the middle of everything?"

Cass pulled him over to her and wrapped her arms around him in a playful hug. "Dad said we're leaving when it's *over,* bud. It's still happening. Enjoy it now."

"I hate when things end," he said.

Wise words for a little dude. I couldn't have agreed with him more.

Monday, Cass was a no-show for swimming. I tried to focus, put in a good workout—that was what I was there for: to swim, to get stronger, prepping to go back into the ocean. *Stroke, breathe, stroke, breathe, blue bikini.* Gah. I swam until my arms stung, then got the noodles to do my blissed-out floaty thing, as Jena and Cass called it. While I tried to breathe, just let go and imagine I was in the ocean, I got the feeling I was being watched.

I opened my eyes.

Wade. He leaned against Jena's lifeguard perch, which she didn't mind at all. She twirled the cord of her whistle around her forefinger while beaming at him.

"Hey, who knew you could get up this early," I said.

"Ha, funny. Like I've been able to sleep at all after what you told me."

"Huh?"

"I'll meet you at the other end," he said, pointing to where I kept my wheelchair. I wasn't quite ready to finish; there was still some time and I was holding out for Cass to arrive, but an up-early Wade was a Wade with something on his mind. I put the noodles back by the lifeguard stand, thanked Jen, and swam to the end of the pool where he was waiting.

"You're looking really strong, Bry. Think you'll be ready to swim on field day?"

"Field day? Nah, too much to pay attention to with the

kids, but you know . . . soon. Hey, have you been surfing with Matt and those guys?" I pulled myself up, spun, and sat, unhooking the clips on my pull buoy.

Wade tossed me a towel and sat down, hands clasped around his knees.

"Dude, you can tell me if you go, I don't care," I said.

"Ah, yeah, only once or twice. I *am* trying to hold out until you're ready, and you look pretty ready, dude."

"You don't have to do that."

"I want to do that."

"Have you seen Matty with my fish?"

"Your red board? Nah. Just the longboard. Why?"

"He just . . . he used it and he hasn't returned it. I know I'm not using it, but—I think he wrecked it and he's afraid to tell me," I said.

"I haven't seen him with it, but I've only been out with them a couple of times. I don't think he'd wreck it."

I wanted to believe it. I'd been doing some online research on how to adapt a surfboard. I wasn't sure if I was going to do it, but it was nice to think about being on the fish again. I ran the towel across my head.

"So why haven't you been able to sleep?"

"Check this . . . so the other night, this hot tourist chick comes into the restaurant and we just hit it off. She's with her parents but at the end of the meal she gives me her number. Do you want to know what I did with it?"

"Do I have to ask?"

"Nothing. Nada. *Niente.*"

"Really?"

He leaned back on his hands. "You and your *so do something about it*. Like what, Bry? Tori's Tori. I can't say I've never thought about her that way, because I have . . . a lot . . . but it scares the hell out of me. It's too real."

"I get it—and then what happens when it all goes bad? Can you really be friends?"

"I'm not worried about it going bad, I'm worried about it going good."

I thought he was kidding, but he didn't flinch or crack a smile.

"That's . . . wow, totally not what I was expecting."

"It takes constant maintenance when it's going good. And I don't mean like Tori's hard to impress or not worth it, it's just work. I've seen the poor schmucks my sisters date and they're like sheep, man. We're going to be seniors. I don't want to worry about anyone's happiness but my own. I know how that sounds, but screw it."

The women's locker room door burst open and Cass came out, wheeling the towel bin. Her face was flushed. She smiled when she saw me and Wade.

"I totally overslept this morning; really could have used a swim too," she said, pushing the bin past us and going to fill up the rack behind us.

“So, Cass is here, like, every day?”

I looked down into the pool, trying my hardest not to grin, but I couldn’t help it.

Wade shook his head and smiled. “Lakewood, you dog.”

THIRTEEN
CASSIDY

I SAT ON MY WICKER CHAIR AND STARED OUT THE window at the big gray clouds that rolled across the sky. The ocean looked inky, even in the early-evening light. Choppy white caps dotted the surface. No magical sunsets for Crest Haven that evening.

The week so far had been rain, rain, and more rain. I was hiding out. Hunter had been going on and on about some new game at the arcade called Whack-a-Shark and I wasn't in the mood. I hadn't heard from Ems since the Fourth, and as much as I didn't want to know what had happened at the Henleys', I kind of did. She had liked my pictures on StalkMe, so I knew she saw. I just wondered what was up. Being ghosted by her was so not cool.

Someone tapped on my door.

"Come in."

Hunter.

I'd been found.

"Hey," I said.

"Wanna go get an ice? It's not raining right now, and Dad said you can take me. It's only a few blocks away."

"Sip N' Freeze? Sure."

Outside, the air was still, like Crest Haven was holding its breath waiting for something to happen. I heard a rumbling in the distance, but couldn't tell if it was thunder or a car. I held Hunter's hand tighter.

"C'mon, I want to get back before it pours."

"I brought my 'brella! Got us covered!" Hunter said, twirling it around his wrist.

We walked the three blocks to Sip N' Freeze and I tried to keep up with Hunter's constant chatter about the slush flavors. He liked root beer but they ran out of it a lot, and cherry was close behind, but not sour cherry because that made his tongue feel like pins were sticking in it. His absolute favorite was blue raspberry because it had the extra-special effect of being able to turn his tongue bright blue, which lasted even after he brushed his teeth. By the time we reached Sip N' Freeze, I was sure I could win a slush trivia contest.

I'd thought the crappy weather would keep the crowds away, but Sip N' Freeze was packed. A line stretched all the way to the sidewalk. The break in the rain must have made everyone want to get out. We stood at the end of the line.

"It's gonna take forever."

"It'll be worth it," I said, ignoring another low rumble in the distance.

My phone went off in my back pocket.

Ems. I picked up right away.

"Omigod, it's about time you called me. How was the pig roast? A disaster, I hope."

Silence.

"Emma?"

"It *was* a fucking disaster. Wanna know why?"

My stomach dropped.

It wasn't Emma.

"Cassidy, please don't hang up."

Tears popped up, *fucking tears*, involuntarily. I'd thought I was finished crying over him, but the sound of his voice . . . *I loved the sound of his voice. . . .* There was always an edge to it, like the next thing he would say was going to be some wild revelation. *Or lie—it could be a fucking lie, remember that?*

I slowed my breathing. Hunter tugged on my shorts to step forward. I didn't hang up, but I didn't say anything either.

"Are you still there?"

"That was low," I said.

"You wouldn't pick up if you knew it was me."

"Emma would never—"

"Emma doesn't know, okay? They're outside in the pool right now. I came in, and she'd left her phone on the counter."

"She'd never do that."

"Okay, I swiped it from her bag. Does it matter? I just . . . I wanted to hear your voice."

"Well, you've heard it. Good-bye."

I made no move to hang up.

"You asked about me. You thought I was Emma and you asked about me."

"I asked about the pig roast, but I guess that's the same thing, isn't it?"

He chuckled. "Okay, I deserve that. I miss you, Cassidy."

We moved up in line.

"What do you want?"

"You. Always you. Come home."

"How can you even be serious right now?" A mom in front of us gave me a once-over and I realized I was talking loud. I leaned down to Hunter. "Do you think you could keep our place while I go over there and talk?"

He looked doubtful, even a little scared. "How about if I just move over here, like two feet away, and I keep moving up with you?"

"Mmmkay," he said.

I stepped away until he gave me a thumbs-up. I turned my back.

"Who are you with?" Gavin asked.

"None of your business. I don't even know why I'm still on the phone with you."

"I think it's because deep down, you miss me too. Cass."

Did I? Hearing his voice stirred up something—feelings, not all bad but not all good. I couldn't answer that. He continued.

"I miss you so much. I fucked up, I get it. I'm not . . . with that girl anymore. I never really was, Cass. Not like with us. Please stop punishing me."

"Me being here is not about punishing you," I said.

"It isn't? Then why aren't you answering my texts? Why are you suddenly posting all these pictures after two months of nothing?"

"Because I have a life that doesn't revolve around you. I have something to post."

"Tell me you didn't post that blue bikini picture just to drive me a little crazy. Tell me, and I'll hang up. I won't bother you again."

My mouth was open, the words right there, *no, I didn't post it for you.* But I couldn't say it. It was a fucking lie. Everything . . . *fuck* . . . everything was still for him.

He sighed. Heavy. Satisfied.

"It worked, Cassidy. You win, okay? I need you. There's so much . . . shit, Emma's coming. Call me. Please. Say you'll at least think about it."

"I'll think about it," I whispered.

"I love you, Cass." The phone went silent.

A rushing sound filled my head; there was laughter and

yells. Hunter jumped up and down, wielding his unopened umbrella like a sword. I was instantly cold and wet. The sky had let loose but I was frozen in place. There I was, thinking I'd forgotten about Gavin. I had a new life, new friends, new job—a little protective bubble by the sea. How could one phone call unravel it? The mom with her two kids who stood in front of Hunter opened up a large black umbrella. She corralled him to come under cover, then waved at me. A raindrop dripped off my nose.

I love you, Cass.

I inched my way toward the woman; by the time I reached her I was drenched.

She smiled. "I hope that was an important call."

She was younger close-up and had a friendly face. The kind of person you could unload your troubles on. I needed someone to tell me that everything was going to be okay. I needed Mom and Nan. I resisted the urge to spill my guts.

"No, it wasn't," I said.

My phone rang. Emma.

I wasn't falling for that again.

By the time we reached the front of the line, I had several texts from someone who I could only assume was the real Ems.

What a prick!

Are you okay?

I'm mad at you!

How could you not tell me about Sugar Rush NATE!!!???

Deetz!!!

Crap. It was my turn to ghost her.

After we got Hunter's slush we moved to the side of the building where there was an overhang. It was a tight squeeze, but we managed. The rain didn't look like it would ever let up.

Call me.

I couldn't. Could I? What purpose would it serve?

"I think my 'brella would cover us."

"Doubtful. It'll let up soon."

A horn beeped, then the car flashed its high beams. Someone waved frantically, but I couldn't see a face.

"Is that for you?" the guy next to us asked.

"No," I said, but suddenly the door opened and a bright-blue umbrella fanned out as a person stepped from the car.

Tori.

"Do you want a ride?" she asked.

"Yes!" Hunter declared.

"Wait there," she said, coming over. Hunter grabbed her hand. I followed. "No, stay, I'll come back."

"It's okay, I'm drenched already."

We walked to the car. She opened the rear door for Hunter, then reached in and handed me a bright-orange beach towel with tropical flowers on it. I wrapped it around my shoulders.

"At least it's something," she said. "Get in."

She held the umbrella up over my head as I ducked into the front seat. The car was small and smelled faintly of stale smoke. A faded air freshener in the shape of a pineapple hung from the rearview mirror. A monster slush sat in the cup holder. This was definitely not Tori's car.

She climbed in, folded the umbrella, and tucked it in the well behind the front seat.

"Are you buckled in, Hunter?"

"Yep. I usually need a booster," he said.

"Buddy, special circumstances, okay? We're only going a few blocks. You know where Ocean Whispers is?"

Tori nodded as she put the car in reverse and guided us out of the spot with ease.

"Thanks," I said.

"Don't mention it."

I pointed at the big cup. "You don't seem like the gallon-of-slush type."

She laughed. "I'll take that as a compliment. Yeah, that's for Nick. He's finally going to give his slush a name; he's throwing a party at Sip N' Freeze and everything."

"Wait . . . his slush?"

"You must be the only person he hasn't told, then—they named a slush after him. Up until now it's been called the Nick Bardot. Pineapple with a cinnamon swirl."

"He must like slush."

"There are four places you can find my brother these days.

The cove, the rec center, our house, or Sip N' Freeze. This mix was his favorite last summer. I think he ordered one every day."

"Well, that's something, isn't it?"

"Yeah, achievement unlocked."

"My favorite is blue raspberry," Hunter said from the back.

"Yeah, I can see that, Blue Lips," Tori said.

We pulled up to Ocean Whispers a few moments later. Dad was on the porch. I reached for the door handle.

"Cass, wait, can we talk a minute?" Tori asked.

"Um, sure. Hunter, will you tell Dad I'll be, like, five minutes?"

"Yep!" Hunter juggled the slush and his umbrella, pretty much a disaster waiting to happen. I watched as he teetered up the paved path to the front door. There were guests on the porch. Dad looked like he was talking to one of them and smiled when Hunter walked up the steps. He took the big cup from him and looked it over, shaking his head, but still smiling. I turned back to Tori.

"So, what's up?"

"Cass, um, I know I haven't been that . . . welcoming. I'm sorry."

"You don't need to apologize to me."

"Yeah I do. I was kind of a jerk on the first day, and I haven't been that much better since then. I miss Liv. And I was a little annoyed that I didn't have a say in her replacement. I shouldn't have taken that out on you though."

I appreciated the apology—would have probably felt the same way if I was in a similar situation with Emma—but I could feel a cry coming on and all I wanted to do was get upstairs to my room. "It's fine. You really weren't that bad."

"Yeah, I kind of was. I told you that Bryan was seeing Liv because I saw the way he . . . well . . . you're just here for the summer, Cass. A summer girl. New. Different."

"Summer girl?"

"You mean you haven't heard Wade go on about tourist girls?"

"I'm not really a tourist," I said. At least I didn't think of myself that way. Was that the way they thought of me?

"No, you're not; the point is, I told you Bryan was seeing someone because he likes you. You must know that, right?"

"I like him too," I said.

"Yeah, but he *likes* you. I just don't want to see him get hurt, he's been through a lot—

"He told me about Shay," I said. "Even Liv."

"He did?"

"Yes. Friends tell each other things."

"I'm sorry. I get a little protective sometimes. I thought Liv would be good for him, but you can't really force something, you know? Just, be careful with him, that's all."

Did she really think I'd do something to hurt Bryan?

"Do you know why I'm here, Tori?"

"What, like on the planet, or here in Crest Haven?"

"I'm here because I broke up with a guy I want to forget," I said, my voice cracking. That was all it took before my own flood started running down my face. I bowed my head and wiped the tears with the back of my hand. I felt weird in front of Tori, but I couldn't stop it.

"Cass, oh . . . hey," she said. She leaned over and opened the glove compartment, rifling through it and muttering the word *pig*, which for some reason made me laugh. She handed me a black bandanna, but just as I was about to take it she pulled it away and flung it toward the backseat. She closed the glove compartment.

"Ew, sorry, I shouldn't have given that to you; it was ripe."

I laughed. "It's fine."

"This should be okay," she said, lifting a corner of the towel I still had wrapped around my shoulders. I wiped my face.

"I didn't mean to make you cry," she said.

"It's not you, it's Gavin . . . that's my ex. . . . He called me when we were waiting in line, and it just, well, made me feel crappy all over again. Things were good—I hadn't been thinking about him much at all, then bam, he calls. He misses me. He hooked up with some other girl, who pretty much flaunted it in my face, and now *he* misses *me*. I came here because he's going off to school at the end of the summer, and I thought I'd never have to see him again. I think I left because I knew . . . I do still sort of care. That's screwed up, isn't it?"

"He sounds like a jerk," she said.

A defense of Gavin popped into my head. *Defense?* Like I could call him a jerk, but she couldn't because she didn't really know him. I hated that that was my first response. Clearly I still had feelings for him. Feelings that putting a hundred miles between us hadn't resolved. Crest Haven was like a beautiful illusion I'd created to distract myself. Pathetic.

"I guess what I'm saying is—I respect your friendship with Bryan. I do. I'm not looking to hook up with anyone. It would be nice to go out once in a while though, with someone other than Hunter."

"You should hang out, Cass. You can call *me* too, you know—it doesn't have to be all work, or scavenger hunts. Maybe we should just forget about these first few weeks and start fresh. Would you be my friend, Benny Barbie?"

I laughed. "I hate that nickname."

"I've come to think of it as kind of an endearment. Even the benny part."

"Okay, friends."

"Also . . . I'm kind of stumped—I want to teach healthy breakfasts for class next week. All I'm finding is really boring stuff, and I figure since you live at a B-and-B you probably have access to cool recipes. Something for the tweens. Maybe a meal they could whip up themselves? I know it's short notice, but—"

"Yes, I'd love to."

"Great."

I got out of the car, pushed open the gate, and ran through the rain toward the porch. I was soaked so the attempt to get to cover faster was a bit silly. *Breakfast.* I could do that. That would be something to think about, to occupy my mind. Maybe Tori would include me in more of her plans if I came up with something good. *Benny Barbie.* I laughed at the nickname. I was back on track, the phone call forgotten.

I love you, Cass.

Okay, maybe not totally forgotten. But I would *not* call him.

I love you, Cass.

The words woke me.

I sat up, looked around the room.

They were only in my head, haunting me from my earlier call with Gavin.

Still.

There's so much . . .

What had he been about to say before Emma came in and interrupted him? There's so much . . . what?

I kept torturing myself with it.

I'd plugged in my phone across the room to charge before going to bed. Hoping, once again, that my trick of out-of-sight, out-of-mind, across-the-room-seems-so-far-away-when-I'm-comfy-in-bed would work. I'd resisted, but now, with my room dark and everything so quiet . . . *I love you, Cass.*

I wanted to talk to him.

I didn't want to talk to him.

Only.

I did.

Why?

Deep down, I did miss him. In spite of everything.

The girl he worked with . . . Kaitlyn. It was easier to distance myself when I didn't think of her name, or her, or when exactly whatever it was that happened between them happened. I never asked how she got the flask—I was too stunned when her friend came up to me, giggling and smirky, and handed it to me in front of school before first bell. I didn't need specifics. I could see it in Gavin's eyes when I gave the flask back to him. He hardly looked at me. *Something* happened. At work, after work, whenever. Not only had I been tagged in a picture of the flask on StalkMe, but a picture of him and Kaitlyn together from her account. Sure, they were side by side; nothing was going on in the photo but they were close, and the look on her face . . . the flashy smile, the way she leaned in, the way they leaned together. Was she the one who sent the *Dimples* card?

He protested. *Why would she tag you if anything had been going on?*

I didn't know, but soon other people around school seemed to.

I'd gone from being invisible to gossip fodder over a weekend, and I wasn't even in the picture. It was torture, feeling that exposed when I'd done nothing. My private life suddenly public. And the question I was left with, the one I still hadn't gotten a satisfying answer for, was *Why?* I wasn't sure there'd ever be one. Gavin hadn't gone to prom either, but shortly after, Emma told me he'd been hanging around with Kaitlyn again.

And yet . . .

He'd been lurking on my StalkMe account.

He said he missed me.

I'm not with that girl anymore. I never really was. . . .

He'd be off to college before I got home. I wouldn't see him again.

He. Called. Me.

I darted out of bed and grabbed my phone. Gavin's number was still in my contacts.

I stared at it.

Then, before I lost my nerve or came to my senses, I called him. I walked over to the bed and flopped down, my hands clammy. One ring . . . then two . . .

If it goes to voice mail, I'm taking it as a sign and won't leave a message.

He answered.

"Cassidy."

"Hey," I said.

"You called."

"I did."

We were silent for a bit, breathing. I didn't know what to say or where to start or if talking to him even made sense.

"I'm sorry about before, Cass. Taking Emma's phone, I just knew—"

"It's okay," I said. "You were right, I wouldn't have answered. What were you about to say before Emma found you?"

"Um . . ."

"You said something like *there's so much* . . . and then she came in. So much what?" I was insane; what did I think he was going to say? He didn't even remember.

"Oh, right. I miss our talks. You listened. I knew I could always count on you to help straighten things out in my head."

I rolled to my side.

"I'm listening now," I said.

"How are you?"

"I thought we were talking about what's going on with you," I said.

"I'd rather talk about you. Why did you leave for the summer?"

"Gavin."

"You could have said good-bye."

"I'm pretty sure I covered that when we broke up."

"Do you like it there?"

"Yes, I do."

"Are you going to say more than single sentences to me, Cass?" There was humor in his voice. "C'mon, what have you been doing, what are you up to?"

I told him about Hunter. Camp. The scavenger hunt. The cooking class with Tori. Little details, no specifics.

"Have you met anyone?"

Ha. Was this whole conversation just to ask that question? I thought about what Emma said—I imagined telling him I'd been with half of Crest Haven then hanging up, but I couldn't lie.

"I've met lots of people."

"I think you know what I mean."

"Gavin, what's the point?"

"C'mon, have you?"

Bryan's face popped into my thoughts. An unexpected rush warmed me. It was nice, but I wasn't about to share my morning swims with Gavin.

"No."

"I want to visit you."

I sat up again. "That's an awful idea."

"Why?"

"I don't have the time. And anything you have to say, you can say it now."

"I'd rather see you, talk to you in person."

"I've got to go."

"Cass, please, just think about it. We could hang out, do

something fun. Remember how we used to talk about going to Ship Bottom? I'd love to go to the beach with you. See you for real in that blue bikini."

I couldn't pretend that it didn't feel good to hear that, that for a split second I saw us together on the beach, the way I used to imagine, but no, it could never be like that.

"Good night, Gavin." I pressed end before hearing his reply.

What can of worms had I opened?

FOURTEEN

BRYAN

"IS IT JUST ME, OR IS THIS SONG DOUCHEY?"

Field day had been rained out and postponed until the following Wednesday, which meant the whole day was unscheduled. Owen had been shuffling between our different groups, assigning us to various places—he'd had a contingency plan, but putting it into action was another thing.

We'd been sent to the multipurpose room to learn the group song with the music director—a sophomore who could play piano—for camp showcase night. Every group was required to do something for the show, I guess to prove to the parents that their money was well spent. The six-to-sevens were assigned "Somewhere Out There." Lesson learned: kids who thought they were going to spend the day at the beach did not enjoy learning show tunes. Not that I blamed them.

And yeah, it was sort of douchey.

On the upside, Wade and I had nothing to do but chill until Owen told us where to go next. We hung toward the back of the room, keeping an eye out in case we needed to step in, but the kids had settled down by the third run-through and it sounded more like a song than random screeching.

"What do you want them to sing? 'Black Parade'?" I asked, popping my chair and balancing.

Wade laughed. "That would be something. Keep the parents awake."

Owen rushed into the multipurpose room, papers on his clipboard fanning as he made his way over to us. He gave a thumbs-up to the kids on stage before calling Wade and me over for what felt like a team huddle.

"You guys are off to free swim next, then cooking after lunch, and we'll probably end the day in here. Maybe a Monty dance party—that's what we were going to do at the beach. The ice cream guy said he'd serve rain or shine, so there's that too. We'll deal with this. First rained-out field day in ten years."

"Monty was supposed to lead a dance party at the beach?" I asked.

"Yeah, only for a little bit. It's too hot for him to be in that costume for long. Have you seen Nick?"

Wade and I shook our heads.

"Well, be ready, Wade—if Nick's a no-show, I nominate

you to be Monty," Owen said with a wink as he left.

"You're kidding, right?" Wade called. "Mr. Beckett?"

"Relax, Nick loves the Monty thing. He's here somewhere," I said.

"He better be or I'll hunt him down. Costumes and jumping spiders, my kryptonite."

"And Tori?" I teased.

"Ha, right. I think we're okay."

"You so rarely sweat, man, it's nice to see you're human."

"You okay going to free swim?"

"Don't know, not sure if I'm up to the *how do you get undressed if you can't stand up* questions in the locker room. It's busy in there today."

"Lake, you should go in. I'll watch the kids while you get changed. You can take all the time you want. I told you Colby still hangs on to the sides of the pool. It might help with you there."

"I'll think about it."

If noise could be used as energy, then the rec center pool would have powered all of Crest Haven for the year. That alone made me rethink going in. Jena was still on duty from the morning, and had two other guards for help, one who walked up and down the side of the pool with a flotation device, and another stationed on the far side. Out of habit I parked my chair at the end of the lane usually reserved for swimming laps. The lane marker was still up, but kids were going up and over it. Wade was at the far end with the kids. He waved.

I put it out of my mind that anyone would be staring and let gravity do its thing, my version of a launch into the water. I landed with a loud splash and swam to the end of the lane toward Wade and our group. The moment I reached the wall, the kids swarmed.

You're swimming!

Cool jump!

Why are you wearing shoes?

Bryan, play Marco Polo!

The last one was from H-bomb, who jumped up and down in front of me. Wade raised his hands. His minions quieted.

"Guys, guys, chill, you're acting like you've never seen someone dive into a pool before. Give Bry some space."

"Hunter, think you could grab me one of those noodles?" I asked, motioning toward the side of the pool.

"Yep," he said, swimming toward Jena's lifeguard stand.

"Not so bad, huh?" Wade asked. I shook my head. Being swarmed by adoring fans didn't suck either. Hunter returned with the noodle.

"Ready to play Marco Polo now?"

I grabbed the noodle and leaned forward over it, putting one end, then the other, under my armpits. "I want to get used to the water, Hunter. Maybe in a bit."

"Anyone who wants to play Marco, come over this way."

The only one who didn't want to play was Colby.

"You okay with this?" Wade said quietly so Colby wouldn't hear. I nodded.

Wade took the rest of the boys farther out into the pool while I stayed with Colby. He was against the wall, lips trembling a bit.

"So you don't like Marco Polo?"

He shook his head.

"Want to swim a lap with me?"

His eyes widened and he looked down the lane before shaking his head even more emphatically. I knew Wade told me he clung to the side, but I didn't realize how bad.

"Well, okay," I said, moving away from him. His eyes remained wide, and I realized my *I'm swimming without you* tactic didn't work. "Can I ask you something?"

He nodded. I didn't want to come out and ask him if he was afraid—that was obvious; I just thought maybe knowing more about it might help.

"Why does the water bother you?"

He shrugged.

A man of few words. We sat there awhile longer, watching the other kids play as Wade was Marco Polo. The kids splashed him, but he was a good sport about it. He yelled *Marco* and dove in the direction of about four of the kids, who laughed like crazy when he belly flopped without catching one of them.

"I don't like to be in the deep water," Colby said.

I turned to him. "Well, they're not in the deep end."

"And I think about sharks being under the water and it scares me."

"Colby-Wan, you do know there aren't sharks in the pool? I, for one, would not be chilling in this water if I thought that."

"I know that, but sometimes I can't help thinking it, and then I kick and can't feel the bottom, and I don't like putting my head underwater."

"Even here? You know, there's music," I said.

"There is?"

"Yep."

"Laaaakewoood." We both turned to see Nick, in his Camp Manatee polo and shorts, standing next to Jena's lifeguard perch. Her eyes were on the pool, but she leaned on her elbow in his direction, whistle poised in her mouth.

"Hey, Nick."

"Looking strong. When we gonna see you at the cove?"

That was a question I hadn't been prepared to answer.

"I don't know. Pool's a lot different, ya know?" I said.

"Your board is looking good. Waiting for you when you're ready."

What did he mean by that? "Has Matt been using it?"

"Uh . . . ," he said, shrugging his shoulders to his ears. "Sometimes. You know, you should just get back to the cove. You're missed. Hey, did I tell you I changed the name of my slush? Gonna have a get-together to celebrate. I'll keep you posted." Jena glanced away from the pool momentarily.

"You have a slush?" Colby asked.

"Yeah. Pineapple and cinnamon, total flavor beast."

Colby's nose wrinkled. I laughed, but pretty much felt the same way about the flavor mix. "Sounds good," I said.

"Mention my name when you go, you'll get a discount."

"Like free?" Colby said. The thought of a free slush trumped fake sharks in the pool, and he pulled away from the wall to look at Nick.

"Maybe for you," Nick said to him.

That gave me an idea. "Colby, could you go grab me another noodle?"

He kept to the side until he reached the stairs, then went over to the flotation equipment and grabbed a purple one.

"Hey, Mr. Beckett's looking for you, Nick," I said. "Monty is supposed to lead a dance party this afternoon."

"Oh, yeah," he said. "Guess I better go mop the floor."

"Huh?"

Nick bent down to get closer to me. "Remember, the kids don't know I'm Monty."

I laughed. He was so serious. "Gotcha," I said.

He stood up and put his elbow on the lifeguard stand. "So, lovely Jena, have *you* tried my slush yet?" he asked, raising his eyebrows at her.

"That sounds perverted."

"I'd be more than happy to bring in a sample for you."

"Stop distracting me." She smiled.

"Fine, fine, duty calls," he said, backing away. Colby handed me the noodle.

"No, buddy, that's for you. I'll make you a deal: you swim with me a little, holding on to your own noodle, and I'll get you any size slush you want—well, if your mom says it's okay."

He looked past me down the swim lane, then nodded.

"We always go to Sip N' Freeze. She'd be okay with it."

"Okay then, let's go."

The noodle shot out a little in front of him and I pushed it back. He grabbed it and started kicking wildly, but at least he was moving forward. I let my own noodle out from under me and swam slowly next to him. Halfway down the lane he stopped kicking and floated for a second.

"You okay?" I asked.

He nodded, took a deep breath, and dunked himself under the water. He rose up sputtering and blinking.

"Dude, hard-core," I said. He grinned and started kicking again.

I swam forward, making it to the opposite wall a good five feet ahead of him.

He kept pushing along, determined, until he finally reached the wall.

"You made it," I said.

He slapped me a high five.

The look on his face said it all.

"So far we have a street name, Monty, a towel, and fireworks. Those seem pretty random to me. I give," Wade said, leaning his head back into his clasped hands. We were in cooking, and Tori and Cass had given the kids an assignment to make cereal collages, while the four of us sat at another long table trying to figure out what the scavenger clues we had so far meant, if anything.

"You said you were going to work at this. I might have to jump ship and join Cass and Bryan," Tori said.

"You know, he's right though, it all seems kind of random," I said.

Wade gave Tori a smartass grin.

Cass sat next to me, the list of clues between us. I kept sneaking glances at her. Her hair was loose and tucked behind one ear. I had studied her left ear so closely I could shut my eyes and still remember every delicate curve. She had three piercings: two small studs, a pearl and a diamond, and a tiny hoop at the start of the outer fold of her ear. Every time she moved the scent of something flowery filled the space.

"Yeah, I got nothing," she said.

"Ugh, my brain is fried—why do you think I'm letting the kids do something as prosaic as a cereal collage? This is left over from making the marshmallow treats. I'm all out of creative ideas today," Tori said.

"Can I make one?" Wade asked.

Tori cocked her head. "Sure, have at it."

"Cool," Wade said, getting up. He came back with four small cups of cereal. Cass reached into one and popped an Apple Jack into her mouth.

"Hey, no eating the art," Wade said.

"But they're my favorite," she said, grabbing another one.

Wade looked at Tori. "What's your favorite?"

"Me? I don't eat that crap."

"You don't eat cold cereal, ever?" Cass asked.

She shook her head. "That's like one of Nick's food groups. I think I'm better off without it. Must kill brain cells."

"That and slushes," I said.

Tori put her hand over her face. "Omigod, my brother the slush king."

"As far as titles go, it's not bad," Wade said, gluing another piece of cereal down on the construction paper.

"Some people go through life never having anything named after them. It's a pretty cool claim to fame," I said.

"Or pathetic, if that's your only claim to fame ever," Tori said. "I have a feeling he's peaked."

"Have you tried the slush?" I asked.

"I think I've been to Sip N' Freeze every day this week to pick up one for him. And oh . . . hell no," Tori said, looking past Cass and me to the door.

We turned. Nick—or rather, Monty—filled the doorway. He shuffled into the classroom waving a flipper. A few of the kids ran over to him, jumping up for a high five.

"Monty, so good of you to stop by," Tori said, standing up. "C'mon, guys, back in your seats. You can see him later."

Monty crossed his flippers, or at least tried to, and shook his head in protest. The kids laughed and instead of sitting down, a few more stood up and went over to him. Only Colby continued with his cereal collage.

"Do something, they're on the verge of being uncontrollable." Tori looked between Wade and me. Wade focused on making his picture.

"They've been cooped up all day, they're entitled to a little anarchy," I said.

"Not here, not now," Tori said.

Cass stood up and clapped. "C'mon, guys, Monty has to save his energy for the dance party. I want to see those collages."

They reluctantly backed off. Monty grabbed Cass's hand in his fin, pulled her to him, and dipped her back. She squealed, but smiled until he pulled her up.

"Seriously, dude, watch the flippers," she said, pulling away from him and straightening her T-shirt. Monty put his flipper up to his mouth and pretended to laugh. Tori escorted him to the door. Cass came back over to the table and flopped down in her chair.

"I think I was just groped by a manatee."

I turned to her. "So, want to get together this weekend, maybe look for the next clue or . . . you know, whatever, just hang out?"

"Um . . . like, the four of us?" Cass asked.

No, just the two of us, me and you, you and me. Us. "Yeah, what do you think? Game, Wade?" I asked.

"I'm working Friday night, but other than that, I'm in. Ha, done," he said, pushing the construction paper away. He'd made a heart out of Apple Jacks and what looked like Cinnamon Toast Crunch.

"Sounds good, then," Cass said.

Tori came back over to us. "Will this day never end?"

Wade presented her with the picture.

"For you, Tori, my heart in cereal form," he said.

Tori looked at the paper.

Her face flushed pink. She opened her mouth but then walked away.

For once, she had nothing to say.

"CASSIDY."

I jammed my eyes shut, ignoring the voice. One Saturday to sleep in, was that too much to ask?

"Cass."

"Hunter, please, another hour at least." I pulled the blanket over my head and faced the wall. For a second I thought it had worked and he'd left, but then I felt the foot of my bed depress as he sat down. He grasped my calf and shook. Couldn't he give me a break? I pulled the covers back, ready to plead, and gasped.

"Leslie?"

She grimaced. "Cass, sorry to wake you, but I need your help."

I blinked a few times and looked at my alarm clock. Six thirty a.m.

"What's wrong?" As I started to wake and Leslie's features came into focus, I could see she wasn't her usual slicked-back-ponytailed self. Her hair was loose and slightly messy around her shoulders. She still wore her nightgown.

"Your father went on a fishing trip—oh, shoot—" She covered her mouth, shot up from the bed, and raced to the small half bathroom right outside my door. Retching noises followed. I got up to see the damage.

"Are you . . ." I didn't have to finish because it was clear she was not okay. She was crouched down in the small space in front of the toilet bowl, pale and gasping. "Is there anything I can do?"

She shook her head and heaved again.

I got a washcloth from my room and soaked it in some cold running water, then crouched down and handed it to her. She dabbed the cloth on her forehead and cheeks before wiping her mouth. She smiled weakly.

"Thanks. Sorry about that. I must have a stomach bug, I feel awful." I helped her to standing and we went back to sit on my bed. I inched away from her; I did not want to catch whatever had made her retch like that.

"I need you to make breakfast."

"For you?"

"For the guests."

"What?"

"I know this is a lot to ask; as soon as this passes I'll be down to help you, but right now the thought of looking at food . . . I just can't. Everything is ready for you—I made the muffin batter; you just have to pour it in the tins and bake, but you'll have to mix up the blueberry pancakes and put out the fruit salad." She put hand over her mouth and ran to the bathroom again.

My brain was slowly beginning to process what Leslie had just asked and was about to push the panic button. Nice way to wake up.

Cooking wasn't the issue, that was a no-brainer—actually something I didn't mind doing at all—but the interacting with a room full of strange adults freaked me the hell out. I'd seen both my dad and Leslie in action, and I did not have the perky, bullshitting, talk-about-the-local-points-of-interest thing down like they did. I stared at my rumpled blanket, the bed calling me back to dreamland. Leslie leaned against my doorframe. The race to the bathroom must have been a false alarm.

"When do I need to start?"

"Now—breakfast begins at seven thirty a.m. We don't have a full house. It's really just a matter of keeping everything replenished. Juice. Butter. Cream. Oh, no." She cupped her hand over her mouth and ran back to the toilet.

"Just go, um, do what you need to do. I'll get ready and head downstairs," I called.

I pulled on some shorts, grabbed a tee, threw my hair in a

ponytail, and slipped into my flip-flops before heading downstairs. The smell of coffee greeted me. At least Leslie had been able to do that. I took a deep breath, trying to quiet the terrified voices in my head that said *you will completely screw this up* and forged onward.

And since when did my father go fishing?

The kitchen was set up for action. Coffee maker sputtering. Various glass cake stands and platters arranged with doilies waited to be filled. Thankfully there was also a to-do list on the counter next to the sink. The steps for a perfect morning at Ocean Whispers were all laid out for me.

Piece of cake.

I started with the strawberry muffins, spooning the batter into the tins and sliding them into the oven. The dry ingredients for the blueberry pancakes were already measured out, and I mixed them together in a larger bowl before getting the fruit to fold in. Everything was going smoothly.

Then I opened the container of blueberries.

They rolled into the batter in one clump. As I tried to fold them in I noticed they were all stuck together in a gray furry ball. I tried to pick some out, to salvage what I could, but the damage was done. My first impulse was to call Leslie. Then I realized giving her a description of rotting fruit pancakes would probably just send her on another vomiting spree. I put the batter to the side and took the fruit salad out of the fridge, trying to pull plan B out of my ass. Too bad it wasn't a number on the to-do list.

It was ten after seven. Twenty minutes until guests could possibly be downstairs, although why anyone in their right mind would get up that early on vacation was beyond me. The timer for the muffins went off and I took them out of the oven and set them on the wire rack to cool. Hunter came bounding into the kitchen. *Did no one sleep in this place?*

"Bud, what are you doing up?"

He looked at me as if that was the most ridiculous question anyone had ever asked. "Where's Mom?"

"She's not feeling right, so I'm making breakfast." *Alone. All me. And I'm completely fucking it up.*

"Can I have some Apple Jacks then?"

"No, I mean for everybody," I said. He didn't comprehend, just pulled out the chair and sat expectantly. A bowl of cereal wouldn't set me back that much. I grabbed the box and bowl and poured, wondering if I put them in a large dish decorated with a doily if they could pass for a breakfast item. Hunter got himself the milk.

Then plan B materialized.

After Tori had asked me to come up with breakfast ideas, I'd gone to the supermarket with Leslie to get supplies to experiment with. I had everything I needed to whip up a sweet version of a breakfast quesadilla. I pulled out the tortillas, cream cheese, and butter, went through the spices (which thankfully were alphabetized), found cinnamon, powdered sugar, and vanilla, and got to work. Hunter munched while I heated up the griddle.

The muffins had cooled enough and I arranged them onto one of the cake platters. I was about to ask Hunter if he could help—he looked presentable enough; his pj's were pretty much shorts and a tee with sharks all over them—but then got an image of him tripping somehow, and realized I'd be completely screwed and serving Apple Jacks. He could manage the smaller things though.

"Hunter, could you bring out the cream and sugar and put it on the sideboard?"

"Yeah," he said.

"Do you think you could help me with some other stuff too?"

"Let me get my shoes!"

I wasn't sure why shoes were an important part of it, but he raced up the stairs and was back in a flash with his light-up shark sandals, ready to serve by the time I'd whipped up the first quesadilla. I eyed the clock. Five minutes until breakfast service.

"What is that?" he asked as I flipped the first breakfast quesadilla onto the plate to cool.

"Don't worry about it, let's get this stuff out there," I said, leading the way.

There was no one downstairs yet, so I put the muffins on the center of the table, and Hunter placed the cream and sugar on the sideboard. Then I realized I'd forgotten to put coffee in the silver urn. We went back into the kitchen. I grabbed the glass carafe from the maker and ran out to fill the urn.

"You need hot water for tea too," Hunter said, pointing at a white carafe next to a box of tea selections.

"I didn't see that on the to-do list," I said, trying not to get burned as I poured the coffee. It only filled it up halfway, which meant I had to make more. "Could you bring that carafe into the kitchen for me?"

Hunter nodded and grabbed the carafe. I followed him back to the kitchen and put the kettle on for hot water. I cut the cooled quesadilla and glanced at the to-do list to check the number of guests again. Eight.

Water boiled, coffee urn filled again—I got to work on two more quesadillas. They were better warm, so I figured this would more than cover anyone out there at the moment, and I could make more as people arrived. Hunter reached for a triangle of the first one. I shooed him away.

"Please don't touch, it's backup breakfast."

"If there's extra can I have one?"

"Sure. Can you take out the fruit salad while I finish making these? Two hands—be careful."

He grabbed the crystal bowl and walked super slow, one foot in front of the other, out to the dining room. I was going to tell him he didn't have to be *that* careful, but then figured best to let him do it his way.

I finished up the quesadillas. They were still cooling, and Hunter hadn't come back yet. Since I hadn't heard a crash, I figured whatever was keeping him couldn't be that bad. I cut the quesadillas into triangles, piled them on a plate with a doily, grabbed the bowl of whipped cream, and headed out to the dining room.

Hunter was regaling two older couples with information on the kinds of dolphins they might see in Crest Haven. Glad one of us inherited the gab gene.

The woman looked at me, which spurred an intro from Hunter.

"This is my sister, Cass . . . she's really my half sister, we have different moms."

Awkward much?

"And what is that you have there?" she asked.

I placed the platter down on the table.

"These are breakfast quesadillas; they're stuffed with sweetened cream cheese and the tortillas are crisped with some butter and sprinkled with cinnamon sugar." It sounded so basic. Why had I thought it would make an impressive breakfast item? I inwardly winced as I waited on a reaction.

"How different," she said, taking a triangle off of the plate.

"There's fresh whipped cream and some preserves if you wanted to spice it up—I guess actually sweeten it up." I brought the silver serving caddy with the jams and whipped cream over to the table. Had I made enough polite small talk?

"I want to try that!" Hunter said. The couple laughed. I watched as the woman dabbed some whipped cream on her triangle of quesadilla and brought it to her mouth. I should have just excused myself, not really wanting to see her reaction, but Hunter and I were glued there, like two grinning idiots. She smiled as she chewed and nodded. Her husband reached for one too.

"It's excellent," she said.

"Thanks." I bowed my head a few times, grabbed Hunter's hand, and went back to the kitchen, hoping my quota of small talk had been filled for the morning, but secretly happy the woman had liked my quesadilla. Or maybe she was just being polite. Whatever. The morning had begun—*four down, four more guests to go.*

"Can I have one now?" Hunter asked, looking at the tortillas with wide, pleading eyes.

"Sure, dude."

The rest of breakfast was uneventful. I kept all the urns and bowls filled, asked guests if they needed anything else; I even recommended a good spot on the beach. Hunter was my sidekick, offering comic relief. He didn't have to do much except smile to get people to talk to him. I'd just started cleanup when Leslie finally came downstairs. I found her in the kitchen, standing near the counter and pouring a cup of tea. She'd dressed in a light-pink sundress, her hair pulled back off her face with a crocheted headband. The color had returned to her cheeks.

"How are you?" I asked.

"Feeling better. I have to do a checkout this morning," she said, putting the mug up to her temple and taking a deep breath. She opened her eyes. "How's it going? I see you had a helper."

Hunter threw his arms around her waist and squeezed. She laughed and held the mug out away from them. Leslie rumpled his hair, then delicately untangled from him, as if the squeeze might have triggered more queasiness.

"Well, no one complained. That I know at least."

"Cass made a breakfast quesadilla! It's so good, Mom, you should have one!"

Leslie's brows raised. I could already sense her question.

"The blueberries were furry; I didn't think you'd want to hear that this morning. So I just kind of improvised with some of the supplies we bought the other day."

She laughed. "Oh, wow, thanks—quick thinking. Maybe I'll have to pick your brain for some fresh ideas."

"Yeah, anytime."

"Hunter and I can finish up here if you'd like to go back to sleep for a while, but if it wouldn't be too much trouble could you help me make up the rooms today? It won't take long, maybe about an hour or two. There's only one room that needs to be completely turned over."

"Sure, I'll help."

I went back upstairs, took a shower, and tried to relax enough to catch some z's. Only my brain wasn't having it. Gavin had been sending random texts since our phone call. *I want to see you. Think about it.* He'd even sent me a picture of us from the winter, when we had a snow day off from school and went sledding down the park. Our noses were red, our eyes bright. That had been a good day. My heart ached remembering how happy I'd been. No inkling of trouble. How we'd gone back to his house and found ways to get warm under the quilt in his room. It was a low blow on his part to send that picture. Unfair. But as Ems said—this was war. I'd thought I had the upper hand. I wasn't so sure anymore.

Did I still care? Maybe it was time to start hooking up left and right and finally let go of Gavin. Although at that point, I wasn't sure what left and right would be. I closed my eyes, mentally going through faces of people I'd met—the random skateboard guys from the Fourth, counselors, Wade, Matt hanging out the car window, Bryan.

Bryan.

The way the water beaded on his chest when he did his blissed-out floaty thing at the pool, his humble smile that always seemed somewhere between happy and sad, those gray-blue eyes. I reached for my phone, scrolled through the pictures of us from the first time we went to the promenade together, and stopped on the one of him tasting the lavender-and-mint-infused lemon ice pop. I laughed, a pleasant tingle building up in my chest as I scrolled through the next set of pics, the ones of the two of us, right before Shay had come up to say hello. *Wonder what Gavin would think if I posted that to StalkMe?*

I sighed. Sat up.

No.

Oh, no, no, no.

I liked Bryan. A lot. The pleasant tingle, the flushed feeling, the way I couldn't stop smiling at our picture together. What did I think I was doing?

I came to Ocean Whispers to forget about a boy, not fall for one.

I sprang up from my bed, pulled on shorts and a tee, and went back downstairs to find Leslie. I purposely left my phone in my room. It was nothing but trouble.

There were five rooms in total to clean. Leslie made the beds; I did the light dusting, emptied the wastebaskets, and made sure each fresh flower arrangement still had enough water. It was the first time I'd spent more than a few minutes in the inn section of the house. Each room was decorated differently in some variation of floral and frilly, with antique furniture and doilies on every flat surface. While not exactly my taste, the rooms were warm and inviting. The fifth room was huge, the only one with a private bathroom and balcony with rocking chairs. It was also the one we needed to turn over.

"This is our master suite, booked every day for the summer and through the fall," Leslie said.

"It's really nice," I said, trying not to imagine what went on in the master suite. The room *was* pretty impressive, with a king-size four-poster bed and an electric fireplace. Quite the love nest. I helped Leslie pull off the fitted sheet and stuff it into the laundry bag.

"So why a bed-and-breakfast?" I asked. Leslie pulled the fresh fitted king sheet out from the linen pile on the rolling cart. She smiled, shrugged.

"It was sort of an impulse buy," she said, her tone casual. She sounded as though she was talking about a pair of shoes. "Your father and I were down here, taking a long weekend one December, and we went on a house tour. Well, I went on a house tour, and dragged your father for as long as he could stand it. You've seen the town at Christmas, right? How magical it all looks? I just fell in love with it. The owner of this place talked about how she was moving to open another bed-and-breakfast in Taos, and we started talking, and before we both knew it, the touring time was over and she gave me her card and it all just . . . felt right. I could see us here." She unfolded the fitted sheet and fanned it out. We started tucking the opposite corners.

"But you had such a cool job before," I said.

She laughed as she tucked the sides. "I guess it was sort of cool, the movie stuff, but that seems like a lifetime ago. My publicity skills have come in handy here. We were both ready to slow down a little bit. Ha, were we in for a surprise! You know, the guests who checked out today said they loved your quesadilla. I'd like to add it to my rotation. You'll have to give me the recipe."

I smiled. It felt nice to hear the breakfast had been a hit. "I don't really write anything down, but I guess I can."

"Would you mind if we put it in the newsletter?"

"Really?"

"Yes, I . . . ooh." Leslie leaned against the bed and put her hand up to her forehead.

"Feeling sick again?"

She nodded. "A little. Maybe I'll go lie down after this. Do you think . . . could you help with afternoon tea, too? That's really just putting things out and making sure they're replenished for the hour. On a gorgeous day like this there might not be many back for tea, but you never know."

"Sure, I'll keep Hunter busy too," I said, anticipating the moment he woke up from his nap, if he'd even taken one like Leslie had suggested.

"Thanks for letting him help, Cass. I should let him do that more often. He really loves having you around."

Before heading down to tea, I raced up to my room and grabbed my phone. My heart lurched when I saw I had a voice mail, but then calmed when I saw it was from my mother. I did owe her a phone call.

Afternoon tea consisted of pitchers of iced tea and lemonade, which I was relieved to find out, because who wanted hot tea when the street was melting? The cookies and fruit salad were already made, and service consisted of checking the table every once in a while to make sure nothing needed to be replenished and it all looked pretty. A lone woman sat on the front porch in a rocking chair, reading a book and sipping some iced tea. Another couple—the youngest I'd seen yet—came up, grabbed some lemonade and a plate of sweets, and wandered up to their room.

I sat down on the top step to call my mother.

"Hey, it's me," I said.

"Cass! We haven't talked in forever, but I take that to be a good sign. How are things?"

"Let's see, it rained all last week, so they canceled field day; Leslie was sick this morning, so I had to make breakfast for the guests. You know, same old, same old."

"Wait, what? Really? What did you do?"

"I whipped up breakfast quesadillas. The ones I make sometimes at home."

"Mmm . . . the ones with the cinnamon? Wow, Cass, I'm impressed. Is Leslie okay? Where's your father?"

"Yeah, she thinks it's just a twenty-four-hour thing. Dad's fishing—some annual teacher excursion or something like that."

“Fishing? I can’t picture that.”

“Me either,” I said. My father’s idea of outdoorsy was firing up the grill. I couldn’t imagine him on a boat trying to catch a living thing.

“So, I thought I’d come down next weekend for a visit; would you be up for it?”

“Yes, definitely. Is Nan coming too?”

“No, but I thought I might let Emma tag along, if that’s okay with you.”

I stood up. “Omigod, really? Emma!”

She laughed. “Why didn’t *I* get that reaction from you?”

“I’ll be happy to see you too,” I said.

“I’m getting a motel room for us, so we can all stay together.”

“You didn’t want to stay here?” I asked.

“There’s no vacancy,” she said. “Thought you might enjoy getting away for a night too.”

“When are you coming?”

“I figure we can come early on Saturday, maybe hit the beach, go out to dinner or something, then I’m sure you’ll want to show Emma around. Sound good?”

“Sounds great,” I said.

Hunter clomped out onto the porch and sat next to me, playing a handheld video game.

“So we’ll see you then, Cass.”

“Bye,” I said, shutting down the phone.

“Oh, wow.” Hunter pointed toward the street. My father

pushed through the front gate holding a large, silvery-gray striped fish about three feet long, still attached to some sort of fishing line. Hunter put his game down and went sprinting toward him. My father grinned from ear to ear, his face ruddy from the sun. I picked up Hunter's game and walked down the stairs to greet him and see what the giant fish was all about.

"Look at this! I wouldn't even let them gut it for me. I have to show this to Leslie, she'll never believe it. I've been on this trip four years in a row and this is the first time I've ever caught anything."

He took off toward the back door before I had the chance to say anything.

"Hey, um, Dad," I said, following him with Hunter at my heels now too. Dad was like a little kid, racing toward the yard with his prize. By the time we reached the back deck, he was in the kitchen. We took the stairs two at a time and followed him inside. Leslie was sitting at the table, cup of tea and magazine in front of her.

"Ta-da," he exclaimed. "Four years and I finally caught something."

Hunter ran his hand along the fish. "Ew, it's slimy."

"Les, what's wrong? I thought you'd be thrilled for me."

Leslie's face contorted. She got up from the chair, leaned over the sink, and vomited.

A couple of hours later, Ocean Whispers was as quiet as its name implied. The offensive striped bass had been taken out somewhere to be gutted, cleaned, and then grilled at home by Dad with some rosemary and garlic and fingerling potatoes. Leslie had turned in early, Dad was busy working on something in his office, and Hunter begged me to watch some special on great whites to kick off Shark Week.

In the midst of all the excitement, Bryan had texted me about meeting up with him, Wade, and Tori at Sip N' Freeze. I wanted to go, I did. The thought of him and his blue eyes made that pleasant warmth rise up again. Definitely not safe. Sure, he would be a distraction, but . . . that's not what I wanted him to be. He deserved more than that. Maybe I was wimping out by staying in, but I didn't care. I was taking Tori's advice. I was being careful with him.

I texted Bryan.

> Helped at inn.
>
> Kind of tired.
>
> See you Monday.

I knocked on the doorframe to Dad's office and wandered in. He was dozing lightly in his office chair, the *Whispers Weekly* newsletter up on his computer screen.

On the first page was a headline for my breakfast quesadilla. I laughed. It made it seem so official. My father startled.

"Hey," he said.

"You put my recipe in the newsletter."

He yawned. "Well, it was all Hunter could talk about. Thanks for today, Cass. Leslie said she couldn't have managed without you."

"It was fun, I guess. Interesting to see how you guys run things. It's tough."

He laughed. "Yes, it can be sometimes. Did you want something?"

"Just wanted to see if you were going to watch that shark thing Hunter keeps talking about. I think it starts in ten minutes . . . I came out to make some popcorn."

"You're staying in tonight?"

I nodded. He smiled.

"Give me a few minutes. I'll be in."

"YOU REALLY WANT ME TO BELIEVE YOU BLEW US off on Saturday night because you were watching shark shows with Hunter?" I said.

"It's Shark Week, did you know that? It's like a national holiday in Hunter's world. And I told you, he helped me out at the inn, I had to do something for him." Cass splashed me. I paddled away, trying not to smile.

"You missed a great time," I lied. It hadn't been awful, but it wasn't the best Saturday night in history either. It was just a night with Wade and Tori and some of the other guys hanging out. Something I hadn't done in a while, and it felt good being around actual people instead of on a raid on *Realm Wars*. What I'd really been looking forward to was seeing Cass outside of camp again. I wanted to know her. And sometimes

I even had the feeling she wanted to know me better too.

She was swimming with me, and that meant something, didn't it? There was a reason she kept getting up early, burning through towel duty, and hanging out with me. Sometimes I even believed it—that she could like me *that way*—but I didn't know how to pursue anything more. One moment I was sure we were friends, and completely content with it, then the next she would pout, or smile, or hell, breathe next to me and I ached for more. I was starting to want it too much, especially if she didn't, and I'd settle for being around her, even if it meant we were just friends.

I grabbed the pool noodles and set myself up to float. Cass still splashed in the other lane, then without warning popped up next to me, spitting water in the air as she broke the surface. I laughed.

"I think I just heard a piano version of 'Pompeii' underwater—please tell me I'm not crazy," she said, blinking the water out of her eyes.

"You probably did; that's Owen's version of being cutting-edge."

"Hey, is there room for two?" she asked, grabbing one end of the noodle.

She needed to stop saying things like that to me.

"You can try," I said.

She put her head back next to mine, but let her legs drift up in the water instead of throwing them over the other noodle. We floated like that for a moment, but it was far from my usual blissed-out solo cooldown. Not that I minded—we were so close, even in the water I could feel the heat coming off her skin.

"Did you know otters hold hands?"

"You sound like H-bomb now," I said.

She laughed. "It's true. Didn't you ever see that video where they're floating and then all of a sudden the one takes the other's hand, like this?"

Cass entwined her fingers through mine. I didn't resist. She pulled us closer together. She was only touching my hand, our forearms kissing, but it felt incredible. A #wheelchairperk of my permanent nerve rewiring. New turn-on zones. My heart pounded so much I was sure it would cause the water to ripple.

"They do that so they don't drift apart when they're sleeping, isn't that the cutest thing?"

Cassidy. Was. Holding. My. Hand.

"Otters!" Jena pointed at us and smiled.

"Yes, like the video; you've seen it, right?" she asked. Jena nodded.

We floated like that for a few minutes, until she finally let go and treaded water next to me.

"By the way, I requested to be in your group for field day," she said.

"Cool. Hunter will be happy," I said.

"Will you be happy?"

"You picked the best group to be with," I said.

"I *could* have helped Monty with the dance party."

"Hmm . . . tough choice, I guess."

"So, what do we do at field day that's so different from any other day?"

"Much more organized fun. At the beach. That's about it."

"Oh, is that . . . will you . . . how will you get to the beach?"

"Think you could give me a piggyback ride?" I said, as deadpan as I could possibly manage. She stood up in the water, brow crinkled, curvy mouth bunched up. I sat there enjoying her face until I couldn't stand it any longer. "No worries, I got it covered."

She splashed me.

Field day was never something I had looked forward to in school. For me, organized sports meant searching for obstacles to grind with my skateboard or a day shredding in the surf. *That* I could get behind, but dividing into teams, playing games with rules and prizes—not so much.

Camp Manatee field day was different though. It was more about spending the day on the beach, and we had a rotation for activities, so only one group would be at one station at a time. We had a couple of planned games, a sand-castle challenge, an organized ocean swim, and the big finale before we went back to the rec center for quiet time was going to be a dance party led by Monty. How Nick was going to pull that off in a-thousand-degree heat I wasn't sure, but it would be fun to watch.

The one part I was dreading was having to use the all-terrain wheelchair, because it required someone to push me around. Maybe I was overthinking it—I'd only been to the beach with my family a handful of times since my mishap. Bottom line: it took effort, planning, special wheels to deal with the sand, and the one thing I'd liked about going to the beach before was that it was a no-brainer. Sometimes it sucked to be invisible, to have people talk over you or around you or about you, like I was deaf instead of para, but the opposite sucked even harder. It was impossible to *blend*. I guess if I were a kid and saw some dude being pushed around in a big-wheeled chair I'd be interested too, it's just—I hated being the center of attention for it.

The kids were over-the-top excited for the beach, moving like little pinballs knocking into each other down the hallway. The beach was only a block away, so we were heading over in our individual groups. Both Cass and Tori were with us. The kids held on to a long rope, so no one would get separated. Cassidy led everyone across the street.

"So where is this four-wheelin' wheelchair?" Wade asked.

"It's supposed to be waiting at check-in—you sure you're okay pushing me around?" I asked.

"Ugh, dude, what a drag," Wade said.

"Can I push you?" H-bomb asked.

I laughed. "You're here to have fun, buddy, not worry about me."

The sun was strong, and we'd been told to take water and sunscreen breaks every forty-five minutes. Water sooner if necessary. We sprayed sunscreen on the kids before heading out to the sand. When I'd gone as far as I could on the wooden walkway, I stopped and waited. There was no other chair in sight. Wade looked from side to side. The kids sort of pooled around me. Sweaty, sticky, and whining—it wasn't even ten o'clock yet.

"Mr. B.'s supposed to be here, right?" Wade asked.

"Yep." More campers arrived, stopping out of instinct at the traffic jam we were causing. I waved for them to go around us. Owen came rushing over, red-faced and slightly out of breath. There was a section of the beach marked off by several large Camp Manatee banners. No chair in sight.

"Wait, guys, you need wristbands," he said. He fumbled around with his clipboard and gave Wade a handful of purple strips. He gave the counselors behind us some too.

"Hey, Mr. B., do we have the chair for Bryan?" Wade motioned with his head to me.

"Yes, sorry," he said, eyeing the growing line behind us. Our kids had wrapped themselves up in the rope they'd been holding and started to spin in a giggly circle.

"It's over there next to the shade tent. Could you get it, Wade? I meant to have it over here. Time got away from me. Sorry, Bry."

"It's cool," I said. Wade handed me the wristbands and walked off to get the chair. I whistled for the kids to cut it out.

"Come here, guys, you need wristbands." They bombarded me with questions.

I hate things around my wrist.

Why purple?

Do we have to wear it all day?

I whistled again.

"Dudes, stop. Do you want to make sand castles? Play giants, wizards, and elves? Then calm down so I can put these wristbands on you—these are your tickets to as much fun as you can handle," I said, motioning for Hunter to be the first. He beamed and held out his wrist while I wrapped it around him and peeled off the adhesive to secure it. "Next."

By the time Wade got back with the beach-access chair, the kids were all wristbanded up and raring to hit the sand.

"Oh, cooooool," they crooned as Wade stopped the chair in front of me. The rec center had zero budget, so they didn't have one of those tricked-out motorized beach chairs. They had your basic beach-access chair, which, to be honest, was goofy as hell to look at, with fat wheels that still sank in the sand. The worst part was I couldn't use it on my own. I needed someone to push me around. Wade shooed the kids away from the chair and studied my face.

"C'mon," he said, crouched down. "I'll give you a lift over."

I held on to his shoulders and he bent lower to grab my legs. In one motion he stood and hoisted me up a little farther onto his back. I kept my eyes forward, not wanting to see anyone's reaction. It was a short walk to the chair. He crouched down again and helped me position myself. The kids actually fought over who could help him push me. Colby handed me my backpack and we moved along to our first activity. Games.

I supervised as they played giants, wizards and elves, but got involved during volleyball, where I didn't need to move from one side of the makeshift court to the other. Cass was on the opposite team and we volleyed a few times.

After a water and sunscreen break, we took our turn at the sand-castle station. I was self-appointed general contractor, with Colby as my right-hand little dude.

"We need more water; the sand needs to stick together better than this," I said, directing them how to build a base. Cass took Hunter and some of the other kids to get more water and to collect shells to decorate. When they got back, she knelt next to me, and stacked sand for a tower.

"You're taking this very seriously," she joked.

"Sand castles are serious business," I said. "It's all about the sand-to-water ratio. Too little water, it'll all fall apart before you even start. Too much and you'll end up getting a shapeless mound. Consistency is key. My dad used to build epic sand castles when we were little, so I guess I'm geeking out."

"It's nice."

"It's nothing right now; we don't have much time so we

have to keep it simple, a few towers maybe."

"No, it's nice to see you so . . . relaxed. You smile differently when your guard is down."

She noticed my smile?

"It's good being out of the rec center, I guess."

"Yeah, something different, right?" she said, stacking another handful of sand onto the pile that was now ready to be shaped into something. "I'll go get some more shells. Let's trick this thing out."

I laughed. "Cool."

She grabbed a pail and asked for volunteers. Five hands shot up.

"C'mon, guys. Hey, Bry, want to sit together for lunch?"

Like she really had to ask.

After lunch and a bathroom break, it was swim time for our guys.

"Do you want to be by the water?" Wade asked.

Did I want to be by the water? I wanted to be in the water, on the water, one with the water. Deep dark blue, with the sun glinting off the waves . . . I could only imagine how good it would feel, that first shocking plunge, taking the edge off. There were too many variables though. I had no control.

"Nah, I'll stick with the shade, I'm getting a little overheated anyway." Another #wheelchairperk—anytime I mentioned a physical issue, people never questioned it.

"Okay."

Wade pushed me over to the tent.

Cass was by the water's edge, Hunter and Colby next to her. Colby kept running away from the surf, while Hunter tried to grab his hand and drag him into the water. At one point Cass took both of their hands to go a little farther into the surf, the waves lapping at their ankles. Lucky kids.

I closed my eyes and imagined I was the one holding Cass's hand, standing next to her, racing out to the waves, pulling her into the water. We could hold hands and float like . . . what was that . . . otters.

"Hey, no sleeping on the job."

I opened my eyes. Cass was there, running a towel up and down her legs. She fanned it out when she was done and sat on it.

"Just chilling for a moment; these little dudes can wear you out," I said.

She leaned on her hands and dropped her head back, stretching her neck. No blue bikini today, but Cass could probably wear a rain tarp and still look amazing.

"So this is what all the fuss is about?" she said.

"The fuss about what?"

"The sun, the sea, the sand—you know, the reason people flock here to roast in the rays and eat fudge."

"Yeah, I guess it doesn't suck," I said.

"You sure you don't want to go by the water? I don't mind pushing you down there," she said.

"I'm cool here, wanted to get out of the sun anyway."

Wade was with Colby and Hunter now. He was kneeling in front of Colby and pointing toward the water. He splashed him with some of the foam from a wave.

"So how was Colby by the water? He gets scared in the pool."

"Yeah, he was a little freaked. Hunter's funny though, trying to get him to go in. I swear, that kid wants to find a shark and ride it. I keep telling him one bite and he's a goner, but I think he's convinced he's the shark whisperer or something."

"You know, if anyone could be, I'd put my money on H-bomb."

"Ha, I think you're right."

"There you are," Tori said, shielding her eyes from the sun and looking at Cass. "We have to hand out the ice cream cups at this dance party. I can't wait until quiet time, I'm wilting."

"You could hang out in the water with Wade," Cassidy said.

Tori stepped under the canopy. "Or I could just stay in the shade. We need to be stationed here, otherwise we'll be handing out cups of ice-cream soup. I'm going to suggest that to Mr. B."

Wade came up behind Tori and shook out his hair, sending droplets of water onto her. She arched her back to get away from him.

"Wade, I managed to stay dry all day. Thanks."

"One word and my minions can do the same," Wade said,

holding his hands out as if the kids were on display.

"You're evil," Tori said.

Wade looked around the tent. "Where's Hunter and Colby? I told them to meet us here."

"Last I saw them they were by the water with you," I said.

The four of us looked between each other.

Cass stood up. "They have to be around. I'll go check by the water."

"I'll look by the games," Tori said.

Wade turned to the kids. "Stay. Here. With Bryan, got that? I'm going to check out that way." He pointed in the opposite direction. I played a game of I Spy with the kids to keep them occupied. Ten minutes later, Cass, Tori, and Wade returned empty-handed. We looked at each other, harsh realization dawning on all of us.

Colby and Hunter were gone.

We'd have to get Owen involved now.

"I'll go tell him," Wade said, trotting over to him.

Cassidy's face paled and she crossed her arms.

I sat there, feeling completely useless. This was an emergency. The exact thing that parents had been worried about, and what good was I? Immobilized. Sitting there, as useful as a freaking sand dollar.

Owen came over to us. The kids were thankfully oblivious, sitting on the blanket and eating potato chips Tori had brought over for them. He drew the four of us into a huddle.

"When was the last time you saw them?"

Wade explained what had happened again, and Owen jumped to action, heading over to the lifeguard stand. Soon anyone who could help was mobilized into action. Cass stood next to me, practically catatonic, and watched as they formed a human chain and walked into the water.

"Why are they doing that?"

"So they can cover more ground in case . . ." God, I didn't even want to say it.

"Do you think Hunter and Colby are in there?" Cass's eyes went wide.

"Cass, I know it looks bad, but they're just doing it as a precaution. I doubt Colby would have even gone in, he's scared of the water."

"But Hunter was getting to him, I saw that. He wanted to go . . . oh, fuck, Bryan," she said, putting a hand across her mouth as she watched the lifeguards launch the rowboat into the water.

I didn't know what to say, I was freaked too. We'd been watching Hunter and Colby. One turn of the head and two kids had vanished. And all I could do was watch as the volunteers dredged the water—they were chest-deep now. I didn't think they'd find Hunter and Colby there, but . . . what if they did? There were always stories of kids getting swept out in some freak accident. There was no rip current though. Maybe I couldn't join in the search, but at least I could try to keep

Cassidy from having a meltdown. *Think, Bryan.*

"Well, as much as Hunter digs sharks, Colby hates them. He was afraid there were sharks in the pool."

"Yeah, but—" She stopped, blinked a few times, features sharpening. "Sharks, omigod, that's it. I think . . . I gotta go, tell them I'm looking in the arcade." She took off running, sand kicking up behind her.

The kids were getting restless.

"Hey," Tori said, clapping her hands. "Who wants to play duck, duck, goose?"

No one really did, but she corralled them under the tent and managed to get them to play a few rounds. Wade came back up to the tent, looking grim, but suddenly his face broke into a wide grin. I turned my head to see what he was looking at.

Cass was in between Hunter and Colby, holding on to their hands for dear life.

"Little dudes, you are in some deep crap," he said, trotting over to them.

Tori ran over to tell Owen. Wade lifted Colby up onto his shoulders. Hunter's eyes were slightly swollen from crying. Cass pulled him under the tent and wrapped her arms around him. She looked over his shoulder at me.

"They were looking at Whack-a-Shark. He's been wanting me to take him to the arcade. He's worried he'll never be able to play it after this," she said.

"You're going to tell Dad," Hunter said.

"Uh, yeah, buddy, I kind of have to—you can't run off like that."

She released him, then Owen came over and took Hunter and Colby off to the side. He knelt down, face stern, but soon had them laughing. Cass grabbed my hand.

"Hey, thanks," she said.

"For what?"

"Helping me calm down enough to think." She leaned over and gave me a quick peck on the cheek, then backed away grinning.

I fucking loved field day.

SEVENTEEN

CASSIDY

THE DAY MOM AND EMS WERE SET TO ARRIVE, I got up early and threw some clothes and toiletries into my duffel bag and went downstairs to see if I could help out. Taking over breakfast duties when Leslie was sick had given me a bit more confidence, and interacting with the guests seemed like less of a hassle and even surprisingly fun. For some reason I was a bundle of nerves; I couldn't wait to spend some time with Ems and Mom. I wanted the day to begin.

When I walked into the kitchen, Dad and Leslie were caught up in a lip-lock in front of the coffeemaker. It was so jarring I nearly tripped over my own feet trying to turn back. They heard my shuffling and broke apart. Seeing them hold hands and give each other moony glances was one thing, but catching them midkiss was just . . . more than I wanted to see.

Especially first thing in the morning.

"Cass, hey, good morning," Dad said.

I came back into the kitchen. Leslie's cheeks were flushed. She smoothed a loose hair and tucked it behind her ear as she went back to pouring cream into a small pitcher. I dropped my bag in the office right off the kitchen.

"I could take that out for you if you want," I said, coming back in to get the pitcher.

"Sure," she said, "but first, Cass . . . we . . . your father and I—" She stopped midsentence to look at him. They were both giggly and weird, and not at all like their usual getting-things-done selves.

"Is everything okay?" I asked. "Mom and Ems are still coming, right?"

"Yes, it's nothing like that," Leslie said.

My father leaned against the counter and put his arm around Leslie, pulling her toward him so they were hip to hip. She laughed, gave him a kiss on the cheek, and they both looked at me.

"We've got some news, Cass," Dad said.

What news they had to tell me first thing in the morning, I couldn't imagine. It didn't look as though they were upset; quite the opposite.

"The other day, when Leslie was sick, it wasn't a stomach bug," he continued.

"We're pregnant!" Leslie said.

The news hit me. Good news. Happy news. I smiled, caught off guard and trying to come up with the correct response. My thoughts went to my mother—did she know? I was selfishly hoping this wouldn't put a cloud over her visit. It shouldn't, but—

"Wow, that's . . . congratulations," I said.

Leslie held out her arms to me. I went over and hugged her lightly, surprised at her rib-cracking embrace. I laughed, then did the same with Dad.

"Does Mom know?" I asked.

"Yes, we called her last night."

That made me feel better, not that I thought it would bother her. I just didn't want to ambush her with it. I mean, it was pretty big news. A new life.

"And Hunter?"

Leslie closed the container of cream, all business again. "We're going to take him out for pizza tonight and tell him, make it special. Of course you would have been a part of that, but we wanted to make sure you knew before you left for the day."

"Thanks," I said, grabbing the pitcher of cream. "I'll take that out."

A new baby.

I wondered how Hunter was going to take it.

"Tell me again why I can't go with you?" Hunter asked.

We sat side by side on the top step, waiting for Mom and

Emma to arrive. The sky was slightly overcast, but the plan was to check into the hotel, go to the beach, get tan, go out to dinner, and then Mom was leaving Ems and me free to do whatever we wanted. I only hoped Crest Haven didn't let Emma down. It seemed like she had high expectations.

"Well, you're sort of punished after your field day stunt," I said.

Hunter frowned. "I just wanted to play Whack-a-Shark."

"I know, and I swear when I'm back and you're not punished, and we have nothing else to do, I'll take you, okay?"

"I guess, but why do you have to go overnight?"

"Because I haven't seen my friend Emma since I got here, and we're going out to do something fun. It's a girls' night, Hunter; seriously, you're not missing anything," I said.

"You're lucky though, you get to stay in a hotel," Hunter said.

"Well, you *live* in a hotel, sort of, how cool is that?"

He shrugged.

Mom and Ems arrived fifteen minutes later. Emma hardly waited for the car to stop before getting out and running toward Ocean Whispers. She threw open the gate and I jumped the bottom two stairs to match her pace. She looked amazing, already tan, with deep-blue and purple highlights running through her dark hair.

"When did you do that to your hair?" I asked.

"Like right after you left. Drew hates it," she said.

"I love it."

We embraced, giggling, then pulled apart.

"What the what with Sugar Rush Nate, Cassidy? Why didn't you tell me about him? Here I thought you were really down with the no-hookup thing, and you hooked up right under my nose."

"I'm happy to see you too, Ems," I said.

"No, really, why were you holding out on me with the details?"

"Can we just stop calling him Sugar Rush Nate, and forget it? I didn't tell you because it was a huge mistake."

"Really? He keeps asking if you're coming back in the fall," she said.

I hadn't even thought of going back to work at Sugar Rush, but they had assured me my job would be waiting for me when I returned. I didn't want to think of it yet. Fall felt like a lifetime away.

"Don't mind me, I'm just the chauffeur," my mother said. I let go of Ems and met her halfway up the path to give her a hug.

My father and Leslie were on the porch. Hunter pouted. I hoped whatever special plans they had later cheered him up, although I had no clue how he'd react to Dad and Leslie's news. Would he be happy? Would he secretly wish his mom would give birth to a shark? I brought Ems up to say hi to the family. I saw Mom whisper her congratulations and give Leslie a hug that lasted a little longer than normal. Then we were off. The prospect of experiencing Crest Haven as a tourist was exciting. There were so many nice hotels along Beach Avenue. I couldn't wait to see which one Mom had booked.

Ten minutes later, we pulled into the very crowded parking lot of the Surf Motel. It was small and, well, shabby. The sort of motel that looked like it must have been nice forty years ago. My mother laughed.

"Well, it's not the Four Seasons, but we were lucky to get this. It was hard to find a place that allowed one-night stays on the weekend."

"We can sleep on the beach," Emma said.

"I'm sure it's not so bad; it's just for a night. It'll be an adventure. Wait here while I check in," Mom said.

"This looks like the kind of place we won't check out of," I joked. The front of the building had tiny rocks embedded into it and a big neon sign in the shape of a surfboard. Fake palm trees stood guard on either side of the door to the office.

"Maybe it's just trying to look retro," Emma said.

Two guys about our age came walking out from the fenced-in pool area. Both were shirtless, tan, jock types, with the sort of abs that almost looked painful. Emma unzipped her beach cover-up and leaned out the window.

"Hey, how is this place?"

The guys smiled at her. The one with the dark hair answered. "Better now that you're here."

"Ems," I said, tugging her back in the car.

"Cool, maybe we'll see you later."

"Maybe," the other guy said.

She sank back into her seat, huge grin on her face.

"This place is perfect."

We fried on the beach for a few hours, then got ready to make our seven o'clock reservation at Gasparro's. Ems and I wanted to bail and get some tacos somewhere without a dress code, but Mom pleaded.

"This place has five stars from *New Jersey* magazine. I need a five-star experience now that I've seen the dump we're staying in. Come on, ladies."

Gasparro's was fancy, but not uncomfortably so. A dark-haired hostess in a silver blouse and black pencil skirt led us to a table in the center of the room. The walls were painted a warm yellow. A trompe l'oeil mural of a courtyard by a rolling hillside encompassed one of the walls. With lots of candles and gentle music, it was the perfect date place.

We'd just opened our menus when a server came over to fill our water glasses.

"Cassidy?"

It was Wade. His unruly man bun was more slicked back. Wearing black pants, a white button-down shirt, and a black apron tied around his waist, Wade was about as far from his camp-counselor surfer-dude self as possible. If he hadn't said my name, it would have taken me a few moments to recognize him.

"This is your second job?"

"Yep, my aunt's place. I pick up a bussing shift here and there," he said, looking around the table. Emma kicked me.

"Sorry—Wade, this is my mom, and this is my best friend from home, Emma. They're here for the night. Wade and I work together at camp."

Wade smiled, holding Emma's gaze a little bit longer than necessary. "Nice to meet you. Your server should be over in a few minutes. Do you want some bread?"

"Yes," my mother said, so eagerly it made me laugh. Wade smiled and disappeared behind an eggplant-colored velvet curtain. He wasn't gone two seconds before Emma started.

"Cassidy, you work with *him*? I don't see how you could have any problem getting over Gavin down here. What are you waiting for?"

Mom took her napkin off her plate and put it in her lap. "Have to say I agree with Ems on this, Cass."

"We're just friends. He sort of flirts with everyone."

"Lucky us," said Emma, grinning.

Wade came back with a bread basket and a small bowl of marinara sauce.

"If you need any recs, I'd be happy to help. I think I've had pretty much everything on the menu," he said.

"Please," Mom said.

"You ladies like mushrooms?"

We nodded.

"There's a mushroom tortellini special tonight that's killer. Usually sells out," he said.

"Thanks," I said.

The waiter came over and took our drink orders. Iced teas for Ems and me. A glass of merlot for Mom. We took Wade's advice and each ordered the mushroom tortellini with shaved truffles. It was one of the best pasta dishes I'd ever tasted, and judging from Emma's and Mom's faces, it was for them too. The grand finale was chocolate soufflé for three, which Wade also recommended.

"They didn't make them like that when I was seventeen," my mother said.

"Mom, ew."

"Nan would be so impressed with him." She took another spoonful of chocolate soufflé. I laughed.

"Nan would be impressed with his taste in dessert," I said, remembering Nan's assessment of Gavin and his dislike of anything sweet.

Wade *was* pouring it on thick. If I didn't know him for his goofiness in camp, I probably would have been just as smitten. He stopped by to see how we enjoyed everything on his way to clear a table that had just emptied.

"That was the best meal I've had in a while," Mom said, sitting back and smiling at Wade.

"Dessert was on me, by the way," he said before heading off to clear the other table.

"He's perfect," Emma said, her eyes following Wade's every move across the restaurant.

"He's flirting," I said.

"Seriously, why aren't you forgetting Gavin with *him*?"

"He's kind of taken," I said, which wasn't a complete lie.

After we paid the check and stood up to leave, Wade stopped by again.

"What are you two doing later?" he asked, looking between me and Emma.

"Nothing," Emma said.

Mom pressed the home button on her phone to check the time. I could see her wheels turning. It was already nine o'clock. At home my curfew had been eleven, which Gavin and I always pushed. Maybe Wade buying us dessert wasn't so innocent. I smiled.

"There's a couple of us getting together at Tori's; I'm headed there after work. I can swing by and pick you up."

"It's kind of late," Mom said.

"Come on, life doesn't really start until ten o'clock," Wade said.

My mother laughed, shook her head.

"Mom, please," I said. "Emma wants to see Crest Haven after dark."

"How can I say no to that?" she said.

We went back to the Surf to change and waited out front for Wade. My mother agreed to a one a.m. curfew, which Emma already wanted to blow off.

"Seriously, why do we even need a curfew—this is such a sleepy little town, can't we just stay out until, like, sunrise?"

"So if we were with your mom, she'd let us do that?"

She smiled. "Of course not, but we're not with my mom. So what's the deal with Wade, why did you say he's *kind of* taken—what does that mean?"

"My friend from camp, Tori, has a thing for him," I said. "I respect that."

"So she's not with him?"

"No."

A huge smile crossed Emma's face.

"Okay, wait, what's the deal, Emma? Why are you so . . . well, you're acting like *you're* not with anyone. First those guys from the pool, now Wade. What's going on with Drew?"

She shrugged. "I'm just having a little fun."

"No, this isn't the same person who couldn't eat dinner with me the night I left because Drew texted her from work. Something's up."

"Okay, tell me if Sugar Rush Nate was a good kisser, and I'll spill."

I laughed. "Why do you care about Nate? Fine, yes, he was really good. What's going on with you and Drew?"

"We had the talk."

I waited for her to elaborate, but she kept looking at cars passing by on Beach Avenue, avoiding my eyes. I wasn't sure what talk she meant.

"Ems, just tell me," I said.

She crossed her arms. "You know the talk, Cassidy. The one where I told him that I planned to begin my own college visits at Penn, how I'd have to stay overnight, how I'd researched bus and train schedules, how by then I might even have a car, that the eight-hour drive would be nothing."

"Oh, Ems."

"And he says—*I was thinking we should maybe keep our options open*. See each other when he was home, but see other people too. That it was unrealistic to try and stay together, blah, blah, blah, blah. And I told him, fine. That I was ready to keep my options open right now, why wait?"

"I'm sorry."

"Don't be, I'm not. You had the right idea, Cassidy, although I wouldn't have tossed the Tiffany necklace. Look at this place," she said, holding her arms out to the sky. "We're going out, at ten o'clock, meeting new people. The ocean is right there. This is paradise."

I still hadn't told her I'd talked to Gavin. I wasn't sure I wanted to—I had the feeling she would give me a lecture about it, how idiotic it was to open that door again. But I didn't really feel like I'd opened a door . . . okay, maybe a crack, but I hadn't responded to his texts and didn't have plans to. My little chat with him was just that, a chat, meaningless, a momentary craziness.

A small white car pulled up in front of the Surf.

"Shotgun," Ems said, racing out ahead of me.

Wade got out and came around to open the door for us.

"So, what time do you have until?" he asked.

"One," I said.

"That's it? Damn, that chocolate soufflé usually buys more time than that," he said.

"And here I thought we were special," I said.

"Kidding. Come on."

EIGHTEEN
BRYAN

"I CAN'T BELIEVE I LET NICK TALK ME INTO THIS," Tori said, surveying the living room of her crowded house. Her arms were folded, face pinched. It looked as if she might have been holding her breath.

"Into what? Having a little fun?" I said.

"He said a few people; to me that means five or six tops. There's about thirty people here now. My mother left me in charge for the weekend. I'm the responsible one and I let this happen. The last thing she needs is some emergency call that her house is on fire while she's at a trade show. She trusts me."

"Tori, what would happen if you just stopped worrying?"

There was a loud crash from the kitchen. And laughter. She sighed.

"That. That's what would happen. Are you okay if I check that out?"

"Since when do I need you to babysit me? Go."

I'd set myself up on the sofa for a bit, my chair missing, probably still out on the patio after Jake wanted to see if he could pop and hop in it. We were about the same height, and after a few times of showing him, he asked if he could practice. The guys were still convinced with the right modifications it would ride the half-pipe like a dream. I'd dared them to take it over to our yard to test out and see what my parents would think of that. I hadn't intended on coming over, but something happened when I logged into *Realm Wars* that night.

I didn't want to play.

No urge to get lost in the game at all. Matt had stopped by my room on the way out and before I even knew what was happening, I told him I'd be over in a bit. After he left, I drained my bladder, grabbed a fresh tee—"Keep Calm and Roll On"—and crossed the yard to Tori and Nick's. I wanted to be around people. I wanted to be around my friends.

That restlessness that had started in the beginning of the summer had only gotten stronger. Why was I waiting for possibilities instead of actively participating? Maybe Nick and the guys had stopped hanging out with me because I didn't meet them halfway. And the worst that could happen at camp—losing a kid—had happened and everything was okay. I didn't lose my job. Parents hadn't freaked out. Colby and H-bomb were fine.

Cassidy had kissed my cheek.

Everything seemed possible.

I felt a breeze on my neck as someone ran fingers through the back of my hair and sat on the arm of the sofa. A long-legged someone wearing shorts and an ice-cream-stained Sip N' Freeze tee.

Shay. Her hair loose and long.

"I didn't expect to see you here," she said, smiling.

"It's not every day Tori agrees to a party; thought I'd come check out this momentous occasion."

She leaned back and waved to a girl who was frantically trying to get her attention from the kitchen.

"Next round," she said, turning her gaze back to me. "I'm so over beer pong."

"Yeah, me too."

"Where's your friend . . . Cass?"

She remembered.

"Her mom's in town."

Shay nodded. "Looked like you guys were having fun that day."

"Yeah, she's cool," I said.

"I'm glad you have someone like that," she said.

My insides reeled. Her inflection on *someone* made me realize she thought I was *with* Cassidy. Shay sounded genuine though, not like she was trying to rattle me, or dig for information. Our breakup wrecked us both, but beneath that was friendship. I could deal with that, but friendship began with the truth.

"We're not together or anything," I said. The words felt heavy. Made me realize how much I wanted the opposite to be true. That I had *someone*.

That I had Cassidy.

"Summer's not over, Bry. You've got time."

"She just broke up with a guy," I found myself saying. "So, I don't know."

"Excuses, excuses," she joked.

"Are you dissing me?"

"You were never this serious. Just, you know, go for it."

"Okay, I will. Problem solved. What should we work on next, poverty? World hunger?"

She laughed. "There you are."

"Shay Foster, get your butt in here!" someone yelled from the kitchen.

Shay rolled her eyes. "Guess they need me. Do you want anything before I go, drink or something?"

"Nah, just perfect your arc shot," I said. She laughed.

"Will do. Talk to you later, Bry," she said, disappearing into the kitchen.

Shay was right. I'd never been this serious. I'd been Matt, hanging out the window, trying to get a girl's attention. I'd had summer-girl hookups like Wade did. Kissing. Fooling around. Not serious. Could I just fool around with Cass? Why did I care that it meant something?

Because it did.

Because I was different.

Because no matter what, hearing *I just can't deal with it* hurt.

I didn't think I could handle that coming from Cassidy.

Even if it was true.

Even if I didn't blame anyone, because, fuck, there were times I just couldn't deal with it myself. But it was my life. I had no choice. But I did have a choice in how it affected me. I was still just me. A little altered, but me.

Not that I thought she'd say it, but if she did . . . would that spoil everything?

Wade walked in through the sliding patio door, saw me, and grinned. Behind him was a girl I'd never seen before, and behind her was Cassidy.

Cass.

I never believed the bullshit of someone lighting up a room, but seeing her made everything sharpen. Every part of me pulled in her direction, wanted her to come closer. She searched the room, and when her eyes landed on mine, she smiled. She grabbed the other girl by the elbow and pulled her over. Wade followed.

"Hey, you're here," she said.

"I'm here."

"This is Emma, my friend from home."

"Hi, Emma, friend from home. I'm Bryan."

"Hey, nice to meet you," Emma said, smiling. She looked over my shirt, brow wrinkling a moment, then her eyes darted around the place as if she was looking for something.

"They're playing beer pong, come on, Cass," she said, pulling Cass toward the kitchen.

"I'll be back," she called over her shoulder.

"Surprise," Wade said, taking a seat next to me.

"Ha, thanks."

"Matty texted me you were here; thought I'd show the girls the wild side of Crest Haven," Wade joked. "It's good to see you out, man."

"When you get a chance, could you check and see what's going on with my chair? Jake took it out to the patio. I just don't want them to wreck it."

"Don't worry, I'm on it."

Emma appeared in the kitchen doorway. "Wade, come on, you have to be on my team. Cass is bailing."

Wade sighed.

"Guess I'm gonna have to show the best friend a good time," he said, getting up.

Cass came through the doorway just as Wade was heading in and they both pulled back and laughed. Cass balanced two cups in each hand as she shimmied past Wade, through the doorway, and over to me.

"Here, Shay thought you might want this. It's a Coke float," she said, sitting down next to me.

I looked in the cup. Coke with a Ping-Pong ball floating in it.

"What a riot," I said, putting it to the side. "I don't drink and drive, long commute next door. Emma seems—"

"—ready for a party," Cass finished.

"She's with the right person."

"Tori won't be pissed, will she? I know she sort of has a thing for Wade," she said.

"Wait, how do you know?"

"That she likes Wade? I knew that from day one," she said. "Emma's harmless, she's just, as I said, ready for a party."

Tori walked out of the kitchen, shaking her head. She perched on the arm of the couch where Shay had been.

"Do you know what those morons did? They stacked a pyramid of beer cans underneath the ceiling fan and then turned it on. Who does that? I'm going to have to mop the floor tomorrow."

"Make Nick do it," I said.

"Yeah, that'll happen. So, Benny Barbie, I see you brought a friend," Tori said.

"Wait, you know she calls you that?" I asked Cass.

"It's the hair," Cass said. "I get it."

"Bry, it's sort of a term of endearment now," Tori said.

"Yes, and that's Benny Emma, complete with colored hair extensions and sunburn. Red party cup optional," Cass said.

"You two are scarier when you get along," I said.

"You should be happy," Tori said.

Sitting there, Cass next to me, friends around, I was pretty happy.

By midnight, the party cleared out except for a few of us. Wade wasn't in sight though and I knew I'd need my chair soon. I'd emptied my bladder before coming to the party, but the twitch in my shoulder was a reminder that I might need to do it again soon. The last thing I wanted was an accident in front of Cass.

"Wade," I called.

"Want me to check if he's in the kitchen?" Cass asked. She stood, picking up a few party cups along the way to help Tori clean.

"He's not there, and neither is Ems," she said when she came back. "Is something wrong?"

"I need my chair; I have to get going," I said.

"Where is it?" she asked.

"It should be on the patio," I said.

"I'll get it," she said. I saw her through the glass doors, looking left and right, and finally disappearing. I took out my phone and texted Wade. He had to be in the house. When I looked up, Cass was pushing my chair into the living room. I gave it a quick once-over. All in one piece.

"Thanks, I can take it from here," I said.

"So, you're leaving?" she asked.

I didn't want to get into the reason why—we hadn't even kissed, I didn't want to talk about my bathroom management—but man, how I wanted to stay.

"Yeah, it's . . . I just have to get in," I said.

"Can I walk you?"

"You want to walk me home?"

She smiled. "Sure."

I let her push me across the yards and up the ramp to the deck. She leaned against the house, eyes on mine. Should I take her hand? Pull her in for a kiss?

"I hope Emma doesn't get into too much trouble with Wade. We have to leave soon too," she said.

"How are you getting home?"

"I'm assuming Wade; that's how we got here," she said. "I guess if he's played too much beer pong we can take a cab. Do cabs run this late around here?" she asked.

"I'll take you," I said.

"You don't have to, Bry, I'm sure we can—"

"I want to," I said. "Can you give me about fifteen minutes, would that work?"

"Yeah."

By the time I came back out, Cass was gone, but there was a commotion on the Bardots' patio. I pushed over as fast as I could. Tori shouted at everyone to leave.

"Just get out."

"Chill, Tori," Nick said.

"No, *you* chill. Tell your friends they need to crash somewhere else because no one is crashing here."

"Not even me?" Wade joked.

"Especially not you," she said. She went back into the house and locked the door.

"What the hell happened?" I asked.

Wade looked down at the ground. Cass had her arm around Emma, who was hunched over, hand to her mouth.

"Screw it, we can stay out here, mosquitos aren't so bad," Nick said, opening his arms up to the sky.

"I'm out," Matt said. "I have a bed waiting for me; see ya."

Jake and Tom headed out too.

Nick followed Matt. "Can I crash with you?"

Cass looked at me. "Can we get out of here?"

"Yeah, come on."

Emma was sniffling. Wade followed us to my car.

"The back will be kind of tight with my chair," I said.

"I'll sit there; I think she needs as much space as she can get."

"She's not going to be sick, is she?" I asked.

"No, no, I'm fine," Emma said. "The worst is over. I don't feel sick anymore."

I was afraid to ask what had happened.

"Emma, are you gonna be okay?" Wade asked.

"Yeah," she said. She pulled away from Cassidy and threw

her arms around him. Cass turned away as they shared a kiss. It didn't take me long to figure out that whatever had made Tori upset, seeing Wade and Emma hooking up didn't help. Tori might have played it cool around Wade and knew the way he was, but seeing it in action was completely different. I texted her.

Me: RU Okay?

It took a few seconds for her to text back.

Tori: Cleaning Benny puke and skunked beer. Just dandy. ;)

Me: Will help when I get back.

Tori: Thnx. I got this.

"Come on, Emma, Bryan was nice enough to offer us a ride home," Cass said. Wade and Emma parted with a few more kisses. Emma walked backward to the car. Wade smiled.

"You have my number, right?" she asked.

"Yep," Wade said, walking closer to the car.

Cassidy turned to him.

"She really likes you, you know."

Wade flinched. "I know," he said.

"Well, you have a stupid way of showing it," Cass said.

And I knew they weren't talking about Emma.

We kept the windows down on the way to the Surf. Emma

put her head back and moaned a few times, complaining about being dizzy. Cass kept a hand on Emma's shoulder. When I put the car in park, Emma opened the door, jumped out, and puked a few feet away. Cass hadn't even moved from the backseat yet.

"Just, can you wait a minute?" she asked.

She stepped out of the car and ran over to Emma. Emma nodded like crazy to whatever Cass said, and she led her over to the front wall of the motel. A woman sitting in the office looked out between blinds. Emma put her head in her hands. Cass came back to the car and slid in the front seat, leaving the door open.

"I'm so sorry, Bryan, this . . . she's not herself. She had a fight with her boyfriend and went a little nuts at the party."

"It happens," I said.

"Yeah, well, I would have liked to stay and help Tori clean up, but I don't think she's too happy with me for bringing Benny Emma around tonight," she said, chuckling. "Why does Wade hook up with other people when he knows how Tori feels about him?"

"I don't know. He's scared, I think."

"That sounds crazy."

"I've told him that," I said.

Emma retched again.

"Oh, God, I have to go. Thanks, Bry."

She leaned toward me, and it was field day all over again.

If I didn't act, she'd kiss my cheek. *Now or never, Lakewood.*

When the heat of her mouth was seconds away, I turned, changing her target without warning. Her lips grazed mine, soft, almost nonexistent. She was about to pull away. I touched her hair, raked it behind one ear, and whispered her name. She leaned into me, her fingers gripping my shoulder.

I was kissing Cassidy Emmerich.

I WAS KISSING BRYAN LAKEWOOD.

I'd meant to kiss him in a neutral place. His cheek, his jaw, his temple . . . as a thank-you for driving us home, for being cool about Emma. That's where I was headed anyway, until he turned toward me, eyes wide, and my lips landed on his mouth. His soft, warm mouth. The shock of it should have made me pull away.

But it felt sooooooo good.

I closed my eyes, my mind on overdrive analyzing everything—the easy way our lips fit together. The kisses: soft at first, then hungry. His hand in my hair, my hand on his shoulder—a total rush. The world beyond his car disappeared, and it was just his lips, his arms. All I wanted to do was climb on top of him.

We finally pulled apart, foreheads touching, breathing heavy.

"Can I see you tomorrow?" he asked.

"You mean later?"

"Yes."

We kissed as confirmation.

Emma hurled again—this awful retching, hairball-on-steroids noise.

"I better go, but yeah, I'll call you when they leave," I said.

He nodded. Pressed his lips together, smiled.

I finally slid out of the car and shut the door, barely aware of my feet hitting the pavement. I had to get Emma inside, but had no idea how to avoid my mother. Our room was tiny, the beds practically on top of one another. And Ems was stumbling without any obstacles in her way; I couldn't imagine how she'd be in a darkened motel room. At least we weren't late—we had that going for us—but I doubted Wade's charm and chocolate soufflé would help us now.

Bryan stayed until Emma and I walked into the motel courtyard. Then he took off into the night. Two red taillights trailing down Beach Avenue. My lips still tingled from his kiss. I couldn't wait to see him again.

"I'm sorry, Cass. You must hate me," Emma said.

The courtyard contained a few round stone picnic tables with umbrellas and some lounges scattered about. I walked us over to a chaise.

"Ems, sit," I said. She flopped back, arm over her eyes.

"I guess you lost at beer pong," I said.

She laughed. "Ya think?"

"Do you think you can pull it together? My mom is probably awake," I said. I saw the dim blue glow of a television screen between the cracks in the curtain of our room.

"I didn't realize he was in a wheelchair," she said.

"Oh, Bryan."

"Yeah, when we came in and you introduced us . . . his shirt makes more sense now, 'Keep Calm and Roll On.' Cute."

"Yeah, he's cool. He's been a good friend, we—"

"Good friend? Shut. Up. I saw you guys maul each other before you got out of his car."

I covered my mouth to stop from laughing. Ems hadn't been as out of it as I originally thought.

She sat up, pulled her knees to her chest. "And that doesn't bother you?"

"What do you mean?"

"The wheelchair thing . . . you never thought, like . . . ," she said, gesturing as if she could pull the words from the air. She leaned back, dismissing her unformed question with a wave. "Forget it, I'm drunk."

I knew what she was getting at—was everything working? My cheeks flushed. The thought had crossed my mind, but it's not like Bryan and I were that intimate with each other. Yet, anyway. Kissing him was a rush. I couldn't wait to do it again. That's all I cared about at the moment. Everything else we'd figure out as we went along.

"Emma, I'm not going to dissect it right now. I'm having fun."

She smiled. "Guess you're officially over Gavin."

Gavin's name was a pin to my Crest Haven bubble. I felt the same flare of guilt that I'd had with Sugar Rush Nate—why, I don't know. There was no reason to feel guilty. At all. I hadn't kissed Bryan out of spite, or to get over Gavin. Maybe my feelings weren't as resolved as I'd thought, but whatever was happening with Bryan was separate. This wasn't a rebound. I kissed him because his lips were warm. He made me laugh. His arms felt good around me. What had I done, though? There was no going back to friendly flirting once someone's tongue had been wrapped around yours.

"Did you have to bring up Gavin?"

"Why don't we call him and share the good news? I'd love to see that prick's ego deflate."

"How about, no. Speaking of mauling . . . what happened? Why did you—"

"Maul Wade after you told me not to?"

"Yeah."

"I don't know, Cass. Please . . . he just . . . I mean, look at him. He's my first surfer dude." She giggled.

"I know, but . . ."

"I wasn't thinking. I'm a selfish bitch, okay? I miss Drew. I fucking miss Drew. And I hate what he said. And I try and be all tough about it, but I just don't get why . . . why I'm not enough."

Hearing Emma say aloud the thoughts that I'd been torturing myself with for the past few months was eye-opening. It was such bullshit—of course we were enough.

I sighed and sat on the edge of the chaise.

"You are enough, Ems. More than that. Being that far apart from someone for so long is hard. Probably next to impossible to maintain."

"It just makes me sad. We were so happy, you know? Why does everything change so fast?"

"I don't know," I said. "C'mon, let's go."

Ems was able to stand by herself, but we walked arm in arm to the room. As I was about to slip my key in the door, my mother opened it and got an eyeful of us. She looked at Ems, then me, and sighed.

"Get in."

When I woke up, Ems was still sleeping, facedown, diagonally on the bed. I pushed back the curtains and squinted. Mom was lounging by the pool in her yoga pants, cup of coffee in hand. I pulled my hair back in a ponytail and went out to sit with her.

"I didn't expect to see you this early," she said.

"Eight o'clock is midmorning to me some days," I said.

"How is Emma?"

"Sleeping."

She nodded, took a sip of her coffee. "Mm-hmm."

I sat in the chaise next to her. Took a deep breath of the

ocean air. Gulls screeched. The sky was blue and endless. No clouds at all.

I kissed Bryan last night.

He was nowhere near, but I felt him all around. *Can I see you tomorrow?*

"What time are you heading out?" I asked, hoping it didn't sound too eager.

"Checkout is noon. I'd like to grab some breakfast before we hit the road. I certainly think Ems could use it."

"Oh, that . . . are you going to tell her mom?"

"I haven't decided yet," she said. "I hope it was worth it."

"We could probably stop by Ocean Whispers and have breakfast."

"Or not."

I realized I hadn't asked my mother how she really felt about Leslie being pregnant. I'd been so caught up in the excitement of her and Emma being here that we didn't get the chance to talk about it.

"Is it because of Dad and Leslie's news?" I asked.

She turned her head sharply to me. "No, not at all. Although, two little ones and a business to run is a lot to handle. I'm happy for them. Your father always wanted a big family."

I wrinkled my nose. "He did?"

Mom nodded and took another sip of her coffee as if she hadn't just revealed a piece of the puzzle I'd been pondering my whole life. This was news to me.

"Was that why you split up?"

"Part of it, I guess."

I let that nugget sink in—if my father wanted a big family, did that mean . . . ? "So wait, you didn't want a big family?"

She inhaled, kneaded the spot where her neck met her shoulder and sighed.

"No. I didn't. I don't. One perfect kid is enough."

"Why didn't you ever tell me this before?"

"How do I explain it without sounding . . ." She paused, shifted in her seat to face me. Elbows resting on her knees, she held the coffee cup with both hands and traced the rim of the lid with her thumb as she spoke. "Marrying your father felt right at the time and we tried. I tried. And it worked for a while, but he wanted to have another baby, and I kept putting it off. Motherhood didn't exactly come easy to me but I don't regret it. I love being your mom. I know it sounds selfish—but I also love the freedom I have now. Not having to answer to anyone, keeping my house as I please. I'm happy. I know I might not be the best at this mother thing, I'm not exactly PTA material and I always order your birthday cake from the bakery, but you know, I try."

Hearing her acknowledge her choice was powerful. Nothing had really gone terribly wrong between my parents—it wasn't that they couldn't make it work. They both wanted different things. Separating had been the right thing to do.

"You're not that bad," I said.

She smiled. "See, perfect kid."

"So if that's not it, why don't you ever want to go there,

Mom? You know, I checked the ledger. There was a vacancy this weekend."

"Cass, what if some couple came to town on a whim and stopped in? If I had taken that room it would be money out of your father's pocket. Besides, I don't want to make small talk with strangers. I'm not exactly a morning person."

"We wouldn't have to, and . . . sometimes small talk with strangers isn't so bad."

"Uh-oh, a few weeks down here and you're a convert."

"I just . . . You and Dad, I mean, you're not like enemies. You get along with Leslie, I don't get why—"

"It's the couples, Cass. I know I just went on about loving my freedom, and I do, but where there are couples and small talk there are always questions about me being alone. And looks. I'd rather my breakfast not be that complicated."

"Oh."

"Maybe before the summer's out, I'll stay there, okay? Bring Nan as my date. Maybe when we come to pick you up."

"Sounds good."

She grabbed my hand. "For now, this is the only couple I need."

The moment Ems and Mom dropped me off at Ocean Whispers I called Bryan. I knew exactly what I wanted to do for our first . . . was it a date? Make-out sesh? I didn't care about labels. I just wanted to spend time with him.

He pulled up in front of Ocean Whispers at seven.

"Hey," he said as I slipped into the passenger seat.

I leaned over and kissed him. Again, I'd intended it to be just a brush across his mouth, but it felt so new, different. Any time it felt like one of us was about to pull away, the other deepened the kiss again. We pulled apart, laughing.

"Where to?" he asked.

"Crescent Beach," I said.

"Crescent? Why?"

"Well, Hunter asked me to find him some Crest Haven diamonds. And I want to see the sunset."

We drove with the windows down, the air rushing through the car, whipping my hair around. When we hit the road that went toward Crescent Beach, he pulled on the hand control and I watched as the speedometer went up sixty . . . seventy . . . eighty. I put a hand against the dash to brace myself as the road came faster and faster underneath us. Bryan's face was joy. He howled before finally pushing forward on the brake. We slowed gradually until we came to the lot where I first met him. He pulled into a spot and cut the engine.

"Do you want to go on the sand?" he asked.

"Can you?"

"I can try," he said. "There's a wooden path that goes past the dunes, then I could probably . . . let's just say I have a way. It's not pretty, but if the end result is sitting with you on the beach, then I'll deal."

"Okay," I said.

Once Bryan was in his chair, I grabbed the blanket from

his backseat and we headed out to the sand. Halfway down the path, I had to push him. The beach was practically empty. The two old guys who'd been fishing the day I tossed my necklace into the waves were there again. A woman walked with her black lab. She threw a tennis ball into the water and he paddled out to retrieve it.

"What now?" I asked.

"Well, find a spot for the blanket, not too far."

I kicked off my flip-flops and walked a few feet away. I fanned out the blanket and set it down on the sand.

Bryan eased himself off the chair and positioned himself so his back was facing me.

"I told you, it's not pretty," he said, propping himself up on his hands. "I call this the butt scoot, and the only people who've seen me do it are my family, and now you."

I smiled. "I'm honored."

He moved backward, putting his hands back, then scooting his butt through. When he finally got to the blanket he collapsed flat, big grin on his face.

"Okay, we're staying here all night," he said. I kissed him lightly on the mouth.

"Here, give me a hand," he said. I entwined my fingers through his and pulled him up. He fixed each leg into a very loose crisscross applesauce, then leaned back on his hands.

"You're okay sitting like this?" I asked.

He smiled. "Yeah, for a bit anyway. One wheelchair perk is if there's sand in my butt I won't feel it, but I'll have to do a longer skin check than usual, make sure it's all out."

"Skin check?" I asked. I pulled my knees to my chest and faced him.

He opened his mouth but stopped, turned his head to the side. "You sure you want to hear this?"

"I asked, didn't I?"

"So has your butt ever gone numb from sitting too long?"

I nodded.

"Mine does too, only I can't feel it. I don't know if you've seen me sort of fidget during the day in my chair, or push up out of my seat for a bit? I need to make sure I don't keep pressure in one area for too long—that can lead to skin breakdown. I have to sort of check myself with a special mirror to make sure nothing's brewing, or in this case make sure I don't have any sand in my butt. Probably not first date convo. . . . Sorry if it's TMI." He blushed a little, then laughed. I put my hand over his.

"I can handle it, you know," I said. He smiled.

"You said you wanted to find a Crest Haven diamond? You might want to get one now before the sun goes down."

"Oh, yeah, Hunter. They're by the water?"

I got up, did a sweep, and found a few of the quartz pebbles along the water's edge. I dried them off on the hem of my shirt and stuffed them into my pocket, then went back to the blanket. Bryan had his eyes closed, kind of like the blissed-out look he got when he floated in the pool.

"What are you thinking about?" I asked, plopping down. I scooted next to him so our shoulders touched.

"You know, there's another beach farther down that you can see the sunset better from; they have Crest Haven diamonds too. Why did you want to come here?" he asked.

"I want a better memory here," I said.

"I can appreciate that," he said.

"That first night you saw me, I threw a necklace that Gavin gave me into the water, kind of a symbolic gesture of good riddance."

"You threw a necklace into the water?"

"Yeah, and then I tried to get it back, but it was gone, and that's why I was crying when you saw me. It all hit me—that I'd lost him, the necklace, that I left home for the summer and didn't know anyone. I felt really alone. Then you asked me if something was wrong with my bike."

He laughed. "I couldn't imagine why you were crying, but I thought you were a little too upset over your bike. I knew it had to be something bigger."

I leaned my head on his shoulder. "What about you?"

"What about me?"

"My father said . . . this is where you had your accident, in the parking lot. If you don't want to tell me, it's okay, but I'd really like to know."

He took a breath. "I mostly don't like to talk about it because it's my own fault."

I put my hand over his again.

"Nick went through a parkour phase and we used to kid him about it, because it looked so lame, you know. There was this parkour club at school, and it's not like the kind you see on YouTube with people flipping off of buildings."

"I've seen some of that, looks insane."

"Right, but not what Nick was doing. This was real basic stuff, like hopping over parking meters, garbage cans, Dumpsters. So one night, we were hanging over on the far end of the parking lot, smoking pot, chilling, and Nick showed us this trick he was trying to perfect. He jumped between the Dumpsters, then flipped around a tree branch, like pulled himself over and landed upright. It didn't look half bad, but we couldn't tell him that, because that would be admitting he'd actually done something right. Then he dared me to try it. So I did. I jumped the Dumpsters, but when I reached for the tree branch my foot got caught and I fell. If I'd gone with it, maybe I wouldn't have gotten hurt, or would've just smashed my face or something, but I tried to correct myself midflight and landed on my back."

"Did you know then?"

"Yeah, I did. I knew it was bad. I felt sort of a crack and a zap, then nothing, and the guys were laughing, because it probably looked hysterical, you know, me flat out. We were all stoned, and it was kind of unreal. And, well, that was that."

I didn't know what to say. I let his story sink in.

"I thought you said it was nothing exciting," I said, elbowing him.

He laughed. "You know, it would have made an epic fail reel, if it didn't turn out to be so . . . tragic, I guess."

"Bryan, I'm so sorry that happened to you."

"Me too, but . . . I don't feel tragic now, Cass. It's taken me a while to say that, but I don't. I mean, this is life, right? I'm sitting on the beach with a beautiful girl, must have done something right."

"Bry."

I leaned in to kiss him.

"You're going to miss the sunset," he whispered.

I turned, nestled against him. He slung an arm around me. The red wafer had barely kissed the water on the horizon line and painted the sky a dazzling orange that faded into periwinkle as it turned dusky.

"Oh, wait," I said, reaching for my phone, ready to take a picture.

"Is this to show someone on StalkMe that you're having the best time in the world without them?" His mouth was by my ear.

"No, not really," I said.

He nuzzled my cheek. I turned to him.

"Then how about just taking a picture here," he said, gently touching the spot between my eyebrows.

"I don't get what you mean," I said.

He kissed the spot.

"I mean, how about making this new, better memory just for you and me."

He took the phone out of my hand and placed it on the blanket. His hair tickled my cheek as he kissed my neck, then my earlobe. I closed my eyes, trying to commit it all to memory, the color of the sky, the purplish tint of the water, the sound of the waves gently lapping at the shore, the feeling of his lips against my skin. When he finally kissed me full-on, I didn't need to see anymore because I felt it. The sun melted in my mouth and shot through my fingertips.

TWENTY
BRYAN

SIP N' FREEZE WAS PACKED. NICK WAS FINALLY christening his new slush flavor, the Bardot Shaka Blast. Even on a night crowded with tourists, he'd somehow commandeered five picnic tables on the side, set apart by fake tiki torches.

Tori and Cass passed out slush samples to the people waiting in line, and Nick, who wore an "I'm Famous in New Jersey" tee and a crown lei, took pictures with anyone who asked. There was a rumor that the local paper was sending someone to do a story. Had to hand it to the guy, he was good at the mascot/front man thing.

"I'm so glad they changed the name of that slush. There was no way in hell I was ordering a Nick Bardot," Wade said. "Think she'll ever get over the Emma thing? She's been weird since the party. Civil, but weird."

"Did you even offer to help clean up?" I asked.

"Yeah, I did. She wouldn't let me in after you guys left. Then at camp it was like nothing ever happened—she didn't say a word about it, all business."

"Dude, I don't know, but you could certainly step up your game—making her a picture with cereal wasn't exactly a shining moment."

Wade clapped a hand over his eyes. "See, when it really matters, I suck at this."

Cass walked slowly toward us, carrying four small cups together in her hands. She intentionally bumped Tori and motioned for her to follow. Tori took two from her and they came over.

Wade might have been down, but I was the fucking sun, moon, and stars as Cass sat on the end of the bench and placed the slush sample in front of me. She brushed her lips across mine, and we laced our fingers together. We'd become inseparable since we made our better memory at Crescent Beach. It was heaven.

She pulled out her phone.

"Why don't we skip the scavenger hunt tonight," I said.

"C'mon, we can multi-task," she said, smiling. I was toast. I'd do anything for that smile.

"Fine," I said.

"I think the clue has to do with this place, listen. *Choose this flavor, but don't have it raw—a formidable opponent, might be a southpaw."*

"What do you think?" Tori asked.

"I think Mr. Beckett was bored out of his mind and purposely came up with something that no one could win," Wade said.

"Wait, read it again," I said. Cass read it.

"It's an ice-cream flavor, don't you think?" I said.

"Yes!" Cass answered. "I'm going to take a picture of the menu board with the ice-cream flavors so we can go over them; be right back." She shot up and practically mowed down Nick.

"Oops, sorry," she said as she continued toward the front of Sip N' Freeze.

"I'm so moving to their team." Tori looked at Wade, who got suddenly quiet. He grabbed the slush sample and was about to drink it.

"Dude, no, I have to make a toast," Nick said.

"It's going to melt."

Nick looked at me. "Matty isn't around. Did he say anything about when he and Jake were getting here?"

"He didn't mention a time. I'm sure he wouldn't miss it."

"Nick, hello, you have to start, these slushes are melting," Tori said. He grabbed one of the extra cups off the table, put his fingers in between his teeth, and whistled. Everyone looked at him. He moved into the center of the tables and stood up on one of the bench seats. Cass came back and snapped a picture of him before putting down the phone and picking up her sample cup.

"Dudes, you know this is a long time coming. I had my first slush at Sip N' Freeze when I was seven years old, tried so many combos, but it was not until last year, when they had a special flavor—Cinnamon Red Hot—that I fell in love and found the perfect match."

"Did he really just use the word *love*?" Tori whispered.

"So tonight, this is a celebration of the newly christened Bardot Shaka Blast." He lifted up the cup. "Long may it give the fine people and visitors of Crest Haven brain freeze." Nick threw a shaka sign and howled before downing the cup.

We all followed. Cass and Wade both had their hands up to their foreheads. Tori took a small sip, winced, then put it down again.

Jake Matson's silver pickup came sweeping into the parking lot and pulled into the last open spot. Matt hopped out of the passenger side and they sauntered across the asphalt. Cass was already talking scavenger-hunt clues again.

"I bet it's cake batter!" she said. "Or maybe brownie batter?"

"Cake," I agreed. "Only now what? How does all of that fit together? I'm starting to agree with Wade."

"Hey, what did we miss?" Matt asked, sidling up to us. His eyes landed on Cass's and my clasped hands. He raised his eyebrows in surprise or approval, I couldn't tell. He gave me an almost imperceptible nod and smile.

Approval.

"Nick just christened his new flavor," Tori said, handing Matt a cup. He took it.

"I thought you were going to wait," he said.

"They were melting, bro, had to do the toast. By the way, Tori, thanks," said Nick.

"For what?"

"All your kitchen experiments have honed my taste buds. Well, that and the 'do you want to be a slug all your life' lectures—the answer is no. Thank you."

Tori raised her eyebrows at him, and I braced myself for her usual sarcastic comeback, but her face softened. "You're welcome, Slush King."

"So have we had enough?" Cass whispered in my ear.

"God, yes," I said, catching a kiss before she pulled away.

"Are you guys heading out?" Nick asked.

"Yeah," I said.

He and Matt exchanged glances.

"Um, hold on," Nick said. He whispered something to Matt and Jake, and the three of them walked off toward Jake's truck. There weren't gone for more than a minute when Wade tapped my shoulder.

"I think they, um, want you to go over there," Wade said.

"What? Why?" I asked.

All I wanted to do was leave and get horizontal with Cass.

I'd thrown a blanket into the car so we could head to Crescent Beach to look at the stars. Make some more memories. Wade looked at Tori. She sighed.

"They just do, come on," she said.

I backed away from the table and navigated the parking lot with Cass, Wade, and Tori following close behind. Matt had his hands on his hips, as he and Nick looked over something in the flatbed. They moved apart as we got closer. Nick opened the flatbed and smiled.

"So, um, I thought since tonight was a celebration, it would be a good time to share some of the love, and, well . . . ta-da . . ." He and Matt reached in and pulled out . . .

The quad fish.

My fish.

But it wasn't my board. At least not the way I remembered it.

There were handles near the top of the board, and the end dipped inward, concave, and it just . . .

Knocked the breath out of my lungs. I should have been stoked. They did this. For me. I looked up at Cass. She smiled, gave my shoulder a squeeze.

"When did you do this?" I asked.

"Dude, look, it's your board, all tricked out, so you can ride," Nick said.

"Ah, yeah, I see that."

Matt fidgeted. "I wanted to do something for you. I didn't think—well, I knew if I asked you, you'd say no."

"But you did it anyway," I said.

He grabbed the board out of Nick's hands and put it back in the flatbed.

"I'm sorry, I just thought if you saw it, you'd want to give it a try," he said. "Bry, we want to help you."

"And if I don't want your help? What if I wanted to sell it? What if I wanted to put it on the wall in my room? What if I wanted to burn it? You . . . you just had no right to take it without asking me."

I turned to Wade. "Did you know about this?"

He pressed his lips together, nodded.

"Bryan, we thought—"

"No, you didn't think, because if you did . . . you wouldn't have done this." I wheeled around, determined to get as far away from the board as I could. I couldn't breathe. My car. Once I got to the Charger I'd be okay. Cass followed.

When we got to the car, I saw that someone had parked their big, stupid rust-colored Hummer over the diagonal lines that designated my space as handicap parking. The vehicle wasn't exactly in my spot, but there wasn't enough room for me to get to the driver's side door. I closed my eyes.

"Bry, man, I didn't think—" Wade was next to me.

"Did I ever say I wanted to surf? Did those words come out of my mouth? I said maybe. I said someday. I don't get why you don't understand that."

My voice was loud, and the others from the party were now

looking over. It felt like the whole line was looking over at me too. An older guy with a beer gut and tan cargo shorts shuffled out of the line. The alarm dinged on the Hummer.

"I'm outta here." I wheeled my way through the parking lot, no idea where I was headed. I'd get the Charger later. I pushed farther away from the lights of Sip N' Freeze without looking back.

"Hey, wait."

Cass.

She crouched down next to me, touched my arm. Her look was soft, sincere. Did she know how much it meant to me that she'd said *I can handle it*? It scared me too. This growing feeling I had for her. I felt like I could tell her anything.

"I thought we were going to look at the stars," she said.

"I can't go back there, not right now."

"Well then, what do you want to do?"

She looked so pretty, smiling at me, hair around her face. This would not end well. I knew it.

What did I want?

I wanted to walk. I wanted to surf. I wanted to feel Cass against me.

"I don't know."

"Okay, come on. I have an idea."

Her idea was a hammock in the yard at Ocean Whispers.

And in spite of everything that had gone down, it was

pretty inspired. Although I had no clue how I was going to get out of the hammock, at the moment, I didn't care. I could sit there for eternity, my hand in her hair, her fingertips grazing my chest under my shirt.

Back and forth, back and forth, she tickled me. I kissed the top of her head.

We didn't talk, and I was grateful. The parking-lot scene was fading, felt less jagged. They should have known better than to spring that on me. They should have known how much that board had meant.

"Can I say something?" Cass asked.

"As long as you keep touching me like that," I said.

She laughed. "Okay."

She ran her fingers across my chest a few more times before speaking.

"I'm sorry for what happened back there."

"Cass. You didn't know about it, did you?"

"No, but hear me out, Bry." She paused, nestled into me some more. "As an outsider, what I see? Are people who care about you. I don't think they meant anything by it, other than wanting to see their friend happy. It's nice, from my point of view anyway. Not everyone has a group of friends like that. I know I don't."

I knew I should see it her way, and deep down, some small voice was saying just that. These guys cared about me, wanted to see me succeed—hell, I wanted to succeed, but I couldn't imagine what it would feel like to surf with my, well . . . limitations. And to see my board with handles? I hadn't asked anyone to do that. As much as I knew I needed to move on, I didn't want to completely forget who I'd been either.

Where I was wasn't bad, only different.

I had friends, a job, a fast car, a girl touching my skin.

"You've got that now," I whispered.

Cass looked up, scooched closer.

"Have what?"

"A group of friends who care about you."

She smiled. "So I'm not just a summer girl?"

I pressed my lips against hers, quick, light.

"Never," I whispered, and kissed her again.

It was midnight by the time I got home. I was about to go through the front way when I heard the scrape of a skateboard. There could only be one person out on the half-pipe this late. I made my way to the yard and wheeled closer to get a look.

Matt.

He had the lights on and was rolling back and forth, pumping hard, kick-turning, and grinding on the coping when he reached the top of each slope. He looked good—he looked damn good actually—but I watched as he wiped out attempting to do a front side one-eighty. He hit the slope hard and rolled down, the board right behind. Ouch.

I slow-clapped to let him know I was there. He jerked his head around, then grinned. He stood up, grabbed the board, and walked over to me.

"How long have you been there?" He sat on the edge of the half-pipe. He had a bottle of Gatorade there, took a swig, and offered me some. I shook my head.

"Long enough to see you wipe out. You were bending your knees too much."

"You could tell that from there?"

"Yeah, you have to make sure your weight is even, then . . ." I had the urge to get up and show him. "It's easier to demonstrate than talk out. You should have Nick show you sometime, he was always good at them."

"He'd be stoked you said that."

I laughed.

"So, you and Cass, huh?" he said.

"Me and Cass," I said.

"She seems cool."

"Yeah, it's nice."

"Just so you know, I wasn't completely down with giving the board to you tonight. I don't know, Nick's a good guy; he thought it would somehow make it more meaningful if we did it that way. I talked him out of presenting it to you in front of everyone."

"Thanks," I said.

He took another gulp of Gatorade.

"And Matt, thanks. It just, you know, took me by surprise. You're right, I probably would have said no, and then what? The fish deserves to be in the water, not hanging in a shed."

"I never rode it, you know."

I looked at him.

"Okay, maybe once before bringing it in."

"Maybe you can save up, buy your own."

"It's not some shit job, either. Steve did it."

"Surf-shop Steve?"

"Yep, glassed it himself too. Bryan, you got lots of people pulling for you. We want to help. I don't know what you're waiting for. I know you want to do it."

"It's not . . . it won't feel the same."

"You won't know until you try."

"Fine. Before the end of the summer."

"Really?"

"Yeah, really."

TWENTY-ONE
CASSIDY

TIME ACCELERATED WHEN I WAS WITH BRYAN. One beautiful Crest Haven day stretched into another, and in the blink of an eye, it was Thursday. Morning swims and crazy car rides. Watching the sunset and hanging at Sip N' Freeze. Talking about everything and nothing and wanting it to never end. Gavin was a memory. He'd taken the hint and stopped texting. Ems had been right—I was over him and finally experiencing the summer I should have been having all along.

I knew, like, really knew, I needed to keep things light with Bryan, but when I was with him, I didn't want to be anywhere else. Neither of us spoke about what would happen when camp was over and it was time for me to go back to my real life. We never talked about staying in touch, but it also felt understood that we would.

At least I hoped so.

Everyone at Camp Manatee was in a frenzy, campers and counselors alike getting ready for Friday's showcase night. Bryan's group had extra practice for their performance, so they were skipping out on cooking for the day, which was fine because Tori and I were figuring out our own game plan.

I'd been happy there was no residual weirdness after Ems had hooked up with Wade. Tori said she'd been angrier with Nick for being so careless than with yet another one of Wade's hookups, but I wasn't so sure. It must have sucked seeing Wade kiss Ems, but I decided to drop the subject. Tori and I had been getting along great.

"All we have to do is bake something to serve the parents, smile, and answer questions they might have about the program, but hopefully they'll be too busy stuffing their faces to talk." Tori paced in front of the classroom, wringing her hands.

"I'm pretty certain you can run a small country. Why are you so worried about this? This class is the best," I said.

"It's the first year, so the thought of feedback makes me want to vomit. I mean, I want it, so we can improve, but what if—"

"Everyone loves it, chill," I said.

"I hope Mr. Beckett wants the class for next year. I have so many more ideas. Think you'll be back?" she said.

I smiled. "So even if Liv is here, you'd want Benny Barbie to be your co-counselor?"

"I guess it wouldn't suck to hang out with you again," she said, joking. "That overnight s'mores oatmeal recipe you came up with for the tweens was perfect. Maybe next year we could each take certain weeks to plan. Alternate coming up with stuff."

"I'd like that," I said.

"So what do you think we should make for tomorrow night? Cupcakes? Everyone loves cupcakes. Or maybe a few different kinds of cookies."

"Or both," I teased.

"Cass, come on, think."

"Okay, cookies—cupcakes have the icing factor, and the paper-liner thing, and cookies you can just grab and go. Less garbage, smaller carbon footprint."

"See, we make a great team. I think we have the stuff for triple-chocolate-chip cookies. We can make them with the kids in the afternoon. I want to try a peanut butter oatmeal no-bake recipe at home. Think you can make something non-chocolate—like sugar cookies; say three dozen for tomorrow?"

"Sure."

After eating dinner and baking three dozen sugar cookies with Hunter, I went for a ride with Bryan to Crescent Beach.

One blanket, a few warm sugar cookies, and us equaled the end of another perfect day. We sat side by side, looking up at the changing sky. I fed him a piece of sugar cookie. He nipped the tip of my finger. I grinned.

"So, do you think I should do it?" he asked.

I rolled to my side and propped myself up on my elbow to look at him.

"Do what?"

He turned his face to me, shielding his eyes from the blinding rays of the setting sun.

"Surf."

"Do you want to do it?"

"I don't know, sometimes I think yes, sometimes no—it's scary to think of all that could go wrong."

"You can't let that stop you," I said.

"Will you be there?"

"Do you really have to ask?" I said, popping another piece of sugar cookie into his mouth. He chewed and stared up at the sky.

"Have we made enough good memories in this place to make you forget about why you came to Crest Haven?"

I smiled. "Yes."

"I wish . . . ," he said, then stopped. I thought he'd eventually elaborate, but he remained silent.

"What?"

"I wish I could stand, hold you against me. I wish the

summer wouldn't end. I wish you'd known me . . . before I fell."

"Bryan, I know you now, and you're pretty awesome," I said.

"So I'm not just a part of proving to someone what a good time you're having without him?"

"Remember that first day, when I saw you?"

"In this parking lot? How can I forget."

"You wanted to help me. You're kind, Bryan. I see you with the kids, with your friends. You've got a wild streak, and these guns," I said, running a finger along the length of his bicep. "I mean, come on. Why would you even ask that question? I think you're . . . incredible. Why are you with me?"

He looked at me. "You've got a cute butt."

"Omigod," I said, nudging him.

He tucked a piece of my hair away from my face. "Because you're sweet when nobody's watching. You make me laugh. You make me think things aren't so shitty."

We kissed. I put my head on his shoulder and looked up at the blanket of sky.

"I wish the summer wouldn't end either," I said.

It was futile to wish, I knew it, but I felt it just the same.

On Friday night, the plan was for Bryan to pick me up so we could go to showcase night together. He'd never seen me in anything dressier than shorts and a lacy tank, and I felt like glamming it up. (At least the beach-bum version of glam.) I'd thrown on the sundress my mom and Nan had sent me in their first care package and put on a sea-glass necklace I'd purchased at one of the promenade stores. I was putting the finishing touches on some beachy waves in my hair when my father appeared in the doorway, an odd look on his face.

"Is he here already?" I asked, releasing a lock of hair from the curling iron. Bryan was supposed to text me when he was out front. I glanced at my phone—nothing from him, but a few from Emma that I'd missed in my fury to get ready.

"There's someone here, but it's not Bryan," my father said.

"What?"

Even as Dad said Gavin's name, I scrolled through Emma's texts—

SOS

G is on his way.

Prick alert!

Hello? Cass?

I couldn't wrap my mind around the fact that Gavin was downstairs. Waiting. For me. I shouldn't have been surprised—it was classic Gavin to show up unannounced. It was something I loved about him at first—his spontaneity—but Mom and Nan had made me look at it in a different way. That spontaneity was his way of controlling the situation; of being able to see me precisely when he wanted. Maybe I knew that by ignoring him, he would pull something like this. The timing, however, sucked.

"Do you want me to get rid of him?" Dad asked.

"No," I said, following Dad downstairs. "I can deal with it."

"He's waiting on the front porch."

I tried to call Bryan, but it went to voice mail. I hung up without leaving a message. If he was on his way, well, there was nothing I could do now. I had to get Gavin to leave. My feet felt spongy and uncertain as I walked toward the front porch. What the hell was Gavin pulling? This dilemma was not lost on my father, who followed me to the front door like a papa bear.

"What are you going to do?"

I shrugged. "See what he wants? Send him away? What time are you guys heading over to camp?"

"Soonish," he said.

"Okay, he'll be gone . . . soonish."

Being angry with Gavin from afar had been easy. I only had to conjure up thoughts of how it felt when I saw those pictures of him and that girl on StalkMe. Being angry with Gavin while he was on the front porch was more of a challenge, and as I got closer to the door, my heart kick-started into overdrive, thumping at the sight of him against my will.

He'd gotten his hair trimmed since I'd last seen him. It was still over his ears and longer in the front, but neater. He leaned against a column by the stairs, facing the beach. His skin was a shade or two darker from being out in the sun. Hands in pockets, forest-green raglan tee on, he looked so natural and calm, like this was nothing out of the ordinary. He could have been waiting outside of biology for me. He turned and shifted so he was standing straight as I opened the screen door. Damn him for looking so good. I wanted to feel *nothing*, but my body had other ideas.

"What are you doing here?" I asked, crossing my arms.

His eyes wandered over me, a slow smile turning up at the corners of his mouth. Those freaking dimples. "It's so good to see you, Cass."

I would not be sucked in. I leaned against the railing, trying to be as casual as possible.

"Why are you here, Gavin?"

He chuckled. "Isn't that obvious? Aren't you even a little happy about it?"

I looked away from him. He came over to me, deliberately putting his face in front of mine, and moving into my line of vision any time I looked away so I was forced to see him. It was something he used to do when we argued, and it would always make me laugh. I relented and looked at him.

"We're over, remember?" I said.

"We don't have to be."

"How can you say that with a straight face?"

"I've been so miserable all summer without you. Don't be

mad at me. Please. I came all this way to surprise you. It's Friday night."

"You can't just show up like this. I had plans."

"Plans can be broken," he said.

"No, these can't. It's a work thing."

"So you'd rather do a work thing than come hang out with me in Ship Bottom? Okay, I get it."

Ship Bottom? Was he really here to take me to Ship Bottom? *Now?* It was about an hour and a half ride from Crest Haven. Before our relationship had all turned to shit, the plan had been for us to spend a week at his family's condo, right after my annual week with Dad. Ship Bottom was farther north, so it would have been on the way home. There was no reason for me to go there now.

"Are you seriously suggesting I leave with you?"

"I'm headed there tonight, thought I'd see if you wanted to come with me. The whole condo to ourselves, like we used to talk about, Cass," he said.

I heard a rumble. The Charger. Bryan was in front of Ocean Whispers. He cut the engine. Any moment my worlds would be colliding, and I felt sick. Sick, sick, sick to my stomach. Maybe I should have had my father get rid of Gavin.

"Gavin, I'm not sure what kind of game you're playing, but I'm—I have to go, it's a work thing, someone is picking me up."

"Do you always wear body glitter to work? Is that the kind

that tastes like cotton candy?" he asked, nuzzling my neck.

Something caught Gavin's attention beyond my shoulder. In a moment, his eyes sharpened with understanding and he looked back at me, smirk on his face. "Wow, Cass, really?"

I spun around. Bryan struggled with the front gate but finally pushed it open and wheeled up the walk. I brushed past Gavin and galloped down the stairs to greet Bryan halfway. His whole face asked *What now?* but he smiled when he saw me. I could feel Gavin close behind, his footfalls on the stairs. This could not be happening.

But it was.

"I didn't know, Bryan, I'm sorry," I said.

Bryan looked beyond me. I didn't have to spell it out for him. His face fell.

"I thought you said . . . you're not together."

"I did, we're not, he just showed up to surprise me," I said. I felt Gavin put his hand around my waist. Bryan's eyes landed squarely on that. I wanted to shut my eyes and pretend it was all a dream I could wake up from. I shooed Gavin's hand away and stepped back from him.

"Bryan, this is Gavin; Gavin, Bryan. We work at camp together. He's, um, my ride."

They nodded at each other.

"Bryan!" Hunter bounded down the stairs, and Bryan looked relieved.

"H-bomb, ready for tonight?" Bryan asked.

"Yes. Who are you?"

Hunter was so freaking subtle. Gavin smiled.

"I'm Gavin, a friend of Cassidy's from home."

"Are you coming to the show?"

Gavin looked from me to Bryan, then back to Hunter. "Show? Sounds fun. All right if I tag along?"

"Not really," I said.

Dad and Leslie stepped onto the porch. Leslie balanced the Tupperware containers of sugar cookies. I ran up to help, relieved I could step away momentarily and think about my next move. I didn't want to make a scene; Gavin clearly had to go, but other than screaming for him to leave, I wasn't sure how that was going to happen.

I took the containers from her. "Thanks."

"Is everything okay?" Dad asked.

"Yes, fine," I said.

When I turned around, Bryan had already made his way back to his car. I raced down the stairs as quickly as I could, balancing the two containers.

"Here, hold these," I said, foisting them onto Gavin as I ran to catch up with Bryan.

"Hey, wait," I called.

I wasn't sure whether he hadn't heard me or was ignoring me, because he didn't pause for a moment. He'd already transferred and was popping one of the wheels off his chair by the time I got there.

"Bryan."

He popped off the other wheel, but it fell out of his grasp.

I reached down to grab it and handed it to him. He muttered *thanks* but barely looked at me. He folded the chair and hoisted it over his shoulder into the back. I thought for a moment he was going to close the door without saying anything, but he gripped the wheel and waited for me to speak.

"Bryan, I didn't know he was going to be here; I'm sorry. I know what he said, but he's not coming to the show."

"So get in, then," he said.

I looked over toward Ocean Whispers. Gavin was with Dad and Leslie now. What could he possibly be talking to them about? Could I just get into the car with Bryan and pretend like it wasn't happening? Bryan snorted at my hesitation.

"I'm not sure what's going on, Cassidy, but it seems like you have unfinished stuff with that guy, so I guess do what you need to do, and I'll see you there."

"Bryan—"

"I'm going to be late, I'll just . . . see you later. Bet you can get a ride from someone else."

Ouch.

I didn't know what to say to that. He closed the door and gunned the engine but didn't move until I stepped onto the sidewalk. Introducing him as "my ride" was shitty, but I'd been caught off guard. I'd felt protective of him and of whatever was happening between us. That was ours, separate from

Gavin. How was I supposed to introduce him?

"Everything okay?"

I spun around. Gavin was there, smirk on his face, holding the cookies. Leslie and Hunter were walking in the other direction toward the SUV. My father came toward us, mouth pressed in a thin line. He looked between Gavin and me.

"Are you coming with us, Cassidy?" he asked.

I didn't owe Gavin anything, but he was there and I got the feeling he was not going anywhere, even if I did take a ride with my family. I didn't want him to step foot in the rec center, but until I talked to him, I knew he'd probably stick around.

"I'll be over there in a bit."

My father nodded. "Okay, then. See you there. Don't miss Hunter's song."

"I won't," I said, turning to Gavin.

"Thank you," he said.

"For what?"

"Letting me stay," he said.

"You can't stay, Gavin."

"You're really going to send me home after I drove three hours to see you?"

"You said you were going to Ship Bottom—don't act like this was some special trip just to see me."

"Cass . . . I'd just like to talk to you. Please, there are things I need to say."

"This better be good."

The rec center parking lot was full. Gavin found a spot on a side street one block away. I looked at my phone. The show started at seven fifteen. It was already six thirty. If I wanted to talk to Bryan I needed to get inside and find him. Gavin, for all his *there are things I need to say,* had not said one word since Ocean Whispers.

He cut the engine. "What's with the guy in the wheelchair? I had the feeling he thought he was more than your ride."

"He's a friend. One of the counselors." *I've been kissing him silly. Silly, silly, silly.* Nan would be proud.

He nodded. "I think someone has a little crush."

"Don't talk like that. You don't know him."

He chuckled, but it wasn't happy. More like an aggravated *hmmph.*

"Who said I was talking about him?" He turned his head and eyed me. "Have you, like, lost your mind?"

"You need to leave, Gavin," I said, getting out of the Jeep.

I slammed the door and didn't look back, racing toward the side entrance of the rec center, where more families were pouring in. As politely as I could, I weaved through the crowd to get to the test kitchen. Tori was there pacing around, her expression stern at first, but when she saw me, her brow creased in worry.

"What's the matter?"

"I need to find Bryan."

"Did you bring the cookies?"

Fuck. I'd left them with Gavin. There was no time.

"I have them, yes, but . . . I need to find Bryan, I'll be back, okay?" I whirled out of the classroom.

"Cass—"

I ran down the hallway to the multipurpose room and poked my head in. Half of the chairs were filled already, with more people piling in. I scanned the room. The back rows were reserved for the campers, so the parents could have seats up front to watch the show. I spotted Bryan with Wade and his group and walked over. Wade saw me first and waved. Bryan's back was to me, but when he saw Wade look beyond him, he turned his head, saw me, then turned back around.

"Bryan," I said, his name getting swallowed up in the cacophony of voices in the multipurpose room. I walked around to face him. "Please, can we talk?" I motioned out to the hallway, where I hoped we could find a quiet corner.

"Do you mind?" Bryan asked Wade.

"No worries, I have the minions under control," he said. The group of boys cheered. Bryan and I wandered out into the hallway and ducked around the corner for more privacy. Neither of us said anything at first. I wasn't entirely sure where to start.

"I'm sorry, Bryan."

"So that was Gavin."

I nodded. "He just showed up, Bryan. No warning. Ems tried—"

"Cass, whatever. I'm your *ride*? Do you know how humiliated I felt back there? The one thing you've never done is make me feel lesser than. Even on that first day, you joked with me, looked at me, leaned in to speak to me. You know how rare that is? It's like you didn't treat me differently because of my chair. You saw me. Until tonight."

"It was a shitty way to introduce you. I'm sorry. I didn't know what to say."

"How about friend? You could have called me *friend*, that would have worked."

He was right. On all counts. I didn't want to see him through Gavin's eyes. Didn't want him to be under his scrutiny. He could have handled it, though. He handled it every day. Why hadn't I just said *friend*?

"So are you getting back with him?"

"No."

"Then why is he even here?" he asked.

"I don't know, Bryan, he wants to talk. I left him out in the car."

"Isn't this what you wanted though? Why else would you post those pictures? It's all a game to you."

"Bryan, no. It's not."

"Just fucking go, Cassidy. Talk to him. Make up with him. We both know where this is headed. You're leaving soon. So, now or later, it doesn't matter, does it?"

His words pierced me. "How can you say that? You do matter to me—"

"Don't you get it? I can't feel like this, I can't fill my head with all this bullshit, when none of it is real. It's only summer. A season. And you're gone."

Someone cleared their throat. We turned.

Wade.

He came over to us slowly, as if he were approaching a bomb about to detonate. "Hey, Bry, I don't mean to interrupt, but we need to get the little dudes lined up."

"I'll be right there," he said. Wade went back.

"Can we hang out later, Bryan, please?"

"I don't know."

"I'm sorry," I said again, but it felt small and silly, too-little words for too big a feeling.

He nodded, and pushed away toward the multipurpose room.

I went back to the test kitchen to face the fallout for spacing out about the sugar cookies. I cursed myself for not grabbing them before I huffed off. It was easier to be angry, to think about those things than Bryan's words. Did he really mean what he'd said? That we were only going to last a season? I'd deluded myself that we had some sort of future, that I was more than a summer girl, but what he'd said was true. When camp was over, I'd be gone.

Tori was setting up a platter of cookies on the front island. She pushed a serving plate with a doily my way.

"Here, it'll go quicker if we both do it," she said. "What in the world happened to you tonight?"

"Nothing, just—"

A knock caused us both to look toward the doorway. My breath caught in my throat.

"Can I help you?" Tori asked, smiling.

"You forgot these," Gavin said, holding up the containers of cookies.

Tori looked at me, eyes wide. I introduced her to Gavin. She grabbed a dish towel and wiped her hands.

"Do you think you guys can finish setting these up? I have to head down to the multipurpose room. Don't want to miss the show. You'll be there, right?"

Tori's voice was all business. She smiled at Gavin, then widened her eyes at me once she was behind him. "Are you okay?" she mouthed.

I nodded. She left us alone.

I opened up one of the Tupperware containers and started arranging the sugar cookies on a plate. Gavin helped, the tension between us so thick it was like a third person was in the room. When we were finished, I snapped the lid back on the container.

"So this is Camp Manatee," he said.

"Why are you really here? Just to stir up shit again? Because I'm over you, you know."

"Cass, please."

The anger I'd pushed aside, the hurt at being rejected, the reason I came to Crest Haven in the first place, fueled me.

"You broke my heart, Gavin. You made me feel like there was something wrong with me. That I wasn't enough. You kissed someone else. Maybe more. And now I'm supposed to drop everything because you're here for me? I—"

"I'm not going to Penn, Cassidy."

It wasn't what I expected to hear. That took all the fight out of me. He kept his eyes on mine. I stepped back. *Not going to Penn?*

"Wait, what?"

"My father and his partners were brought up on charges of tax fraud. They were accused of laundering money for a few of their clients. I knew things weren't good, but I didn't know how bad they were. It still feels unreal saying it, like I'm on an episode of *Law & Order* or something," he said, laughing a bit. I didn't know what to say. Was it real? I didn't think he'd lie about that, and there was something in his eyes, something I'd never really seen . . . defeat, resignation.

"He's been liquidating assets—his car, I lost my phone, and I'm out of town per my mother's orders, so they don't repo the Jeep. She's fighting to keep the Ship Bottom place. Did I mention they're splitting up too? It's a fucking mess, Cass. My old man can be an asshole, but I never knew he was this level of asshole. We were all kind of blindsided. We still have the two weeks she'd blocked out for us at Ship Bottom, and she told me to go."

"And you're not going to Penn?"

"I've deferred, but I doubt I'll even go to Penn in the spring. I never filled out a FAFSA or whatever the fuck it was I was supposed to fill out, and I could probably kiss loans good-bye with my father's record now. It's embarrassing as hell and I just want to disappear, with you, like we always talked about. Forget it for a few days. I've missed you. So much."

His hands were on my waist but I kept my arms folded. A barrier. I could feel myself softening at his explanation. *He wasn't going to Penn.*

Bryan's voice echoed in my head. *Just fucking go. It's only a season.*

Music trailed down the hall. The showcase had started. Hunter's group was going on fourth. I needed to be there.

"I can't go to Ship Bottom," I said.

"Can't or won't?" he whispered.

I let my hands snake around his waist. He was so warm. He sighed, drawing me closer. My cheek pressed against his chest. His heart hammered like crazy. He was nervous. He did care, didn't he? There was always one thing I'd carried away from that first night at Meadowbrooke—the silly thing he'd said about horror movies, about us being the couple who made it out alive. I knew he was goofing at the time, but I liked to think there was weight behind those words. Maybe, even after all of this, we would.

"I want to go," I whispered. *But I can't.*

"Cassidy, I need you."

Before I knew it, Gavin's lips were on mine. I opened to him as if the summer had been a spell his kiss woke me up from.

Just fucking go.

Gavin wasn't going to Penn.

"So you'll come with me?" he asked.

"Yes."

TWENTY-TWO
BRYAN

THE MULTIPURPOSE ROOM WAS AN OVEN. PARENTS used their programs to fan themselves, the kids wanted water every two minutes, and all I wanted to do was go home and throw myself into *Realm Wars*. Screw it all.

Just. Fucking. Go.

That's what I'd told her. And her eyes, damn. It had been a precision hit just as I'd intended, but seeing her deflate felt almost as shitty as seeing that able-bodied asshat put his hand on her waist. And I'd meant it. It had felt great to say it. At least in that moment. I couldn't hold on to the mirage that was Cassidy Emmerich any longer. It didn't matter what we whispered to each other in the night. How I felt when her hair brushed across my face, or my hands ran along her body, or my lips touched her warm skin.

She was a summer girl and the end was inevitable.

Sure, we'd stay in touch, maybe even a lot in the beginning, but somewhere around Halloween, we'd both suddenly get too busy, we'd get caught up in school, in life—or maybe only one of us would, leaving the other hanging. And I knew which person I'd be in that scenario.

"Bry, you okay?" Wade whispered.

"Yeah, fine," I said, putting a finger to my lips and motioning to the stage, where a group of tween girls was doing a routine to "California Girls," only they'd changed it to "Crest Haven Girls" and were in a very uncoordinated but comical kick line at the moment. Wade almost looked annoyed at being shut down, but what did he want me to say? I wasn't fucking okay, but I had to man up, or at least keep it together until the night was over.

The door to the multipurpose room opened. Tori crept in, alone, holding the door until it finally shut behind her. She moved over to the wall, arms folded. Our eyes met.

"Cass?" I mouthed.

She shook her head and shrugged. What if she'd listened to me? Was she somewhere talking to that guy? Were they making up? If Tori knew, she wasn't letting on. I was about to go over to her when I felt a hand on my arm. Colby.

He cupped his hand around my ear and whispered, "I don't want to sing."

"Dude, you have to," I said, not in my most sympathetic

inside voice. Even Wade noticed. Colby blinked hard, sucked in his bottom lip. *Nice, Bry.*

I motioned for him to follow me, pulled him over to the side. As the guy who'd become the one to talk him off the ledge, I had to be cool in his hour of need. These were big stakes to the little man.

"Sorry, that was harsh. Why don't you want to sing?"

"There's too many people, my heart feels like it might explode."

"First off—your heart won't explode. That would be really gross. Second—your mom and dad are here, right?"

"Mom and Grams are here. My dad doesn't live with us anymore."

Oh, fuck. How did I not know that? He said it so matter-of-factly. He wasn't embarrassed, or even sad; maybe it bothered him sometimes, but in that moment it didn't. He stared at me, wide-eyed, waiting for words of wisdom, or for me to tell him it was okay to bail. He trusted me.

"I bet Grams and Mom really want to see you sing. They're sitting in this boiling room, all for the two minutes you'll be up there."

"What if I forget the words?"

"Just move your mouth. No one is going to know."

"Really?"

"Yep, chill, you got this," I said, making a shaka sign. He grinned and did the same thing. The audience applauded for the Crest Haven Girls. Wade stood up, herding the kids together. Colby gave me one more freaked-out look but I nodded at him. He took his place behind H-bomb, and Wade led them up to the side of the stage to be announced.

"You're good at this, you know," Tori said, crouching next to me.

"Ah, it's easy."

"No, actually, it's not, Bry. I don't know how you spend so much time with the little ones. I'd lose it twenty times a day. You're a rock star to these kids, anyone can see that," she said.

I'd never thought being a counselor was rough. Maybe that's how the best jobs were supposed to feel. We watched as Wade ushered the boys up the stairs to the stage and into position, along with the other groups of six-year-olds. My neck tensed—I was nervous for these little guys. Hunter put his hand over his eyes, looking over the audience. Was he searching for Cassidy? He would be bummed out if she missed it.

"Is Cassidy coming to this?" I asked.

"I left her in the classroom, she was putting out the cookies, but . . ."

"But what?"

Tori's gaze dropped to the floor.

"I know about the dude who was with her, if that's what you're worried about telling me."

"She seemed sort of upset after talking to you. What the heck happened?"

"I told her to leave," I said. Tori's eyes widened. "Actually, I said *just fucking go*. I meant it at the time, I didn't think—"

"Shit, you said that to her?"

"I was pissed off."

I reached into my backpack for my phone, hoping I'd find a message from her, but there was nothing. My heart sank. I pressed the video button on the phone and set it up to record.

"If she was here, she wouldn't miss this," I said, positioning the camera for a good view.

The music started. Wade hurried off the stage and leaned against the wall by the front. None of the kids could stand still. A few fidgeted. Some tried to do the hand motions that were supposed to go along with the song. Colby looked out at the audience and waved, I guessed at his mom and grams. The kids sang softly at first, with bursts of loudness. They were slightly off-key and had to strain at the high notes, which made a murmur of laughter roll across the audience, but our little dudes were killing it. Colby, who had been petrified moments earlier, was now up there, singing, laughing. Brave. Somewhere between the swims, and kickball, and whining, these kids had managed to get under my skin. Maybe I'd be a blip to them when all was said and done, but this was a summer I'd never forget. They were a part of that.

The audience went crazy after they were finished. I held up my hand to slap a row of high fives as they returned to their seats. Wade stopped and saw Tori.

"You clean up nice, Tori," he said.

Tori played with a piece of her hair, twirling it around her finger. "Really, so what? Every other day I look like crap? Thanks, Wade," she said, smiling and then walking off.

He groaned and slumped down in the seat at the end of the aisle next to me. "Did I not just tell her she looked pretty?"

"Um, no—you said she cleaned up nice. There's a difference."

"I don't have any problem hitting on girls; why am I having a tough time with her?"

"So you're hitting on her now?"

"No, you know what I mean. I like her, Bryan. Are you sure she really likes me, you know, that way?"

I laughed; it was nice to see Wade off his game. "Don't try so hard, but, you know, try."

After the last number Monty appeared and attempted to get the parents involved with a group dance. Some were game. Others looked uncomfortable. Lots were suddenly interested in their phones. One incredible #wheelchairperk—begging off awkward dance fun if I wanted. I wheeled over toward the side of the multipurpose room. Even though there were still two weeks to go in camp, showcase night was traditionally the night parents came to meet and tip the counselors. It wasn't a given, or expected, but after the dance we corralled the kids and waited for their parents to pick them up so they could go check out the special electives together.

There were lots of "great job," "he loved it," "already talking about next summer." It felt good, especially knowing that some parents had had reservations about me in the beginning of camp. Colby ran out to meet his mom and pulled her over to us.

"Bryan?" she asked, looking between Wade and me. I waved.

"That's me," I said. An older woman came up behind them.

"This is Bryan, Gram," Colby said, grinning.

"So *this* is Bryan. It's always, Bryan said this, or Bryan did that," she said.

His mom smiled. "You should know you've made quite the impression on him this summer. It's been nice seeing him come out of his shell. He keeps mentioning something about you owing him a slush."

I laughed. "Oh yeah, I do—it was sort of a swimming bet. I'll make good on it, buddy."

"We have you to thank for that too. He's always been a little skittish in the water and now he's doing great. Thank you," she said, handing each of us an envelope. "Take care; say good night, Cobes."

"Thank you," I said. "See you Monday."

Colby made a shaka sign. Wade laughed. "Little dude."

Mr. and Mrs. Emmerich came up to us next, thanking us for a job well done.

"He wants me to call him by his nickname, H-bomb; have

to say it suits him," Mrs. Emmerich said, tousling Hunter's hair.

"Have you seen Cassidy?" Mr. E. asked.

"She's probably with Tori in the test kitchen," Wade said. Mr. Emmerich looked at me. For all I knew Cass was with Tori, helping out like she should have been. Hopefully she was there. What if she had made up with that guy after all?

"Great, we'll head over there now. Keep up the good work, guys, only a few more weeks until school starts," Mr. E. said.

"Thanks for the buzzkill, Mr. E.," Wade said. The multipurpose room emptied out. Wade and I hung back, fooling around with the other counselors while we stacked the folding chairs. Nick took his Monty head off. His hair was matted down with sweat. One of the group leaders poured a bottle of water over his head, and Nick tried to chase after him, tripping and ending up on the floor, a hysterical headless manatee.

"C'mon, let's go see if Tori's got any cookies left," Wade said.

There were still a few straggler parents and kids in the test kitchen, so Wade and I sat at a table near the back. He went up, sheepishly grabbed a few cookies off a platter, then sat across from me and opened his envelopes. He handed me a sugar cookie. *Cass.* I put it to the side.

"Don't you want to count your tips?" he asked.

No—I wanted to see Cass. The fact that she wasn't there made me edgy.

"There's still parents here," I said.

"C'mon, they're not even paying attention to us," he said.

The envelope from Colby felt thick. I carefully opened it, trying not to rip it. Along with a twenty-dollar bill, there was a clumsily folded piece of paper, which I undid slowly. I smiled. Colby had drawn a picture of the two of us: me in my chair, well, me as a stick figure in a wheelchair, and him as a stick figure next to me. We were holding hands and raising what looked like slushes high in the air. I showed Wade.

"Wow, he drew you like a terminator—look at the picture he made for me. My shades are the biggest part."

"Kid knows what he's doing," I said.

Tori pulled a chair over and sat down, put her face in her hands, and sighed.

"Tough night?" I asked.

"Nope, it went pretty well. I wish Cassidy hadn't bailed on me. Does that mean I can keep her tips?" she said.

"What do you mean, Cass bailed?" Wade asked.

Tori and I looked at each other.

"You explain it to him," I said.

"Cass's ex showed up. I think they went somewhere to talk. I texted her before but I haven't heard from her. I can't believe she'd ditch you like that, even if you did tell her to *just fucking go*."

"You said that to her?" Wade said.

There was a knock on the doorframe. We turned. Mr. E.

came into the classroom. He had his hands in his pockets, a grim look on his face.

"Hey, Mr. E.," Tori said.

"I didn't want to say anything in front of Hunter, Tori, but can you tell me when the last time you saw Cass was?"

We didn't need to ask any more questions.

We could all see the truth in his eyes.

Cass was gone.

TWENTY-THREE
CASSIDY

THERE WAS MAGIC IN THE WORD *YES*. I FELT IT AS I took Gavin's hand. A surge that made everything sharper. Like the first time we ran through the woods. It was so thrilling I wouldn't have been surprised to see a glittery trail on the air behind us, our own private Milky Way, as we raced out of the rec center. Our smiles contained it. I felt it when I slid into the passenger seat of the Jeep and Gavin said, *Let's go.*

Nothing mattered. The last six weeks a speed bump as we tore out of sleepy little Crest Haven, with its horse-drawn carriages and quaint houses and fudge shops, windows down, wind in my hair. The feeling consumed me, made me giddy.

And it lasted all of about twenty minutes.

It was at that point I started to think about Hunter. What would he think of me leaving? They probably wouldn't tell him right away. Would he notice me missing after the show?

Would he overhear something, perceptive little kid that he was? He just took everything in, even when you didn't think he was listening. I'd never taken him to the arcade to play Whack-a-Shark.

I turned to Gavin. He chewed his upper lip in thought, nodding along with the song that was on the radio. Driving for him was a way to get from point A to point B. So different from Bryan and the way his face lit up when we drove fast, the way his eyes had darted to me, then back to the road. His howl. I felt like I'd caught a glimpse of a secret part of him. Gavin didn't have the same joy on his face as we drove into the night. We hadn't spoken since we left.

We left.

I'd missed Hunter's song.

Tori was probably pissed I wasn't there to help her.

Leslie.

Dad.

Bryan.

His words stung. *Just fucking go.* He'd been hurt, and rightfully so. Running away from him wouldn't change that. It wouldn't change anything. Why was I doing this? How was I going to make it right?

Gavin had done it again. One look in those eyes and I'd caved. It was my own fault, my desire to dive headfirst into adventure, as if he was the person who could lead me there. What had felt good in the moment—that after everything he still chose *me*—had worn off. It didn't matter that he wasn't going to Penn. I didn't want this anymore. I didn't want him.

I was about to speak up, when Gavin placed his hand on my knee. "Have to make a pit stop," he said, giving it a squeeze.

I nodded. "Sounds good."

Twenty minutes later we pulled up to a rest stop for gas. Gavin asked the attendant for twenty dollars' worth. I had to make my move.

"Hey, um, I'm going to head inside." I reached for the door handle.

"Sure," he said, leaning over for a quick kiss, "everything okay?"

"Yeah, fine, I just have to go to the bathroom."

I slipped out of the car and made my way toward the rest stop.

A man carrying a cardboard tray of drinks held the door open for me. I walked into a wall of frigid air. The sudden drop in temperature made me shiver. The line for Starbucks stretched across to the small gift shop. I cut across and went into the ladies' room.

A stall opened up. I went in, locked the door, and leaned against the wall. I still didn't know how to tell Gavin; maybe I could just hide away and forget about it. We were only forty minutes away from Crest Haven. Could I even depend on him to drive me back?

No.

He'd start the sweet talk, the one that would make me think about all I'd be missing. He'd somehow justify going to

Ship Bottom, like he did for skipping out of school, or blowing off dinner with Mom and Nan, or any of the other times I chose him over something else in my life. Maybe he would surprise me, but I doubted it.

A good ten minutes passed before I finally left the bathroom. Gavin was across the hallway, leaning against the wall next to a crane arcade machine that contained small stuffed bears with "I ♥ NJ" shirts and fluorescent rubber balls. His eyes were on me, and he stood up straight as I walked toward him. My stomach clenched. He had a Frappuccino in his hand and held it out as I got closer. The whipped-cream peak sagged.

"Java Chip. Your favorite. It looked better ten minutes ago."

I took the drink from him. He slipped his arm around me, kissed the top of my head. We took a few steps toward the exit.

I stopped, turned back, shrugged off his arm.

"Cass, c'mon," he said.

I shook my head, looking at the drink instead of into his eyes. "Gavin, I can't go."

He put his arm around me again, gently ushering me away from the flow of people heading out.

"What's this about now?" he asked.

I forced myself to look at him, which was a mistake. Memories, the best ones, flooded me. I loved our story. That run through the woods that started it all. Gavin was my junior year, and it had been incredible—until it wasn't. It would never be the same. Why couldn't I let go? I picked his hand off my shoulder, stepped back.

"I'm sorry all this shitty stuff is going on with your father," I said, "but it doesn't change anything, does it?"

He ran a hand through his hair and looked past me, shaking his head.

"How many times am I supposed to say I'm sorry before you believe it."

"That's just it. I'm not sure I ever will."

His face scrunched in confusion and he leaned against the wall again, leg bent, one foot up.

"What's going to happen when we get to Ship Bottom?" I asked.

"Does it matter? You, me, the place to ourselves, anything can happen," he said. And I could see it, God, I could see it, feel it, it's what I'd wanted, but I could also see the fallout now, clearer than before. That any moment my father would realize I'd left with Gavin. How long would it take him to call my mother? Would Nan worry? Leslie and Hunter? How would I get home? The fact that none of that mattered to Gavin was more apparent than ever.

"I can't. I need to get home."

"C'mon, I don't feel like backtracking, Cass."

"Don't worry, I already called someone to pick me up," I lied.

He didn't know what to do with that information. He sort of huffed and walked away, but then came back.

"Who? Your ride from before?"

"He's not just a ride, Gavin. I shouldn't have introduced him like that. His name is Bryan, and yeah, he's a friend. He's more than that actually; you were right. I do have a crush, so does he. And he's an incredible kisser."

He laughed. "Really, and what's going to happen when the summer is over, and you're home? What are you going to do then?"

"I don't know, really, but I know it won't involve you. It doesn't matter that you're not going away."

His hands clenched into fists.

"Why would you do this to me? I drove three fucking hours for you, and it's still not enough," he said.

"No, you did this . . . to us. Good-bye, Gavin," I said, turning fast before he could say anything else. I tossed the drink in the nearest trashcan, and then called the one person I knew who'd pick me up, no questions asked.

I grabbed another drink, then sat down at the far end of the rest stop by the Burger King. People came and went, families, groups of kids. I took out my phone for something to do while I waited. There was a text from Tori.

Everything okay?

Where RU?

I smiled. She cared. I had a place to go back to. Friends. Family.

When I looked up, my ride entered through the doors at the far end. He didn't see me at first, and I was caught off guard by the expression on his face. I'd expected him to be angry, but he looked . . . scared. Worried. He moved quickly through the crowd, head turning from the gift shop to the bathroom. I wanted to call out, to end his search, but the words wouldn't come. His dark eyes found mine. My insides crumbled. Tears of relief flooded my eyes as we moved toward each other. He looked uncertain, but I could see he was relieved too. He opened his arms and I buried my face in his shirt.

"Are you okay?" he whispered.

"Yes, Dad. Please take me home."

Gavin is out of my life.

That's the first thing I thought when I opened my eyes in the morning. I wondered if he ended up going to Ship Bottom, and then realized I really didn't care. Thoughts of him didn't dig into me as much as they had. Maybe one day they would stop altogether. I grabbed my kimono and went downstairs. It was ten, the very end of breakfast service. Leslie had made cinnamon buns, and there were a few left on the glass cake stand on the counter. She burst through the kitchen door just as I was about to reach for one.

"Morning, Cass. Go ahead, I put those aside for you," she said. I grabbed a cinnamon bun and peeled off a flaky piece. Pregnancy had not slowed her down. She placed a tray of empty coffee cups next to the kitchen sink.

"Thank you," I said. "Where is everybody?"

"Your father took Hunter down to the beach to see the dolphins. We thought we'd let you sleep in. How are you doing this morning?"

"Great," I said, and it sounded like I meant it. "I'm sorry about last night, Leslie. Did Hunter realize I was gone?"

She shook her head. "No, Cass. He did notice you weren't there for his song, but six-year-olds are pretty forgiving."

"I think I owe him a trip to the arcade," I said.

"He'd love that," she answered.

We were interrupted by a knock on the back door. Tori waved before coming in. Her dark hair was pushed back with a pink bandanna and she carried a cardboard tray with two drinks in it. She smiled in greeting.

"Hope it's okay I just barged in," she said.

"Leslie, this is Tori," I said.

"I know Tori," Leslie said, smiling. "I meant to ask you about your mother last night. How is she doing? Business must be great this summer."

"She can't complain," Tori said. Leslie looked at me.

"Tori's mom owns Hope Depot, a sort of . . ."

"New-age gift shop. She does angel readings and stuff. I know, horrible corny name. I've been trying to get her to change it for a few years now."

"Why don't you two hang out on the side porch; it's a gorgeous morning. We're supposed to get rain later, so you might as well enjoy the sun while it's shining," Leslie said, heading back out to the dining room.

Tori followed me to the side porch. There was a couple sharing breakfast at one of the small tables. I smiled in greeting as Tori and I found two open rocking chairs in a quiet corner. We sat side by side. I curled my feet up beside me and took a sip of the mocha.

"So, you really missed a bitchin' time last night," Tori said. For some reason we both found this hysterical.

"I'm sorry I bailed like that, Tori, I just . . . went a little—"

She held up a hand. "Apology accepted. I handled it pretty good; the parents loved me," she said.

"How's Bryan?"

"Oh, you know, he thinks you're a total benny skank and never wants to talk to you again."

She laughed at my horrified expression.

"Cass, come on, you could puke in the guy's lap and you'd still rock his world."

"I screwed up, big-time, in so many ways."

"That's why I'm here," she said. "We're hitting the beach this afternoon. Bryan wants to surf."

"He does?" I asked. "When did he decide that?"

She shrugged. "He said something about being inspired by Colby, that if he could get up and sing and not lose it, he had nothing to lose either. Following his own pep talk advice. I'm just happy he's trying it. I stopped by to invite you."

"I'm not sure he'd want to see me."

"Cass, believe me, he wants to see you. So we'll be there around five-ish, sound cool?"

"I'll be there."

TWENTY-FOUR
BRYAN

I COULDN'T REMEMBER THE LAST DAY I'D SURFED. Sometimes it bothered me because it seemed like something that should have left more of an impression. Had I known it was my last time in the water on two feet, would I have paid more attention? Would I have spent as much time practicing my bottom turns? Or would I have ridden as many waves as I could? I didn't have one distinct snippet, like barreling or a particularly awesome cut back, that stood out.

Instead, the memories ran one after the other, which wasn't as awful as it sounded because it was like one long, uninterrupted dream. Kind of like the ocean. What I remembered was cutting school with Wade to catch September swells. The stoke when everything aligned and it was me and the wave and nothing else. I used to be fearless with it. I knew the danger, but it didn't matter. Even when I wiped out, rag-dolling, not knowing which way was up or down, I'd trusted the ocean. Trusted myself. Loved that hard-earned tired feeling that came from a day in the water.

Fear, though, was real this time. I hated it. Bit it back. It didn't help that my mother—who imagined everything from a jellyfish sting to me ripping my foot open on the ocean floor—made me wear my full suit with Reef booties. *Should we put him in a shark cage?* Matt joked. Mom shut him down with a glare. I begged my parents not to come with us—I didn't want fanfare. I just wanted to go in the water. Wanted it to be normal, natural. It was after five, regular beach hours over, the tide coming in. They came anyway, along with Owen, set up beach chairs and an umbrella a little bit away from where we'd put our gear. They were there but not with us. And I guess I was a little grateful to see them, cool to admit or not.

Nick and Wade were surfing too. Matt was going to help propel me from behind when the wave broke and Tori and Jena, who was there on Nick's invite, were on the shore to help if I needed it. Jena had her board with her but sat out for now, I think waiting, watching, in case I needed rescuing. Those feelings of vulnerability, of not wanting help, were still there, but I fought them too. My friends weren't gawking at me, they were here to experience it with me. We'd borrowed the all-terrain wheelchair from the rec center. Nick carried my board. I was piggybacking on Wade again.

"So I'll carry you beyond the breakers; think you can paddle out?" he asked.

"I can out-paddle you, bro," I said, holding on to him. He laughed.

"Can't wait to see you try."

Nick held the board steady as I grabbed the handles. Wade sort of hoisted me and helped position my legs so they were in the concave dip and wouldn't flop around. The waves were small but it was different than being in the pool. It was a rush, being there, the water surrounding me. The water was alive, active, ready to play. *Why had it taken me so long to do this?* I paddled out with them—my swim training had paid off—and waited, getting used to just being there. Nick grabbed a smallish wave first.

"How does it feel? You okay?" Wade asked.

"Yep," I said, watching a swell grow beyond him.

"Any time you're ready, Bry, or we can just hang out today, if you want."

Instinct took over.

"Come on Matty, push," I said, paddling a bit. I felt the lift of the wave. The urge to pop up was so strong, as if I'd just been in the water yesterday. I held on to the handles and used my shoulders to turn into the wave as best I could. It was rough, and small, and over before it started, and more like boogie boarding, but I'd done it. I got caught up in the white water, but Jena was there to help me turn around. Matt met me halfway, and helped me back out.

No, it wasn't the same.

But it was still freakin' awesome.

Wade caught the next wave. Nick, Matt, and I watched as he rode down the line.

I'd missed it. So much. Why could my friends see that and I couldn't? I thought about what Nick and Matt had done, the night at Sip N' Freeze. How I'd reacted.

"Hey, guys," I said.

"Yeah," Nick and Matt said at the same time.

"Thanks."

Matt grinned.

"No worries," Nick said, and gave me a shaka sign.

I tried a few more times, once actually wiping out, and Jena and Tori were right there.

"I can swim, you know," I said. Jena smiled, giving me a hand.

"Hey, someone else stopped by to see you," Tori said, helping me back on the board. She motioned behind her. Standing in the surf, hands covering her mouth, eyes wide and thrilled, was Cassidy. Whatever had happened, whatever jagged feelings I'd had from last night, were forgotten. She was there.

I may not have remembered the last day I surfed, but that day, I etched in my memory.

Later we sat on the beach, watching the others surf. I'd taken off my wet suit and was in my board shorts, wrapped in a towel. I sat in the beach wheelchair, while Cass was cross-legged next to me on a blanket. Now that I'd finished with the scary surfing part, my parents and Owen had left in search of a lobster dinner. The others were juicing every last second out of the sunlight, but looked ready to pack it in soon. Cass and I were alone. Neither of us had brought up the previous night so far. Maybe there was no real need to, but I didn't want to leave anything unsaid.

"I'm sorry about last night, Cass."

She looked up at me. "What? Why? You didn't do anything, Bryan."

"But what I said—"

"You had every right to say that. You were angry. I did treat you differently with Gavin around. I chickened out. I'm the one who's sorry. The whole thing caught me off guard; I didn't really know how to handle it."

"Yep, pretty awkward, but . . . you're here . . . so I guess . . ."

"I'm over him. No games. Nothing. I actually have a crush on this cute surfer guy with a hot black car."

I let that sink in, but tried to play it cool.

"For what it's worth . . . I told him you were more than a friend to me."

"Really?" The corner of my mouth had a mind of its own, totally blowing my "I'm going to be a cool aloof guy" cover.

"Yep."

Tori stood by the surf as Wade jogged out with his board. He stopped by her and shook out his hair, like a dog. Tori yelped and backed away. Cassidy laughed.

"So, when do you think those two are going to realize they are madly in love with each other?" she asked.

"Ya think?"

"Uh, yeah, totally," she said. "Not much rattles Tori except Wade."

They began walking toward us. My moment alone with Cass was fading. "So, this guy in the black car, have you told him yet how you feel?"

She shifted and stood up, leaning across the chair. Her eyes looked amber in the setting sun, like they had a light all their own. I placed my hand in hers and she wrapped her fingers around mine.

"I'd rather show him," she said, leaning over to kiss me. I put my hand on her shoulder, pulling her closer. She leaned into me, mouth soft and open. When she pulled away, there were tears in her eyes. Not exactly the reaction I'd expected.

"What's wrong?"

"How is this going to work, Bryan?" she whispered.

"I thought it was working pretty well. What do you mean?"

She sat back on her heels, swiping a tear and putting on a smile for Wade and Tori as they got closer. "This. Us. Summer is practically over, but this . . . you and me, it feels like we're just getting started."

"It's not like you live halfway across the world, right? What are you, three hours away?"

She nodded.

"I drive; there's phones, email; you can visit your dad, right? Or you can post pictures on StalkMe to show me what a good time you're having without me."

She laughed. "I wouldn't do that to you."

We kissed, but pulled away as Wade and Tori approached.

"You don't have to stop on our account," Wade said. Tori elbowed him.

The others came back from the water. Jena trotted up to the blanket and dropped her board. As she dried her hair with a towel, she grinned and pointed at me and Cass holding hands.

"Look at you two love otters."

We laughed. The others looked at her like she was crazy.

"Otters? What do you two do down in that pool?" Wade asked.

I squeezed Cass's hand.

"Don't let go," she said.

"Never."

THAT NIGHT, ALONE IN MY ROOM, I SAT IN THE dark by the window, entranced by the storm that Leslie had mentioned earlier in the day. Rain pounded on the roof. Brilliant flashes of lightning lit up the inky dark. Thunderclaps rumbled and rattled the house. The storm was violent and alive.

I grabbed my phone to review the last scavenger-hunt clue, the one we hadn't figured out yet.

Sparkle in the sun
Rough in the sand
Lucky is the person
Who finds one in their hand

Mr. Beckett was not exactly Shakespeare with the clues. *Rough in the sand?*

A massive boom cracked and set off a car alarm. A lightning flash lit up the room and I shrieked. A small figure holding a stuffed shark stood in my doorway.

Hunter. *He had to stop doing that.*

"Hey, buddy, sorry, are you okay?" He shook his head and padded over to me, burying his face in my shoulder. I hugged him.

"I hate thunder," he said.

"You? Hate thunder? And here I thought you weren't afraid of anything."

"I'm not afraid, I just don't like it when it's this loud. The house is shaking. Could I stay with you?"

"Yeah—how about we go down to your room; it's cooler there," I said.

A red spaceship night-light was all that illuminated Hunter's room. I swallowed a scream when I stepped on a Lego, but managed to navigate our way to his rumpled bed, ignoring the throbbing pain in the arch of my foot. He slid onto his star-scape sheets. I pulled the blanket up around him and handed him his shark.

"Can you lay down with me?"

"Okay, shove over," I said, picking up the cover.

We lay side by side, Hunter clutching his stuffed shark, Eddie. And me, hands above the blanket and clasped across my stomach. The storm raged on for a while, but finally began letting up, the booms becoming more distant. I let the clue play over in my head again.

"You think that baby is going to change everything?" Hunter asked. I'd thought he'd fallen asleep. I tried not to laugh at the way he said *that baby.*

"I guess. Babies kind of come in and change things, but maybe not everything. What are you worried about?"

"I like being the little brother. I don't want to be a big brother," he answered.

"Well, you'll always be my little brother, but then you also get to be someone's big brother. That's pretty cool that you can be both."

"Will you be the new baby's half sister too?"

I hadn't given it much thought, but when I heard him say it, it sounded odd. The fractured family I was part of was growing. I had Mom and Nan. Dad and Leslie. Hunter. And now I was going to be half sister to a brand-new human being. My family was going to need my help, and I wanted to be there for them. Maybe it called for more weekend visits throughout the year. I couldn't imagine how crazy next summer might be with a baby around. I wanted to be there for everything. I smiled.

"Yes."

He sniffled. I turned. In the red glow of the night-light I saw a single wet stream rolling down his cheek.

"I just like you being mine."

I nudged him. "Aw, Hunter, don't be upset. You know, babies aren't much fun at first. I won't be able to play

Whack-a-Shark with it. Or take it for slushes."

His sniffling turned to giggles. "Babies don't drink slushes."

I went with it. "Of course not, but someday the baby will want a slush, and you're going to have to help. How else will it know that sour cherry makes your tongue feel like pins are sticking in it?"

"Or that blue raspberry makes it turn bright blue."

"See, there you go," I said.

He snuggled his head against my shoulder.

"Cassidy?"

"Yes?"

"Can I just call you . . . sister? Not half sister?"

His voice was so innocent, my heart melted. I gave him a kiss on the forehead.

"As long as I can call you brother," I said.

"Deal."

He shifted over to his side. I turned to my side too, so we were back-to-back. The rain slowed down to a light patter. His breathing became deep and even. My eye caught the collection of items at the base of his night-light. A shell. Some sea glass. His great-white action figure. A peg-legged pirate. And the Crest Haven diamond that I'd found for him. A souvenir from the night Bryan and I made our new better memory. I reached over and picked it up, held it between my thumb and index finger so the red light sparkled through it.

Sparkled.

That's it! The answer to the clue!

I reached for my phone, but realized I'd left it upstairs.

I sat upright, nearly pulling the covers from Hunter. He shifted his position, smacked his lips a few times, but thankfully remained asleep. I slipped out, tucked the blanket around him, and tiptoed upstairs to my room. I grabbed my phone from the chair where I'd left it and plopped down onto my bed. I read the clue again.

Crest Haven diamond made perfect sense. Now how did it fit with the others?

Without thinking I texted Bryan.

Got the last clue! Crest Haven diamond!

When he didn't reply I texted again.

Hello?

My phone rang. It startled me momentarily, but I answered before it sounded again.

"Hello?"

"You know it's two in the morning, right?"

Bryan. The sexy, gravelly, sleepy voice of Bryan.

"What are you doing calling me then?" I asked, grinning in the darkness.

"You started it."

"But I only texted."

"About scavenger-hunt clues. At two in the morning."

"Did I wake you?"

"Maybe."

"You think I'm nuts."

He laughed.

"No, Cassidy Emmerich, I think you're a trip."

"So we can go over them?"

"I'm up now."

Bryan and I talked until the sun began to lighten the sky. I didn't want to hang up, but at some point either he or I did, because when I woke, my phone had slid off the bed onto the floor, and there was a small circle of drool on my pillow. We hadn't made much progress with the clues, but we had talked. And talked.

It felt like the beginning.

Baseball.

All of the clues led to baseball, or a baseball game. Specifically, the last Saturday-night home game of the South Jersey Leviathans in August.

When I finally figured out we needed to be paying more attention to the "batter" part of *cake batter ice cream*—it all clicked into place. The one clue that had given us the most trouble was the first one—and in the end it was Bryan who realized the cabanas were at the foot of Cartwright Street, and

Cartwright was the last name of Alexander Cartwright, aka the "father of baseball." Total team effort. We weren't the only ones who guessed correctly, but it was our names that Mr. Beckett pulled out of the sand pail on the last day of camp.

We decided to take Wade and Tori, who seemed to need some scavenger-hunt clues of their own to discover that they were into each other. It was a gorgeous night. I didn't really like watching baseball on television, but being at a live game was different and sort of exciting.

"Do we really have to stay until the end?" Tori asked.

"Yes," Bryan and I said together. I turned and kissed him, ignoring Tori's exaggerated groan at our PDA.

"Don't want to miss the fireworks, Tori, the best part," I said.

"Why can't they just shoot them off before the game begins? Wait, I know, because they need incentive to keep people in the seats during the mind-numbingly boring parts."

"I'm having fun," Bryan said, entwining his hand in mine. We were in accessible box seats along the first base line. The Leviathans were up by three in the middle of the seventh. It was seventh-inning-stretch time, the groundskeepers dragging mats to smooth out the clay along the infield to the tune of "Mony Mony" and trying to get the crowd clapping along.

"Chill, Tor," Wade said.

"Fine, but I'm going to get a caramel apple before concessions close—want anything?" she asked.

Wade grabbed her hand. "Wait, don't go yet."

"They're cleaning the field; I'm not missing anything. I'll be right back."

"No, really, stay," Wade said.

"Why?"

"Look, they're doing trivia on the Jumbotron," he said, pointing to the big video screen out past center field.

"That's great. I don't know baseball trivia."

"They're also wishing kids happy birthday."

I turned to Bryan and he looked away fast, a small smile on his face. When he looked at me again, he laughed. "What?"

"What's going on?" I asked.

He shook his head. "Nothing." Then he looked back toward the Jumbotron and covered his mouth as he shook with laughter.

"You did not do this," Tori said.

I turned to see the screen and gasped.

TORI, PROM?

Calm, cool Wade was anything but, as Tori glared at him in his seat.

"It's August," she said.

"I know, I know, it's just—

The crowd cheered as the picture on the Jumbotron switched from the words to a live video shot of Wade and Tori bickering. Wade stood up now. A chant of *prom, prom, prom* started around us.

"Did you know about this?" I asked Bryan.

"Yep, I dared him to do it."

Wade took Tori's hands. "Even if it's no, just say yes for now, please. Everyone's looking."

Tori laughed. "I'm kind of enjoying making you squirm."

She finally nodded, the crowd cheered, and the Jumbotron went on to wish someone named Cindy a happy thirtieth.

"Do you mean it?" Wade asked.

She let go of his hands, stepped back. "Maybe."

Wade put his hands on his hips, looked up to the sky. Tori turned away, determined to get her caramel apple, but Wade touched her shoulder.

"Tori, I like you, okay? I like the whole sundress-and-Chucks thing you got going on, and I like that you don't take crap from anyone, especially me, and your cake pops rock, and I don't mean that in a sexy way—you're a good cook, or baker, or whatever you call it, and I want to worry about your happiness and I just, well, I like you. There. Should have asked you to prom last year, so I'm getting a head start now."

Tori remained silent, arms folded. Wade's face was probably just a more intense version of mine and Bryan's. Eyes questioning, chin lowered, he blinked, waiting.

"Wade, I like you too, okay? Always have. You're full of yourself, but it's endearing somehow, and you smell like coconut oil, and the man bun is even sort of growing on me, so yes, I guess I'll go to prom with you, but maybe you can buy me a caramel apple first," she said, then grabbed fistfuls of his T-shirt and pulled herself up to him, planting a kiss on his mouth. Wade's arms momentarily flailed out in surprise, but he quickly regained composure and wrapped them around Tori. She pulled away, a big grin on her face.

"Let's get that apple," she said, leading him out of the aisle.

I put my head on Bryan's shoulder.

"So you told him he was crazy?" I asked.

"Yep—I mean, prom is months from now; anything could happen."

"You're right, I guess, still—it was sort of sweet."

"Now that she said yes, but man, there were a few moments I was sweating for him."

"So . . . you would never do anything like that?"

"I'm not really the prom type, you know; all this hardware sort of makes for an awkward night on the dance floor."

"Yeah, but . . . really? You looked like you had fun last year." I didn't want to sound disappointed. He squeezed my hand.

"So let's say I hypothetically asked you to prom, even though it's eight months away and you could get sick of me or I could get sick of you or a giant wave could come and wipe us all out, would you, if you had to answer tonight, would you go with me?"

I wished I could see into the future, which was about as impractical as a wish could get. Bryan was right. The odds were against us. It was months away; anything could happen. Making plans that far in advance seemed like a pretty ridiculous thing to do.

But.

The night was perfect, and the magic of summer was still in the air and in Bryan's eyes, and if I had to respond, that night, I knew what I would say.

It was a leap of faith, with only one answer.

"Yes."

This. Book.

I'm wary of the term *book of my heart*, mostly because that's a lot of pressure to put on one story. This novel, though, is special to me in so many ways and I'm beyond privileged to be able to thank the following people who helped me along this wild ride.

First and foremost to my readers—whether I've met you in person or if you've felt the urge to drop me a line or Tweet or message—thank you. Your kind words and enthusiasm make this writing gig the best job in the world.

A million thanks to my agent, Tamar Rydzinski, for pretty much everything. So blessed to have you and LDLA in my corner.

Thank you to Donna Bray for your belief in this story and your guidance, and for asking the questions that always seem to light the way.

Many thanks to the excellent team at Balzer + Bray/HarperCollins, including Viana Siniscalchi, Caroline Sun, Nellie Kurtzman, Alexei Esikoff, and Michelle Taormina.

Thank you for all that you do, whether it's apparent to me or not—your hard work is much appreciated.

Thank you to Meg Wiviott, Sarah Aronson, and Jessica Love—all of who either offered words of wisdom or advice when I first began shaping Cassidy and Bryan's story. Many thanks to Jennifer Moore, licensed and certified recreational therapist, who generously offered her time and expertise and allowed me to pick her brain on more than one occasion. And thank you to Brock Johnson, board member of Carolina Coastal Adaptive Sports and founder of "Wheels to Surf," for sharing a bit of his own experience and for helping me sound like a surfer.

This writing life is often solitary, but I'm lucky to have such wonderful colleagues, many of whom I call friends. The following lovelies inspire, enlighten, listen, or are just plain amazing—Jaye Robin Brown, Lynne Matson, Cindy Clemens, Laura Renegar, Amy Reed, Amber Smith, Judy Palermo, Vivi Barnes, and Christina Farley. Continued thanks to my One Four family—still a sounding board and virtual clubhouse when life gets particularly crazy. And a special shout out to Madcap Retreats (and retreaters) for providing a safe space to create and kvetch without judgment.

Thank you to my family and friends—your continued support means everything to me.

And last but not least, to my own personal Team Constantine—thank you for keeping my feet firmly on the ground and for putting up with my weirdness. Love you, always.